TEARS OF THE DRAGON

CYNDI FRIBERG

Tears of the Dragon

ISBN 978-0-9883001-4-9

Electronic book Publication, January 2013
Trade Paperback Publication, January 2013

Praise for Beyond Ontariese
Taken by Storm

"Taken by Storm had it all–tense action, suspense, erotic sex, humor and a wildly imaginative plot. " *The Romance Studio*

"Unplug the phone and put the kids to bed; once you start reading Taken by Storm you won't want any interruptions!" *Fallen Angel Reviews*

"For a story that will delight, entertain, and keep you on the edge of your seat, I highly recommend TAKEN BY STORM and award it RRT's **Perfect 10**." *Romance Reviews Today*

Operation Hydra

"I highly recommend **OPERATION HYDRA…**it's one of the best science fiction romances I've ever read**." Perfect 10!** *Romance Reviews Today*

"Outstanding! This segment only whetted my appetite for more. The heat between Kyrsta and Trey could cause a nuclear meltdown" *Simply Romance Reviews*

City of Tears

"WOW! **City of Tears** by Cyndi Friberg is one amazing blend of science fiction at its best and romance at its hottest…" *eCata Reviews*

The Legend

Listen little children to my tale
About a Fairy lass and human male.
Fair Fiona frolicked through the trees
There she felt the stir of love's cruel tease.
He was handsome, but could he be true?
That's the question left for me and you.

Fair Fiona offered him her heart.
And he promised they would never part.
His hateful words soon brought her to her knees.
"You meant no more to me than all of these,
Who offer up themselves trying to please."

Fearsome Dragon planned the massacre
But Fiona drew his eyes to her.
"The pain of this betrayal will one day fade."
Then, turning to the man, this curse she made:

"'Til the Lady finds the fate that once I sought,
Disappointment, pain and death shall be thy lot!"

Then from this world Fair Fiona stepped,
And from the skies above the dragon wept.

Prologue

Pendragon Castle
Northwest of Dover, England
1213

Fair Fiona hovered over the sleeping girl, searching her face and longing for the innocence reflected in her delicate features.

"Is she the one?" Fearsome Dragon asked carefully.

Floating nearer, Fiona continued to assess the newest Lady of Pendragon. Her thick eyelashes had dried into sooty spikes, and even in sleep an occasional shudder disrupted the cadence of her breathing. This was not a blissful bride.

"I cannot be sure," Fiona admitted.

"Then we must remain."

The dragon sounded so dejected that Fiona glanced his way. A shimmering silhouette, trapped between two worlds, he was just as anxious to return to the Fairy realm as she.

"'You created this debacle, Fiona,'" she mimicked Oberon's imperial tone, "'so you *will* see it through.' I have no choice, my friend. I must be certain."

The dragon accepted her statement with a regal nod, and Fiona wanted to scream. He should be with his mate. He should be guarding his hatchlings, but instead he stayed at her side, faithful and obedient to the end.

A scuffling sound drew her attention to the bedchamber door. Automatically, she cloaked her presence and joined her guardian on the far side of the bed.

Low and mournful, a groan filled the chamber. The door eased open, and Fiona started forward. Fearsome Dragon extended his wing, silently reminding her of her promise to Oberon, her father. She must release these people from her curse and interfere in their lives no longer.

The stench of ale and unwashed flesh assailed her nostrils. Fiona fisted her hands to keep from cleansing the air. A man lumbered into the room, unsteady, obviously drunk.

"I do not believe this!" Her musical voice was no longer audible to human ears and her eyes began to glow. "This...*creature* is to be her husband? This cannot be. She must love him or we will be trapped here forever!"

"You cannot interfere. It is forbidden," Fearsome Dragon reminded firmly. "She is his bride; this must be done."

Fiona shook with foreboding. The drunken oaf would brutalize his lady wife. Violence emanated from him in heated waves. This was not a gentle lover, come to woo his timid bride. This beast had come to conquer.

Moonlight spilled through the open window, illuminating the high bed and the bride sleeping there.

The girl stirred restlessly and the man paused beside the bed. With a soft gasp, she sat up. "Gaston...my lord. You startled me."

"It matters not." His words slurred slightly, but still managed to convey authority. "You are my wife. This is your duty."

Rowena knelt on the bed, clutching the coverlet to her chest. "Mama told me I must... I will..." Her lips trembled. "I'm frightened, my lord."

He snatched the covers from her hand and jerked her forward. Fiona vibrated with fury, tortured by her choice. She could watch him molest this child or break her solemn vow.

He ground his mouth over the girl's in an abomination of a kiss. His hands moved over her body as she squirmed and shoved against his chest. Jerking his tunic off over his head, he thrust his erection toward his terrified bride.

"Please," she cried out. "Not like this. I—"

Cutting off her protest with a vicious slap, he shoved her to her back and yanked her hips toward the edge of the bed. Rowena shrieked and flailed, her terror polluting the air, making it painful for Fiona to breathe.

The Fairy surged past Fearsome Dragon and flew straight into Gaston's sweaty face. He screamed as her aura seared him, but her fury was not yet appeased.

She stung him again and again, driving him to the floor, while his yelps and curses filled the room.

Pulsing with destructive energy, Fiona paused to look at the girl. She stood beside the bed, the man's tunic balled in her hands. Though her thin body trembled with terror, defiance burned in her gaze.

Rowena tossed the tunic at Gaston and said clearly, "You vowed to honor me, to love and cherish me! By breaking your vow, you've freed me from mine."

Fiona punctuated the girl's claim with an especially vicious sting, very near the juncture of his thighs. He screamed and scuttled toward the door.

"When you're ready to treat me with kindness, sirrah, I will honor my vows to you."

He called her several vile names and scrambled from the room, not bothering to don his tunic.

Fiona danced in the air, exhilarated by their triumph, but the girl covered her face with her hands and sank to her knees. Her soft sobs tore at Fiona's heart until tears trailed down her own cheeks.

"You're safe, little one. He will not harm you. No one will harm you now."

Fearsome Dragon intercepted the words before they reached Rowena's ears. Fiona glanced at him, surprised by his angry expression.

"This bit of glamour is going to cost you," he said. "When will you learn that rules must be obeyed?"

"I should have let him —"

"I didn't say that, but your father will —"

"My father will learn to accept me as I am, or he will never see me again," she vowed.

Chapter One

Five Years Later

He emerged from the darkness like a specter, moonlight glistening off his chain mail and the massive black horse beneath him. His hand rested upon the hilt of the lethal-looking sword strapped to his side. The gesture should not have been so intimidating, given the distance separating them, but Lady Rowena of Pendragon trembled all the same.

"If you persist in this foolishness, I will lay siege to your castle," the dark knight called out in strong, articulate Norman French.

Rowena squared her shoulders and pressed her hands against the stone ledge of the battlement. She had been summoned to the forward tower some moments before by the frantic urging of one of her castle guards. One would think Satan himself had appeared at her drawbridge, not this one knight with a handful of men.

"Pendragon Castle has never succumbed to a siege, and many have tried. You don't frighten me!"

"I don't want your fear, my lady. I want your cooperation. Storming your defenses will give me no pleasure, but I've orders from—"

"I understand your orders," she interrupted. "It's your misfortune that your needs are incompatible with mine. I *cannot* leave Pendragon Castle at this time."

"Milady."

Rowena glared impatiently at Farrell, her steward. He stood behind her, his expression a potent mixture of anxiety and fear. She couldn't fathom what had him so distraught, but she stopped his interruption with an upraised hand.

"Lower the drawbridge, so we can discuss this like civilized people," the dark knight tried again.

"There is nothing to discuss. You've requested that I accompany you on some fool's errand, and I've refused. That is the end of it."

"Milady," Farrell repeated more urgently. "You should—"

"I should what? Allow myself to be duped by one of Edwin's tricks?"

"Lady Rowena!" The stranger's bellow demanded her attention. "The night is chill, and I am weary of your stubbornness. Lower the bridge!"

"If I allow you in, you will only have to leave come first light. I am not going anywhere with you." Though shaken inside, she did her best to sound assertive. Edwin had tried all manner of intimidation over the past few weeks, but this felt different somehow.

"You *will* accompany me regardless of your preference. If I must, I shall complete my mission with you bound and gagged over the back of my horse. Now open or pay the price!"

Rowena didn't respond well to ultimatums. "Seek shelter in the village and be off my land by Prime!"

Not waiting to hear his response, she turned from the opening in the guard tower and shoved her way past several stunned soldiers. The long-distance conversation was only straining her voice and fraying her nerves. She descended the narrow stone steps, emerging in the lower bailey.

"Was it wise to dismiss him out of hand?"

Rowena glanced over her shoulder and found Farrell half a step behind her. A steward was a valued member of any castle's staff, but Farrell was more than just her steward. He was her mentor, her advisor and her friend. "What else could I do?"

"Invite him in, serve him mead, and explain your position."

She smiled and slowed her pace just a bit. "Did you hear what he said? He threatened to abduct me if I continued to refuse him. Edwin has tried some despicable things in the past, but this—"

"Edwin did not send this man. I tried to tell you in the tower."

"Tried to tell me what?" Rowena faced Farrell.

"Did you look at the message he sent you earlier? Did you study the seal before you broke it?"

Chagrined by his gentle reproach, Rowena asked, "What of it?"

"He claims to be Dominic of Chapstow."

Farrell's tone implied she should recognize the name. Anxious energy set her in motion. They climbed the stone steps of the keep together, and she glanced at him while he pulled open the heavy door. "I remember his name, Farrell." Stepping past him and into the great hall, Rowena moved to the hearth in the center of the room.

"If his claim is true, you should have invited him in."

"Who, pray tell, is Dominic of Chapstow? And why does his name ensure him better treatment than other men?"

"Have you heard the name William Marshal?"

Biting back a sarcastic retort, Rowena took a moment to unfasten her ermine-trimmed cloak. She handed the garment to a passing servant then continued the conversation. "William Marshal is the regent of England, Farrell. I have heard his name a time or two."

"William is also the Earl of Pembroke and Lord of *Chapstow* Castle."

"Sir Dominic is William Marshal's man?" Her heart sank. "Oh my, I should have let him in."

Farrell smiled but made no further comment on her blunder.

"Edwin has me so off balance," she whispered. "I thought only to protect what's mine."

"He will not retreat, milady. He will most likely present himself again at daybreak, and I suggest you let him in. You have already introduced him to the Shrew of Pendragon, perhaps on the morrow he can meet Lady Rowena."

If Farrell knew how badly it stung each time she was called the Shrew of Pendragon, he'd never have repeated the unwanted title. But she carefully hid her feelings, maintaining an unshakable composure. No one must ever guess the fear concealed beneath her fire and bluster. "I pray you're right. I don't need another enemy."

"I'll return to the tower. If Sir Dominic is still in sight, shall I send for you?"

"Aye. What a muck I've made of this."

Inclining his head, he moved away.

Rowena stared into the fire, which had been carefully banked for the night. The hall was quiet and clean, but it hadn't always been so. She could still remember the neglect and disorder that greeted her five years before.

Large iron wheels filled with costly candles hung suspended by chains from the massive oak trusses. The candles were only lit for special occasions. Their real purpose was to impress visitors. On ordinary days, smoky torches, one at each corner of the hall, provided inadequate lighting. Sprigs of lavender and mint had been scattered among the rushes covering the floor. The scent was pleasant but subtle. Numerous long tables had been dismantled and stacked against the outer walls, making room for the villeins and workmen to bed down for the night.

Stepping away from the central hearth, Rowena moved toward the head table at the far end of the hall. The head table couldn't be dismantled and it rested upon a low stone dais. An enormous, elaborately carved wooden chair dominated the center of the arrangement. Rowena's eyes automatically gravitated to the chair.

Gaston's chair.

But this was *her* hall!

Rowena had made it hers through long hours of hard work and determination. And Edwin would not take it away, not while breath still stirred within her body.

The door at the other end of the hall banged open, snatching Rowena from her thoughts. Farrell stood framed in the threshold.

"Come quickly, milady," he called. "He has breached the castle walls."

"What?" The word burst from her, propelled by disbelief. "'Tis impossible."

Shouts and pandemonium greeted them as they reached the lower bailey. Farrell rushed on to explain that the drawbridge had been lowered without the proper order, a guard had been found dead and the portcullis had risen, seemingly of its own volition. None of it made any sense to Rowena, so she focused more closely on the scene surrounding her. Archers had manned the walls, and the castle knights were rushing about with no apparent order or direction. She scanned the area for Ludlow, the captain of the guards.

Before she could locate him or comprehend the chaos, an eerie hush descended over the bailey. Like thick, cloying fog, the tension became palpable. She heard a horse nicker, and then the line of her best knights parted, as if directed by some unseen hand.

Destriers were always large and intimidating, but never had Rowena seen a horse so mammoth or magnificent. Its long, glossy mane gleamed in the moonlight. Condensation rolled from its nostrils like smoke. The solid black coat made it appear as if the beast had been fashioned from the darkness itself.

Raising her gaze to the rider, she forgot all about the horse. From the guard tower, he'd looked much as any other knight, a large man concealed beneath chain mail and a thick surcoat. But now the moonlight provided dimension and detail. Rowena felt her world tip out of balance. His metal helm was tucked beneath one massive arm while the night wind played through his long, dark hair. Even in the dense night shadows, Rowena couldn't miss the flash of his gaze.

"Dominic of Chapstow is also called Undaunted," Farrell whispered from beside her.

Rowena didn't respond. She couldn't take her eyes from the invader. How had he gotten within the walls of her castle? Why had someone not launched an arrow through his neck as soon as he uncovered his head?

Because no one wanted to start a war with William Marshal. She hadn't known this man's reputation, but thankfully her knights had.

From the impressive proportions of his body to the fierce arrangement of his features, he emanated power. With lithe agility, he dismounted, his heavy mail apparently no hindrance to the fluidity of his movements.

His men rode in behind him, quickly forming a menacing circle. In an instant, she and Farrell were trapped within the ring, face-to-face with the dark knight. He tossed the helm to one of his soldiers, striding directly toward Rowena. Her insides quivered and throat constricted. He was huge—and obviously furious.

His mail-covered hands closed around her upper arms, jerking her violently forward. She collided with his chest. He shook her once, hard, and then glared down into her upturned face.

"I have killed men for far less insult than you dealt me this night. Never has my simplest request been met with such discourtesy." After sneering the words directly into her face, he shoved her away.

Rowena stumbled backward, barely catching herself before she fell to the dirt at his feet. "You accuse me of discourtesy and insult, but you are the one issuing threats." With quicksilver speed, anger evaporated her fear. "I've explained that I am unable to leave my castle. That is all the explanation any honorable knight should require."

He rejected the statement with a harsh laugh. Rowena planted her fists on her hips. Heat burned her cheeks.

Farrell smoothly stepped between her and Sir Dominic. "Might I suggest we move this conversation into the hall? Surely, you'd both be more comfortable having this discussion over a tankard of mead or ale?"

Remembering Farrell's earlier words, Rowena reined in her temper. She still had no intention of going anywhere with this beast, but she must find out how he'd breached her defenses. If he could get in, so could Edwin.

"Farrell is correct," she said softly. "Shall we away to my hall? I would be honored to extend my hospitality."

Another burst of laughter assured Rowena he hadn't missed the possessiveness in her invitation.

"Farrell, please ask Ludlow to see to the needs of Sir Dominic's men." She turned back to the knight. "If you will follow me."

She didn't wait to see if he accepted her invitation. Spinning on the ball of her foot, she maneuvered between two of his soldiers and marched toward the keep. Never before had she been this angry — or this afraid. Her world was coming unraveled and this man was gleefully tugging the string.

Rowena jerked open the door, stomped past the center hearth and gestured toward the head table. "Please be seated. I'll see to your refreshment." She tossed the words over her shoulder and headed toward the service rooms at the lower end of the hall.

Her angry façade slipped just a little when he could no longer see her face. *What was she to do?* How had this been accomplished?

And who had died that he might succeed?

She'd have to find out from Ludlow which of her guards had given his life. Her people depended on her. It was her responsibility to keep them safe. She'd reacted with pride and anger — and one of her people had paid the price. It was a bitter brew to swallow, but Rowena accepted her failure.

Before she secured bread from the pantry, she entered the buttery, unsure what beverages she would need. An odd moaning reached her from one darkened corner and Rowena stepped backward.

"Who goes there?" she demanded. Her eyes adjusted to the darkness and she saw the shadowy outline of a person, or persons.

The quick shuffling of clothing and a familiar chuckle instantly soothed Rowena's fear.

"So sorry, milady." Thora stepped forward into the light spilling in from the hall. "Didn't mean to frighten you."

Thora's hair was down around her shoulders. The laces of her gown had been loosened and the chemise beneath bunched at one shoulder. Milton, the castle marshal, stepped up behind Thora and awkwardly tugged his forelock.

"We've visitors, Milton, and the visitors have horses. You do still oversee my stables, do you not?"

"Aye, milady. I beg your pardon. I'll go there now."

He shuffled past Rowena and made a hasty exit.

"I didn't mean to interrupt your evening tryst, Thora." Rowena allowed a hint of reproach to harden her tone.

"What are you after, milady?" the servant asked, apparently unashamed to be caught at her amusement.

"I need refreshment for one of the visitors as quickly as possible."

"I'll see to it."

Amazed that her attendant didn't grill her with questions, Rowena turned back toward the hall. She made it to the doorway and then paused. "Redress your hair before you serve us."

Rowena smiled for the first time that night as she left the buttery. Thora was one of the few rays of light at Pendragon Castle, all the rest had been hardship and strife.

The smile proved to be short-lived. As Rowena stepped back into the great hall, she stumbled to a halt. Sir Dominic sprawled in the master's tall-backed chair, his muddy boots propped on the head table.

Dominic knew he was going out of his way to provoke the lady, but he couldn't seem to stop himself. She stood motionless in the stone archway leading to the storerooms. He stared at her, hiding his reluctant admiration behind a hostile glower.

Her bright green eyes narrowed in a nearly angelic face, the lush fullness of her mouth compressed into a grim line, and her hands clenched into tight little fists.

God's blood, she was adorable!

She didn't want him here. Every movement she made, every word she uttered, illustrated her displeasure. But he couldn't understand her attitude. Why did she perceive him as a threat? William Marshal had invited her to court, not scheduled her execution.

Dominic watched the subtle sway of her slender hips while she crossed the hall. She kept her shoulders squared, her bearing regal. A fluttery wimple framed the pale oval of her face, held in place by a golden fillet. He wondered if the hair hidden beneath was the same dark brown as her highly arched brows. Was it long and silky or wild and curly?

She looked far too young to be entrusted with the vast Pendragon holdings. The thought made him suppress a smile. William Marshal knew how badly he wanted holdings of his own. He'd not aspired to anything so grand as Pendragon Castle, but… Could it be his liege had an ulterior motive for this errand?

"Thora will be with us directly," she informed stiffly, her gaze hostile.

Dominic swung his legs to the stone dais and leaned forward, resting his elbows impolitely on the scarred tabletop. He was hot and uncomfortable in his heavy chain mail, and this chit was the cause of it all. He'd worn the hauberk more for effect than any suspicion he'd need the protection.

This was supposed to be a quick, simple errand. William needed to speak with this girl, and Dominic was to bring her to Windsor Castle. Yet she'd refused not only William's summons but the simple hospitality customarily extended to any knight.

"How did you get beyond the curtain wall?" Her momentary attempt at civility fell away like a cheap costume.

Dominic laughed. How could so tiny a creature possess such indignation? She reminded him of a feisty kitten, hissing and spitting at the world, with no concept of her true size or limitations. "I rode across the drawbridge."

"Who lowered the drawbridge? Who raised the portcullis? How did you get a man inside my castle?"

She stood before the dais, glaring up at him, but he was in no mood to soothe her. "Join me." He motioned toward the empty chairs at his right with a lazy nod of his head.

Stiffly, Rowena moved around the table and took a chair, leaving one empty between them. "How was it done, Sir Dominic?"

"I'm weary, thirsty—and annoyed. Can we simply pretend to be friends for a moment?"

"Fine," she sneered. "Shall we discuss the weather? The upcoming harvest? A recent skirmish? The merits of Magna Carta, perhaps?"

"You really are in need of—"

His comment was interrupted by a throaty, feminine laugh. "I could tell you exactly what Lady Rowena is in need of, but I don't think she'd thank me for the suggestion."

Dominic glanced toward the speaker and smiled. Now *here* was a woman. Her simple woolen gown and the crude pattern to her harshly accented French placed her among the lower class. Rarely could a commoner speak the language of the nobility, however coarsely. Who was she?

Her bright blonde hair and curvaceous form were pleasing indeed. Amusement sparkled in the depths of her wide blue eyes, and Dominic switched to English, hoping the lady wouldn't understand. "Tell me, fair damsel, what does the lady need most?"

The servant glanced quickly at her mistress and then placed the small tray on the table in front of him. "A good long tumble with a man who knows what he's about," she returned in English with a pretty smile.

Dominic waited for the lady's outraged gasp or harsh remonstration, but her expression didn't change.

"Pour the wine, Thora, and then be off," Rowena instructed in French.

Dominic studied the lady's delicate features while the servant filled their cups and quietly slipped away. Could Lady Rowena not control her own people? It hadn't seemed so, until now, but what a bold comment for a handmaiden. Even if the lady hadn't understood —

"I'd know the reason you've forced your way into my home." Rowena's insistent tone cut through his confused thoughts.

"Forced my way into your home?" he challenged. "I remember no siege. I employed no battering ram. There are no holes in the walls of your castle."

Rowena happily pictured herself dumping the contents of her cup over his head. "Why are you here? What do you really want? *How* did you get in?" She had no patience left where this man was concerned. He was rude and presumptuous, and she was terrified she wouldn't be able to outwit him.

"I'm here because my liege lord bid me come, and I want a hot bath."

Rowena closed her eyes, knowing he'd see her exasperation. Then she looked directly into his face. His eyes were blue. Not brown, as she'd first thought. They were a rich midnight blue.

Scrambling to remember the issue at hand, she finally said, "If we can have done with this foolish conversation, I'll see to your bath myself."

"An intriguing proposition. And I have one in return."

"A proposition?"

He nodded. "I'll answer your questions one at a time. But for each answer I give, you must provide the answer to one of my questions."

"Agreed. How did you get within the walls of my castle?"

"I rode my charger." He chuckled. "How long has your husband been dead?"

Rowena seethed. This was a game to him! "He died on All Hallow's Eve." Even as she spoke the words, Rowena found it hard to believe she'd been free of Gaston for nearly a year. "Did one of your men kill my guard?"

"Aye." He smirked, obviously enjoying the game. "Who is Edwin of Llangly?"

Rowena smiled. If he hadn't been told the details of her relationship with Edwin, then this game could be far more interesting than she'd first thought. "My father."

"But I thought—"

"The next question is mine. Who killed my guard?"

"Ephraim." Dominic offered no more information.

His expression was thoughtful. Rowena was sure he was deciding how best to phrase his next question.

"Is Edwin of Llangly your mother's husband?"

"Aye." He'd never puzzle through that tangle. "What position does Ephraim hold within your household?"

"He's my squire. Why is your mother's husband challenging your marriage to Gaston of Pendragon?"

"For the obvious reason. He wants Pendragon Castle and all of the other holdings that came to me upon Gaston's death." If Ephraim was Sir Dominic's squire, and it was this squire who'd killed the guard, then it stood to reason Ephraim also raised the portcullis and lowered the drawbridge. "How did Ephraim get within the castle walls?"

"He climbed up the chute of your garderobe," Dominic explained with another quick grin.

"That's disgusting! You ordered your squire to climb up through the latrine? That is vile."

Dominic chuckled. "Ephraim will be well compensated for his trial and apparently the ploy was effective, for here I sit within your cozy hall."

"I never thought to fortify the pit of the garderobe. This is too much. Must I station guards outside the privy door?"

"The next question is mine, but if you'd prefer I answer that, I'll allow my questions to accumulate."

"Nay." She waved away the suggestion. "I wasn't posing a question. I was thinking aloud."

"Why have you been so reluctant to cooperate with me?"

Rowena lost interest in the game. "Edwin of Llangly has been a thorn in my side longer than I can remember. After Gaston's death, he determined to have my holdings, but I'm just as determined to retain them. A widow is afforded many rights other women are not. I'm in the rare position of controlling my own life, and I intend for it to remain so."

"How does Edwin hope to gain control of Pendragon? On what grounds is he contesting the marriage? Has he blood ties to Gaston? Is your mother still alive?"

Rowena laughed and pushed her chair back from the table. "I've no more questions for you. So, I've no reason to answer yours."

"Then keep your own counsel," Dominic grumbled. "But know this. I've been instructed to bring you to William Marshal in a timely manner—and I fully intend to do just that."

"I understand." Rowena stood. "I'll go see to your bath."

* * * * *

"How *dare* you insult me in front of the knight. What were you thinking, Thora? I should have you flogged!" Rowena anxiously paced in front of the crackling fire in her solar, her private sanctuary above the great hall.

"I was thinking what I've been thinking for nigh unto a year. You need a man in your bed. Why not Sir Dominic?" Thora's wide blue eyes revealed concern, but the hint of a smile tugged at one corner of her mouth.

If the buxom blonde were not her dearest friend, Rowena wouldn't tolerate her insolence. But Thora had been Rowena's only ally since she arrived at Pendragon Castle, a terrified bride of fifteen. "Your solution to a great many problems can be found upon the surface of a bed."

The servant's smile departed entirely. "I'll not deny my fondness for bed sport, but this situation is a bit more complicated than the need for pleasure."

"Do you think I don't comprehend the situation?" Rowena snapped. "Edwin needs only prove my virginity and all is lost. My maidenhead must be gone before I'm presented to the regent. But how do I go about this? Where do I turn?"

Thora studied her thoughtfully. "I think what Edwin really wants is to wed you himself."

"What he wants is irrelevant. Brother Leland assured me that such a union would never be allowed. Edwin was wed to my mother. It would be considered incestuous were we to wed. How could I share the bed of a man I once called father?" Rowena shuddered. "Edwin knows 'tis impossible. But if Sir William finds out the truth, he will recommend that the Church annul my marriage."

"If you took a lover, even for one night, Edwin would have no grounds on which to pursue the annulment."

"I know, but this secret is too damning. How can I trust anyone—and what if I conceived a child?"

"We would retire to one of your other fiefs and return to Pendragon with *my* child."

She squeezed the older woman's shoulder, warmed by her loyalty. "I couldn't do that to you, Thora,"

Rowena said quietly. "I couldn't do that to a child born of my body."

"Is it better to submit yourself to Edwin and surrender Pendragon Castle?"

"I'll never surrender." Determination surged through Rowena.

"And every person I know is grateful. Edwin is vile! We have to keep him from Pendragon no matter the cost." Thora paused, her expression cautious. "There is only one way to fight this. You must seduce Sir Dominic."

Rowena laughed until she realized Thora didn't share her mirth. "Surely, you jest."

"Nay, I do not. I think Sir Dominic is perfect for this task. Who better to rid you of this unwanted obstacle? He's strong and handsome, and he's honor bound to protect you until you've been delivered to William Marshal. He's sitting naked in his bath even as we speak."

"This is madness. If Sir Dominic realized the truth, he would be 'honor bound' to reveal my virgin state to William Marshal."

"That wouldn't happen. Men see what they expect to see. If he thinks you're a lusty widow, deprived of her husband's attentions, then that's what he'll find. Even if he did realize the truth, you'd only need to weep pathetically, explain all you've suffered at Edwin's hand, and you'd have an ally. It's worth the risk. Edwin must be stopped!"

"I cannot," Rowena said, but there was no conviction in the protest.

* * * * *

Dominic allowed the soothing heat of the bath water to ease the tension from his body, but no power on earth could have relaxed his turbulent thoughts. One stubborn slip of a girl had nearly bested him. The realization stuck like a fishbone in his craw. He'd battled England's enemies for longer than he could remember and never had he been so close to defeat.

Her delicate face and flashing gaze materialized within his mind, so Dominic opened his eyes. He didn't want to think about how appealing he found her features. He refused to wonder if her lips were as soft and pliant as they appeared. Instead he looked about the chamber. The room was not large but the furniture was stout, the floor clean. Was Rowena responsible for the orderly environment or did— His thoughts ended abruptly when he heard an odd creaking sound.

His eyes snapped toward the door. It inched open and four slender fingers curved around the wooden edge. The door eased inward and Lady Rowena stepped into the room.

Dominic felt his heart slam into the wall of his chest and blood flooded his groin.

Damn the wench! What was she about?

She closed the door but didn't move farther into the room. Firelight touched her face, making her smooth skin glow. He imagined that same flickering light dancing over her naked body and groaned. The golden flecks in her wide green eyes seemed to sparkle with metallic brilliance. Dominic's hands gripped the rim of the tub so tightly his knuckles turned white.

Had William realized what he was doing when he set this woman in his path? Dominic smiled. Silly question. Of course he knew, the wily old goat!

"I promised I'd see to your bath. I'm a woman of my word."

Her voice held far more confidence than her expression. She'd somehow managed to repress the fear he'd seen moments before, but her hands trembled. If she was afraid of him, why was she here?

"I'm quite comfortable," he said. "You need not tarry."

She clutched a small vial in her right hand. "I've an ointment that will soothe your muscles and help you relax. May I apply it?"

Dominic *had* been relaxed—until she stepped into the room.

Just before Dominic left Windsor Castle, William had insisted he vow not to touch Rowena intimately. Dominic had been confused by the conversation, but he was beginning to understand the reason for the odd request. Had tales of Rowena's exploits reached the ear of William Marshal?

Old bitterness and past resentment surged through Dominic, extinguishing his building desire. Rowena looked so young and innocent, but appearances could be deceiving. Dominic had learned that lesson a long time ago.

Curious to see how far she'd carry the game, he sat up and beckoned with his hand. "Come. Soothe me."

Rowena was amazed that her wobbly legs supported her weight. Sir Dominic's naked body left her shaking and breathless. His broad shoulders and brawny arms rested along the rim of the wooden tub, every ripple and curve of his chest and abdomen available for her inspection. Thankfully the water was clouded with soap, or she might well have crumbled to the floor — or flung herself into the tub.

Strangling a ridiculous giggle, Rowena quickly crossed the room. There was less to see from the back, but the view was no less spectacular. His back was wide and corded with muscles.

You must be bold. You must seem eager for his embrace. Nay, she corrected herself, *you must be eager for his embrace.*

Setting the vial on the floor, she raked her fingers through his sodden hair, drawing it into a mass at the nape of his neck. The heavy thickness felt wonderful tangled around her fingers. She twisted his hair into a tight coil that trailed down along his spine.

"Why do you wear your hair long? Most soldiers keep it short so it fits more easily beneath their helm." She needed something to distract herself from the heat and tingles flaring to life all over her body.

"For the same reason I scrape my whiskers."

She laughed, leaning in until her mouth hovered over his ear. "Are we beginning another competition of words?" A shudder raked his body, and she smiled.

"Nay." He fidgeted, leaning slightly away. She could hear his ragged breathing and feel heat radiate off his skin. "Most men wear beards and cut their hair. I prefer my hair long and my jaw clean. I've never been overly concerned with social convention."

"I see." She lifted the vial Thora had given her and poured a small amount of amber oil into her cupped palm. Warming the oil with her body heat, she smoothed it over his broad shoulders.

A soft gasp escaped her throat. She'd not expected his body to be so hot—or so hard. The muscles beneath her fingers felt as if they were sculpted from stone— warm, living stone. She squeezed and stroked, fascinated by the slick slide of her hands over his flesh.

She kneaded his corded shoulders and worked the ointment into his thick upper arms. The side of his neck seemed especially tight, so she rubbed the area with her thumbs. She wanted to touch more of him. She wanted to touch all of him. Her fingers splayed across his shoulders and stretched downward, caressing his chest.

Suddenly, he grasped her wrist and dragged her in front of him. Anger and something even more intense drove every trace of gentleness from his features. Rowena wanted to run, to scream, but she needed him to act upon the lust smoldering in his dark blue eyes.

He grasped her upper arms and yanked her forward. The tub bit into her abdomen and tepid water splashed her skirt.

"I am not soothed."

His voice sounded harsh and needful. Rowena fought through her terror and forced herself to meet his gaze. She let her lids droop slightly as Thora had showed her, and she remembered to lick her lips. "Then let me soothe you. Tell me how. I will do—"

He shoved her backward so forcefully she landed hard on her bottom. Tears blinded her as failure loomed on the horizon.

"Get out."

He spoke the words with such finality that Rowena wanted to crawl beneath the floorboards. She scrambled to her feet and flew from the room.

Tears streamed down her face by the time she reached her bedchamber. She threw herself onto the bed and wept. All of her old insecurity crashed over her like storm-swollen waves.

You are unfeeling and frigid, Rowena. No man will ever find solace in your bed! Gaston's hateful voice echoed from the grave.

He had not wanted her.

Just like Gaston, Dominic had not wanted her.

Chapter Two

Damn the man! Fair Fiona glared down at the dark-haired knight from her hiding place in the corner of his room. Was he partial to other men? What was wrong with him?

It had been no simple task to convince Rowena to come here. How dare he reject her out of hand!

Vibrating with destructive energy, she prepared to dive.

"Don't even think about it," Fearsome Dragon warned.

"There was no reason for him to be so cruel. Rowena is passing fair. Why would he hesitate?"

"Perhaps he doesn't wish to be manipulated by a meddlesome Fairy."

She flew right through her guardian — knowing it annoyed him — to get a better look at the knight. "We must have more time. I know I can find a man worthy of our Rowena, but first we must thwart Edwin."

The dragon's laughter rumbled, sounding very much like thunder. The knight looked around, confusion bright in his vivid blue eyes.

"Be careful," Fiona whispered. "He heard you."

"Has masquerading as a human taught you nothing about them? Rowena doesn't belong to us. For the moment, at least, we belong to her."

"And we will *ever* belong to her, if she cannot break my curse." Floating in a lazy circle around the human, she went on. "One step at a time, my friend. We must stop Edwin then we'll plan the rest."

"Without the knight's cooperation, how do you intend to protect Rowena from Edwin's plot?"

She flew through the thick stone wall. Pausing to make sure the corridor was empty, she transformed into Thora.

Tossing her hair over her shoulders, she said to the unseen dragon, "I'll think of something. I always do."

* * * * *

Rowena didn't see Sir Dominic again until midmorning the following day. The great hall bustled, everyone preparing for the main meal to be served. Rowena joined the assembly, hoping she didn't look as anxious as she felt.

Dominic's rejection left her with no option but to attempt one final, dangerous bid for freedom. She intended to extend him every courtesy, play the role of charming hostess to the fullest, and then become violently ill. The ruse wouldn't work for long, but she only needed one day, perhaps two, before she would be able to present herself to William Marshal.

Farrell met her at the foot of the stairs, his expression reflecting his anxiety. "What transpired last night? Was Sir Dominic reasonable?"

A heated blush blossomed across her cheeks as the memory of Dominic's nude torso materialized in vivid detail. If he'd been reasonable, she'd have spent the night in his arms and in his bed. "Reasonable can be hard to define."

The steward smiled then his eyes grew serious, intent. "You must be very careful in your dealings with this man. The stories surrounding him are many. I spent the last few hours listening to those who know him best recount unbelievable acts of violence and mayhem."

"He's a knight, Farrell. Violence and mayhem are his vocation." Fear fluttered in her stomach.

"Nay. It's more than that. They spoke of..." His voice faltered, and Farrell glanced away.

"He is here. I cannot change that fact," Rowena commented when he did not explain what he had overheard. "Gossip naturally accompanies anyone with notoriety. And you said yourself that Sir Dominic is well known."

"You're right, of course. We'd be wise to focus on the situation at hand. Were you able to come to an understanding? Are you going to accompany him back to William Marshal?"

"A very good question, steward," Sir Dominic cut in. "I'm curious to hear the answer."

Rowena turned, thinking she was prepared for the sight of him. Her breath caught painfully in her throat and she forced her eyes not to widen. He was tall and commanding. His broad shoulders, thick upper arms and deep chest needed no padded gambeson or chain mail hauberk to appear powerful.

And his face… Rowena had never seen features so fiercely handsome, so savagely appealing until she met this man. He'd pulled the unfashionable length of his raven black hair straight back from his forehead and bound it at the nape of his neck. Without the softening contrast of his loose hair, his cheekbones appeared even sharper. His dark blue eyes gleamed back at her with brutal intensity.

Lying had never come easily to Rowena, so she chose her words carefully. She could feel his gaze move lazily over her features, even after she averted her face. "Is there no alternative? Can I not send your lord a message explaining the details of my predicament?"

"And if he has questions after reading this message, am I to come scurrying back for your reply?" His tone was dry, mocking. "I think not. You need to accompany me."

"Then can you ensure the security of my castle in my absence?"

"Are your castle guards so inept? Have you never ventured beyond the castle walls before? You seem to have very little faith in the competency of your own men."

"It's not their competency I doubt," she admitted. "It's their loyalty. Some would prefer to swear fealty to Edwin."

"That is not true," Farrell defended her passionately. "The men are loyal to Pendragon Castle, and you are the Lady of Pendragon."

"Among other things," Rowena muttered. "Let's join the assembly. Everyone is anxious for the meal to begin." She motioned toward the head table with a graceful sweep of her hand. The lesser tables had already filled with people. Dominic's men had stayed largely together, dominating the long table closest to the hall's main entrance.

"By all means," Dominic agreed.

They took their places upon the dais and Dominic casually picked up the small round loaf that sat beside each thick bread trencher. Breaking off a piece, he handed it to Rowena. "You should be commended on your keep. Seldom have I seen a hall so clean and well organized."

"My thanks." She nibbled on a small bit of bread while the first course was served.

Servants moved between the tables efficiently. Spit-roasted chickens and mutton were distributed in bowls throughout the hall. Then boiled cod with parsley sauce. Apple fritters and boiled greens were served to accompany the meat dishes.

"How soon can you be ready to travel?" Dominic asked as Rowena began to fill the trencher set before them.

She chuckled, setting aside the serving dish. "Are you always so tenacious?"

"Always." He didn't smile, but a suspicious twinkle came into his eyes.

"How long will I be gone? Where is Sir William?"

"He'll receive us at Windsor Castle, and the duration of your stay will likely be determined by your willingness to cooperate."

She didn't miss the subtle reprimand in his softly spoken words. "Then I suppose I can make ready by the morrow. Will that satisfy you?"

His gaze narrowed and his lips pressed together. "You need not concern yourself with my satisfaction. I was sent here for a specific purpose. You would do well to remember that fact."

He sounded annoyed, but his velvety blue eyes took on a soft, distant quality. Was he remembering what it felt like as her hands slid over his flesh?

"I've not forgotten your reason for being here. But you must understand, I've been defending my position at Pendragon nearly from the day I laid my husband to rest." The conflict at Pendragon Castle began long before that, but Sir Dominic didn't need to know her entire history.

"Against this Edwin? Or are there others with a mind to be Pendragon's lord?"

"What did Sir William tell you?"

"Just that Edwin of Llangly has petitioned the crown to recommend the annulment of your marriage. William thought it odd, being that Gaston is dead, and a third party submitted the petition. He sent me to deliver his summons and escort you to Windsor Castle."

"How long have you served Sir William?" She smoothly changed the subject.

"My father was William Marshal's vassal, so I was sent to be fostered with his sons. A rival baron murdered my parents and burnt our keep to the ground, so I became his ward." He spoke in an emotionless monotone.

Rowena's hand flew to her mouth. She'd only meant to distract him. How could she have guessed that he'd reveal something so horrible? "I'm so sorry, sir," she whispered.

"I've had many years to accept the loss."

"Was this person brought to justice?"

"King John saw my father's death as an opportunity to seize back the land he'd granted to my family. I was too young to fight the injustice. William approached King John on my behalf, but the king wasn't interested in his opinions or objections."

Rowena couldn't meet his gaze. Fiddling with her food, she said, "I remember stories of his outrageous liberties. King John was not a good king."

Dominic laughed. "Truer words may never have been spoken. The Barons Charter was designed to curtail his rash behavior, but he had the document invalidated nearly before the ink dried."

"So, are we better off with a boy king?" She hoped to lighten the conversation.

"Sir William is a good and just man. King Henry couldn't ask for a better regent."

"But King Henry is a child. For many years yet, he'll be vulnerable to the influence of others."

He nodded. "That's why the regent must be strong, his character above reproach."

"You admire him greatly," Rowena said.

"King Henry?"

"William Marshal," she clarified, then seeing laughter in his dark blue eyes, she smiled.

As the servants began to clear the tables, Rowena remembered the role she needed to play. Easing back against the tall, wooden chair, she closed her eyes and rubbed her temples.

"Is something amiss?" Dominic asked.

"Just a bit of a headache. If you'll excuse me…"

Dominic rose smoothly and pulled back the heavy chair. Rowena hadn't expected him to follow her, but there was no mistaking the heavy fall of his boots. How long must she indulge him before she could retire to her solar?

She reached the ramparts before she acknowledged his presence. "Do you intend to follow me around until we depart?"

He stepped up beside her and leaned one shoulder against the stone fortification. Rowena allowed her gaze to move leisurely over his handsome features. He was far too comfortable with himself.

He smiled. "The thought had occurred to me."

"Why? Do you fear I'll climb down through the latrine and escape your evil grasp?"

He chuckled. "Are you always so prickly?"

The temptation to trust him twisted within her. Oh, to abandon her rash plan and enlist his aid. If he understood what she'd suffered, would he make love to her slowly, tenderly? Would he awaken her senses with patience and skill, or was he a brutish clod like —

It didn't matter! Sir Dominic had made his position clear.

Turning her face away, she stared out over the bailey, to the village beyond the river. He hadn't wanted her. He'd sent her away.

"I've no reason to escape you, Sir Dominic. I don't want to leave the castle, much less start a game of cat and mouse."

"How long were you married?"

She glanced at him suspiciously. Why would he care about such things? It was common knowledge. "Five years."

"Really?" He sounded skeptical. "How old were you when you wed?"

"Older than some but not nearly as old as I would like to have been."

"What sort of answer is that?"

"The only sort you'll get if you persist with these personal questions," Rowena told him. "You were ordered to escort me to William Marshal, which gives you no right to pry into my personal affairs."

"Why are you so defensive? Was your marriage so very unhappy?"

"My marriage does not concern you." She spun and walked off along the battlement, the wind whipping at her veil. He made her feel vulnerable, exposed, and she didn't like it.

"What are you so afraid of?" he called.

She kept right on walking.

* * * * *

Church bells pealed, announcing Sext. Rowena pulled the hood of her cloak up around her face and hurried toward a cottage nestled in the shadows of the mighty curtain wall. Brother Samuel would be in the church, singing the midday mass, which left Brother Leland alone.

Constructed of waddle and daub, the cottage appeared similar to all the others in the crowded village of Pendragon, but Rowena knew a sanctuary lay hidden within. She shifted her basket to her elbow and rapped on the door, listening carefully for a response.

"Who goes there?" Brother Leland's familiar voice called out.

"'Tis Rowena, Brother Leland. May I join you?"

"Please do."

Brother Leland sat in a chair near the fire, a blanket wrapped around his frail shoulders, his sightless eyes staring in her direction. Though sparse on top and rather shaggy, his hair was snowy white, a dramatic contrast to his stark gray robes.

"You look so pale." Setting her basket on the table as she passed, she pressed the back of her hand to his forehead. "I brought more of Cook's willow tea. Did it bring you any relief before?"

"I'm an old man, my lady. My earthly body has simply worn out. You needn't fuss over me."

"I enjoy fussing over you." She crossed to the table. "You brought me comfort more times than I can count. Now it's my turn."

Rummaging through the basket, she found a small bundle and returned to the friar. "Cook made her spice cake, so I stashed some away for you." She opened his hand and placed the treat in his grasp. "I'll heat the tea while you partake."

"I heard about your standoff with the knight." He began to nibble. "Will you never learn temperance?"

There was no real rebuke in his question, so Rowena didn't take offense. "I thought Edwin had sent him, and I'll fight Edwin with my dying breath."

"And what of this knight? Will you fight him as well?"

Pausing in her task, she glanced at Brother Leland. So often his questions weren't meant to be answered but to bring order to her thoughts. "Do you know who he is?"

The friar raised the cake to his mouth, hiding much of his face. Rowena turned back to the tea, shaking her head. Of course he knew. Sometimes it seemed that Brother Leland received information from God himself.

"I can't go with him, yet I don't know how to avoid it." She moved a chair near the fire as she went on. "When Fair Fiona appeared on my wedding night, I was ever so grateful. But now — "

"You still believe that a *Fairy* frightened Gaston away?"

"Do you believe that I, alone, could have held a knight at bay?" Rowena returned.

"Nay," Brother Leland conceded. "No woman I know of could."

She rose and swung the kettle away from the fire. "He wasn't wrong to expect... I would have submitted… I only wanted him to offer some show of compassion."

"There was no gentleness in Gaston." He sighed. "He didn't deserve you—and apparently your Fairy friend agreed."

Rowena smiled. Brother Leland likely knew more about the Pendragon legend than anyone alive, but she was never certain if he believed in it or merely found it all amusing.

She poured tea into a cup and handed it to him. "Well, my 'Fairy friend' has left me with quite a predicament."

"And you've concocted some rash and reckless solution, no doubt."

"Now when have you known me to be either rash or reckless?"

He choked on his tea. "I know you all too well, my lady. That's what frightens me." He held out his hand, and Rowena brought his thin fingers to her cheek. "I officiated at the wedding, child. Gaston even displayed stained bed linens. Anyone here at Pendragon will testify to having seen them."

"Bed linens can be faked. Everyone knows this."

He chuckled and turned his face toward the fire. "Aye, but generally they are faked because the bride is *not* a virgin. Let Brother Samuel write a message to William Marshal explaining the senselessness of Edwin's petition. I can still manage my signature."

"I welcome your support," she said, and gently released his hand.

But she knew a written reference would never be enough. Edwin would demand an examination. There was no help for it. She must take a lover before she arrived at Windsor Castle.

* * * * *

Knowing Edwin of Llangly watched her closely, Titania made each movement slow and titillating. Firelight licked her naked flesh while she lifted the pitcher and poured tepid water into a shallow bowl. After wetting a square of toweling, she raised the cloth to her naked breasts, subtly pivoting on the ball of one foot so Edwin could see her better.

She guided his scrutiny with the cloth, drawing his attention to each curve and hollow. Careful not to obscure his view, she circled her nipples and teased her feminine curls. When she reached one smooth hip, she pivoted again, presenting Edwin with her softly rounded bottom.

"Must you leave at dawn?" She glanced over her shoulder.

He reclined across his huge bed, naked, arms raised, hands locked behind his head. His long legs crossed at the ankle and, much to her disappointment, his shaft remained placid against his thigh. His dark blond hair was tousled from their recent tumble. Male appreciation shone in his wide blue eyes, but no great passion had ignited within his gaze.

"Aye, but the night is not yet over."

His words pleased her, even if his physical reaction did not. She didn't want to use magic to compel him unless it was absolutely necessary. Each time she drew energy from the Fairy realm, she risked her husband sensing the withdrawal.

She rinsed the cloth and approached the bed. "Shall I bathe you, milord?"

"With that rag or your wicked little tongue?"

"Whichever would please you more." She crawled onto the bed, remaining on her knees as his gaze moved over her body — or rather the body she currently occupied. Lissette had fallen from her horse at the most opportune moment. The chit had been meant to die. Titania was simply prolonging the inevitable.

Titania had been monitoring Fiona's progress from the Shadow realm, but inhabiting a human allowed her to influence the situation without risking discovery. Ever since her conception, Fiona had been a thorn in Titania's side. She loved Oberon, and he loved her with a passion few understood. Still, many obstacles had complicated their relationship, and Fiona topped the list.

Barren was such an ugly word, yet childless sounded so pathetic. Titania had blithely blamed the lack on Oberon until his mistresses began to conceive. Fiona was his firstborn, his heir unless he named another.

"The rag will do, for now."

Edwin leaned back, expectation clear in his blue eyes. Knowing she could kill him with a thought made submitting to his arrogance bearable. She washed his chest and torso, teasing him with her gaze as much as the cloth.

"Have you heard back from the regent? Will he recommend the annulment?" She bent closer, fanning his abdomen with her breath.

He grabbed a handful of her long blonde hair, drawing her face away from his flesh. "I must be absolutely certain of the information you've given me."

She let out a childish sigh and flopped back onto the mattress, knowing the sudden motion would set her breasts to bouncing. "I told you only the truth, and I told you all I know."

"Gaston *never* touched Rowena?" He'd questioned her many times. Were all humans this annoying?

Displaying her exasperation with another petulant sigh, Titania recited the facts. "Gaston came to me on their wedding night, babbling about golden lights and magic powers. He was convinced Rowena was some sort of witch. The bed linens were faked. Rowena is a virgin."

"And he didn't attempt to bed her again?"

She slowly licked her lips and rolled up onto her side, resting her hand on his thigh. "He was afraid to." She laughed. "The battle-worn Lord of Pendragon Castle was terrified of his wife. If it weren't for her rich dowry, he'd have tossed her back to you. Besides, he had me to entertain him. Why bother with that frigid shrew?" *Because without Rowena, Gaston couldn't produce an heir.* The thought made Titania bristle. The frustration was all too familiar.

"No other man has managed to pry her thighs apart?" Edwin remained focused on the elements of the tale she needed him to understand. A subtle Fairy compulsion ensured his obsession.

"I slept within the walls of Pendragon Castle every night until we learned of Gaston's death," Titania said quietly. "*No man* has gone near Rowena. I'm not sure if it's fear or distaste that keeps her far from them, but Rowena has no interest in men. Were it not for her temper, she'd make a splendid nun." Titania laughed. "I, on the other hand, lost my fear of men years ago." As if to prove her point, she straddled his hips. She leaned forward and brushed his lips with one turgid nipple.

Edwin chuckled, filling his hands with her warm resilient flesh. "You'd better be right. If she's taken a lover — for even one night — our case is lost."

* * * * *

Rowena stared at her reflection in the looking glass and felt fear coil within her belly. Ladies didn't venture out without their heads covered, but her hair hung loosely to her hips. Thora had braided a thin section on each side and pulled it back with a ribbon. A simple woolen bliaud laced up the front and the wide scooped neck bared the upper swells of her breasts. Thora had added a braided leather belt, accenting the distinct indentation of Rowena's trim waist.

"The orchard is secluded enough. You shouldn't be interrupted," Thora said, fussing with Rowena's hair. "Wear my cloak. Yours is far too fine. My hood is wide and deep. It will conceal your face."

"I know what needs to be done, Thora."

A long, strained silence followed. Thora's obvious worry increased her own. She'd be in danger until this was done. Any number of things could go wrong, but the alternative was unthinkable. Pendragon must be protected.

"Do you remember the story we rehearsed?" Thora asked.

Rubbing the bridge of her nose, she nodded.

"I'll go with you," Thora said suddenly. "At least that way—"

"Nay," Rowena cut her off. "It would be too suspicious. You must tend me in my sickbed."

With a heavy sigh, Thora nodded. "I wish I knew this man, but Milton assured me his cousin will be gentle."

"And he has no idea who I am?"

"Of course not. He is visiting Llangly until Michaelmas, and he has never been to Pendragon."

Rowena turned from the silver looking glass and asked, "How did you explain this to Milton?"

"I told him the same story he told his cousin. A dear friend of mine is being forced into a nunnery and wishes to know a man before she weds with God. He gallantly offered his own services, but I set his thinking to rights."

Smiling just a little, Rowena could almost picture the scene. "I'll just bet you did." She blew out a breath and reached for Thora's cloak. "I'll return as soon as I can."

"You should be able to make it to the orchard and back before nightfall. It's not safe—"

"You're clucking like a mother hen, Thora. I know what must be done." Rowena's show of spirit was entirely for Thora's benefit.

Thora draped the long, hooded cloak around her shoulders, and Rowena made her way to the stables. The day had turned out rather blustery, so Rowena pulled the cloak tightly around herself as she entered the stable yard. Thora had requested a palfrey for her use. When the stable boy merely tugged on his forelock and didn't move to help her mount, Rowena smiled.

Afraid the wind would uncover her head, she didn't mount until she crossed the final drawbridge. Llangly lay to the east and the orchard was on the outskirts of the village. Rowena mounted and put her heels to the horse's sides, anxious to have this errand finished.

* * * * *

"How long have you served Lady Rowena?" Dominic asked as the steward led him toward the entrance of the great hall.

"I was born here. My father was steward to Sir Edgar, who was Lord Pendragon before Gaston. Gaston's mother married Sir Edgar and when my father died Gaston made me steward. I've served Lady Rowena since Sir Gaston's death."

Dominic nodded, shooting the other man a sidelong glance. He was in his mid-thirties, Dominic supposed. His features were regular, his hair, mustache and beard were all dark, as were his eyes. "How did he die?"

"Who?"

"Gaston," Dominic clarified. "Your lady's husband?"

"In the lists. He was knocked from his horse and broke his back."

He winced. Injury and death were an occupational hazard for a knight. "I noticed the chapel, but I saw no rectory. Is there no cleric in residence?"

"There is a small monastery in the village of Pendragon, but it's beyond the castle walls and across the river. The old monastery up in the hills is abandoned, but it's a fascinating building. It was literally carved into the side of the mountain."

"For what reason?"

"It was the perfect defense. There is only one way in or out. A single man could hold off an entire army from the elevated entrance. While the monastery was in use the monks kept all sorts of treasures hidden inside their mountain."

"I'd like to see this wonder before I depart," Dominic said thoughtfully.

"Give the word and I'll arrange it."

Dominic chuckled. If only Farrell's lady would be so accommodating. "You have my thanks for the tour. I believe I'll check on Lady Rowena's progress."

"Her progress?"

"Aye. She had better be preparing to depart on the morrow."

Farrell didn't comment. He bid Dominic farewell and went on about his business.

"Dominic!"

Turning around on the stone stairs to the keep, Dominic watched his best friend hurry across the inner bailey. He and Ezra had fostered with William Marshal and served together ever since. Ezra was the fourth son of a minor baron with little chance of inheriting wealth from his father. Their needs had been similar, so Dominic and Ezra set out together to win fortune and fame with their swords.

Dominic had managed to accrue a small fortune, but his most passionate desire still eluded him. A fiefdom. It didn't have to be large or well developed, but Dominic longed for a holding of his own.

Ezra had found success as well. After saving the life of one of William Marshal's sons, Ezra had been granted a marcher castle on the border of Wales. Ezra was anxious to complete his service to the regent and claim his new holdings. Dominic understood his friend's restlessness but envied the reason for Ezra's unrest.

"Have you seen the mews? She has the most beautiful falcons I've ever seen," Ezra said as he reached Dominic on the stone stairs. His short blond hair was messy, and enthusiasm shone in his bright blue eyes.

"There is much at Pendragon Castle I find impressive. Even Sir William does not live better."

"Unless he's at court," Ezra pointed out.

"Aye, there is always court. Did you do as I asked, or were you so captivated with the falcons you forgot?"

Ezra followed Dominic into the hall before he answered. "The castle is in no danger that I could see. The guards are well armed and practiced. The design of the fortification makes it easy to defend. I cannot tell you why Lady Rowena is so fearful of attack."

"She mentioned something about loyalty. Did you perceive any rebellion among her men?"

They crossed the hall and stood before the central hearth. Ezra extended his hands toward the fire. "I spoke at length with Ludlow, the captain of the guards. He said the men are more content serving Lady Rowena than they were her husband. From what I gather, Gaston had a passion for war. When his sword was not needed for a battle already begun, he would simply begin one. And if all else failed, he would turn to the tournaments."

"And the lady? What had Ludlow to say about Lady Rowena?"

"He spoke highly of the lady, praising both her compassion for her villeins and her management. According to Ludlow, the manor has never run more smoothly."

"It's odd." Dominic faced his friend. "But the threat must be real. Lady Rowena doesn't strike me as the type to be easily intimidated."

"Ludlow did mention a curse," Ezra said with a short laugh.

"A curse?"

"Aye, it would appear some Pendragon ancestor infuriated the Fairies, and the line has been doomed to die without issue ever since."

"Then the line would have ended with the first generation."

"The bloodline did," Ezra told him. "When the first Lord of Pendragon died without an heir, his widow's second husband became Lord of Pendragon."

"There is nothing unusual in that."

Ezra nodded. "But Ludlow also told me that every generation since has birthed only girls or died without issue altogether."

"Gaston was not born a Pendragon?"

"I didn't ask the specifics." Ezra rolled his shoulders and glanced about the hall. "I might be tempted to take on a Fairy curse for this castle."

"And face down the Shrew of Pendragon?" Dominic teased, with an easy smile.

"She managed to keep you at bay."

"Not for long."

Ezra stared at him for a moment.

"Are *you* thinking of wooing this woman?"

Dominic laughed. "Even if William rules in her favor, I don't think Lady Rowena will welcome a wooing, in any form."

"If you have the backing of William Marshal, will it matter what the lady welcomes?"

"That question is a long way off. One step at a time, my friend, one step at a time."

Ezra pressed him no further. "When do we leave?"

"Tomorrow at dawn."

"And she has agreed to accompany you without incident?"

He sounded skeptical, and Dominic couldn't blame him. "Aye, but I don't know how far I can trust her. She may be up to something. I was on my way to check her progress."

"Is that not her handmaiden?" Ezra nodded beyond Dominic's left shoulder.

He turned and saw Thora trying to creep past them. "Indeed it is. I'll speak with you later."

He hurried toward her.

"Sir Dominic," she said casually, and continued toward the door.

"Where are you bound?" He caught her sleeve just above the elbow.

"The kitchens," Thora replied. "My lady is not well. Something she ate earlier has twisted her entrails. She's retched continually for the past few hours."

Suspicion surged through Dominic. She was lying. Her expression was sincere, her voice convincing, but Dominic knew she lied. "If she is vomiting, then what would you need from the kitchens?"

"Cook also brews potions. She knows herbs and medicines. My lady is really not well."

"I would see her."

"That is cruel," Thora chided. "She is lying in bed, too weak even to hold her own head while she vomits, and you want to interrogate her? Do you think she ate something apurpose to make herself ill?"

"I would see her, not interrogate her."

"It's impossible. She is not presentable, and she would have my head if I were to allow you to invade her privacy thus. Would you care to be viewed while you bend over a slop bucket?"

"I don't trust the lady. I'll only stay long enough to determine whether your claim is true."

"You doubt my word?" she objected. "You call me a liar? What could she possibly gain by postponing the journey? She has already agreed to go."

Each of her points was valid, but Dominic had relied on his instincts for far too long. "Have done, damsel. Take me to her." His hand moved from her sleeve to encircle her upper arm. He pulled her toward the stone steps that led above to the lady's bedchamber.

"I will not do this!" She snatched her arm from his restraining hand. "If you're such a boor as to invade a lady's sickroom, then you'll be doing so alone. I'll have no part of it!"

Each of her objections only fueled his determination. He grasped her arm again and continued toward the stairs. She screeched and dug in her heels, but he ignored her protests.

As they reached the stairwell, the irrational woman darted past him and planted herself squarely in the middle of the first stair. Dominic nearly collided with her.

She leaned toward him, a come-hither smile parting her lips. Her blue eyes lit with a familiar intensity. "It'd be much more interesting to visit my bedchamber."

Under different circumstances, Dominic might have been amused, but he saw through her ploy. He grasped her by the waist and lifted her out of his way. She tugged on his tunic all the way up the stairs.

"Please, my lord, you must listen to me."

"When you're ready to speak truthfully, I'll listen."

He marched across the solar, but Thora arrived a step ahead of him. She leaned against the door to the bedchamber and looked up at him through her lashes. "She's ill, milord. Let her rest. I'm sure we can find something entertaining to pass the time until she mends."

"Doubtless we could. But I believe your lady has recovered enough to leave her bed." As he spoke, he shifted the latch and opened the door behind her. She stumbled backward. He stepped past her and into the bedchamber. The curtains were open, the great bed obviously empty.

Glaring at the lady's empty bed, he demanded, "Where has she gone?"

"You don't understand." She spoke calmly, but her sky blue eyes were bright with cunning.

"Then enlighten me. Where is your lady, and why is she pretending to be ill?"

"No harm will come of her errand." She took a step nearer, her eyes wide and inviting. "Just wait until she returns." She laid a warm hand on his upper arm. "There is no reason to fret."

Shaking off her hand, he grasped her shoulders and dragged her up against his chest. Their faces were mere inches apart. "Are you quite certain of that? Would you wager your life on her safety?" He shoved her away and pressed on. "Has she left the castle compound? Tell me now!"

She remained resolute. "She'll return before night falls."

He moved closer again. "I hold you personally responsible for anything that befalls Lady Rowena. Are you sure she is safe? Where has she gone?"

Dominic admired Thora's loyalty, but uncertainty crept into her expression. Finally, he would have answers.

"I cannot tell you."

She turned away from him. Before she could regain her composure, he advanced, driving her back until she pressed against the wall. "Has she left the castle? If she's beyond the curtain wall, she's in danger."

"She'll return before nightfall."

"So you say." He pressed his palms against the stones on either side of her, caging her with his body. "You are too stubborn for your own good." She averted her face. He gripped her chin and captured her gaze with his. "Tell me where she's gone, Thora. I'll not harm her."

He saw surrender in her eyes.

"You promise?" she asked. "No harm will come to her?"

"That is why I'm here."

A silent moment passed. Tension built and Dominic's hands clenched into fists against the cold stone wall. Would she yet withhold her secret? Stubborn wench.

"She's gone to the village of Llangly, to the orchard on the outskirts of town."

"Why?"

Thora squirmed, refusing to meet his gaze. "She's going to meet a man."

"What man? For what purpose?"

"I don't know his name, but he's said to have information about Sir Edwin."

"Sir Edwin?"

"Aye," Thora affirmed.

"What information did Lady Rowena require before she could face Sir William?"

"She didn't explain. You'll have to ask her when she returns."

"How long has she been gone? Who escorted her?"

Thora's calm expression slipped a bit more. "She departed shortly after she left you on the wall walk."

"And who accompanied her?"

Thora closed her eyes and whispered, "No one."

Chapter Three

Rowena curved her fingers around the molded handle of the dirk tucked into the belt at her waist while she warily scanned the orchard. The weapon was simple, easily concealed, and the cool weight against her palm gave her comfort, made her brave.

Never again would she be a victim. Never would people she cared about suffer. Not when it was within her power to intervene. Only as their Lady could she protect Pendragon's people, so she would do what must be done—and not look back.

Hearing hoofbeats in the distance, Rowena crouched behind a tree. She watched the rider approach and dismount. Thom. Thora had said his name was Thom. Neither handsome nor homely, ordinary features ruled his lean face. Late afternoon light dappled his shaggy brown hair.

"Missy?" he called. "Are you here, girl?"

She pressed against the tree. Her hand tightened on the dirk. A bird trilled merrily, mocking what Rowena must endure. Could she really do this? Could she...she had to! There was no other way.

Cleansing her mind with the crisp autumn air, she stepped into view.

"There you are." Thom laughed, his dark eyes crinkling at the corners. "I was beginning to wonder if Milton was amusing himself at my expense."

She wrapped herself protectively in her guise, flashed a quick smile and lowered her lashes. "Milton's tale is true, kind sir. My parents gave me an ultimatum, and I don't respond well to ultimatums."

He ambled toward her, his dark gaze frankly assessing. "Did you wish to stay here, or is there somewhere else you'd rather go?"

"My father is still at the inn, and I'm not familiar with the area. Here will have to do." She pushed back the hood. "I can't be gone long or he'll come looking for me."

She unclasped the cloak and swung it off her shoulders, gripping the material to disguise how her hands trembled. His dark eyes narrowed. Rowena nervously licked her lips.

Was he pleased by her appearance? His gaze lingered on the swell of her breasts and the indentation of her waist. Still, five years of insecurity battled with the appreciation she read in his expression.

You're emotionless, Rowena. Cold. No man will ever find pleasure between your thighs. Why couldn't she banish Gaston's hateful voice? He was moldering in his grave, yet his voice haunted her.

"Are you sure you want to do this?" Thom asked.

"I'm certain." The words tasted like ash in her mouth. Folding her cloak over her arm, she smiled and focused on the warmth in his dark eyes.

Please, just let him do this quickly.

His calloused fingers stroked her cheek. She controlled the need to pull away. He would touch far more than her cheek before this day was through.

With growing dread, she watched his face descend. A veritable stranger was about to bestow her first real kiss. Tears gathered in her eyes as another romantic dream evaporated like gossamer mist.

The distant thunder of horse's hooves snapped his head up. Rowena followed the direction of his stare and released her pent-up breath. Not recognizing the horse, she twisted away and turned to flee.

He caught her arm. "Be calm. It's only my brother Jack. Give me a moment and we'll be rid of him."

"Nay," she said urgently. "No one can know I'm here."

"Then—remain out of sight."

She melted into the trees, moving stealthily toward her horse yet remaining close enough to hear their conversation. This was likely her last chance. She dared not squander it if there was any possibility of salvage.

Jack was a younger, darker version of Thom. Though Thom stood taller and appeared more heavily muscled, the calculating gleam in Jack's eyes made Rowena shiver.

"You're daft, man," the younger brother snapped. "There's no one here. Milton…"

She lost the rest of his sentence.

"Then whose... I told you she..."

Only snippets of Thom's response made it to her ears. Jack's voice dropped even lower, and Rowena couldn't hear him at all. If Jack wasn't leaving, she was!

"Go home!" Thom ordered. "I know how you... She's not..."

Thom's words were sporadic but they were enough to solidify her decision. Careful not to draw their attention, she crept through the trees.

In the meadow, at the far edge of the orchard, her horse grazed patiently. She bent, fumbling with the knotted reins. A hand grabbed the back of her skirts and yanked her off balance. Her hip hit the dirt and she yelped, more from surprise than pain. "Leave me be!"

Jack swatted the horse's rump, sending the animal bolting across the meadow.

"Why are you doing this?" She scrambled to her feet, edging back toward the heart of the orchard.

"Maybe my brother's not such a dolt, after all." Jack smirked. He stalked her, eyes bright with cunning. "You're about the prettiest piece I've seen in a good long while. Let's spread your cloak right here, so God can watch me mount His virgin bride."

Wadding the cloak into a thick ball, she threw it at his smug face and ran. She darted between the trees, changing direction without warning. Crunching leaves and snapping twigs warned that he followed. She didn't pause to look.

A sparkle of gold flitted in her peripheral vision.

Yes! Fair Fiona, help me! Help me now!

64

Where was Thom? Would he restrain his brother — or assist him?

Something tangled in her hair, bringing her up short. Rowena screamed.

"Why so shy, sweeting?" Jack sneered. "You were willing enough to spread your thighs for my brother."

She jammed her elbow backward, desperate to strike something vital. He jerked on her hair. She cried out. "Get your hands off me!" Fury and panic deluged her senses. Bile burned her throat. Her stomach cramped.

His arm banded her waist, trapping her arms against her sides. She kicked wildly, unable to see her target.

"Jack! Let her go. There are willing women aplenty. There's no call for this."

Thom's angry voice came from somewhere behind them, and Rowena sobbed. Please, God, please, let him be rational. Let the kindness she'd glimpsed in his eyes save her now.

"She made you an offer," Jack argued. "I'm just seeing she delivers."

"She made the offer to me, and I say let her go."

"If you're no longer interested, be off. If you're staying, let's begin."

Rowena threw her weight forward then slammed her head back, connecting forcefully with Jack's chin.

Grunting, he cuffed the side of her head. "You stupid bitch!"

He pushed her violently, tumbling her to the leaf-strewn ground. She landed on her hands and knees, but he flipped her over. Breath whooshed from her lungs, and she stared at him in silent horror.

Thom grabbed his brother's arm, glaring into his eyes. "She's a virgin! Leave her be."

"You're a fool!" Jack shook off his brother's hold. "What virgin would seek out the likes of you or me? This is a game. She's a whore."

Thom's dark gaze searched her face, and Rowena watched her last hope die. He believed his brother.

"Please," she cried, reaching for him. "I'm not a whore." Jack shoved her down. "Just leave me here. I don't want—"

Jack silenced her with the back of his hand.

Thom moved a few paces away and turned around. She sobbed. This couldn't be happening! Where was Fair Fiona?

Her head pounded, the pain nearly blinding, but she forced herself to focus through the haze. If she wanted to survive this day, it was up to her. Easing her hand along her side, she searched for the handle of her dirk. There! The familiar shape pressed into her palm, and she slipped the blade from her belt.

Come on, you bastard. Just a bit closer.

He knelt between her legs, grabbing her skirts with both hands. Rowena reared, driving the knife toward his chest. His forearm deflected it at the last moment. The blade sank hilt deep, but too far to the side to pierce his heart. He howled and toppled backward. Following him over, she jerked the knife from his flesh.

She raised her arm for a second strike, but Thom caught her wrist. He viciously twisted, and her fingers went numb, the dirk slipping from her useless grasp.

Jack wheezed and coughed. His arms grabbed Rowena, dragging her down against his blood-soaked chest. She screamed, writhing and shoving frantically.

"If he dies, you die!" Thom snarled, flinging her from his brother's gasping body.

She hit a tree with a sickening thud and reality faded for a moment. Pain sliced through the stupor and she grasped her head.

Thom knelt beside her. She blinked repeatedly, trying to bring him into focus. He raised a dagger, and she shrieked, instinctively covering her face with her arms.

Without speaking, he sliced her bliaud nearly to the waist and hacked away a large section of her shift then returned to his brother. Bandages. He'd only needed bandages.

Terrified of drawing attention to herself, she stayed quiet and still. Would he kill her once Jack was tended? He obviously didn't care that she'd been protecting herself.

He returned a few minutes later, his dagger covered with blood. "Know this." He leaned down and meticulously wiped the blade against the pale skin of her chest. Rowena closed her eyes, waiting for the searing pain, the icy sting of death. He pressed the point of his dagger against her breast, waiting until she opened her eyes. "If my brother dies, I *will* find you."

Huddled against the tree, she watched him gather Jack in his arms and bear him toward their horses.

Tears streamed unchecked down her cheeks, but she was unable to make a sound.

She was alive!

What had happened to Fair Fiona?

Why had no one helped her?

She had fought this battle alone.

With no one but herself to depend upon—she had managed to survive.

* * * * *

High in the trees, Fair Fiona trembled. "I hate this," she lamented, her voice undetectable to the woman below. "How can Father be so cruel? She needed me desperately."

"Nay, this is encouraging." Fearsome Dragon spread his wings, sheltering the Fairy with his power. "She is beginning to understand."

Fiona blinked back tears, her heart still aching for her friend. "Aye. She has glimpsed her own strength, but how do we make her see her true beauty?"

"We cannot make her see anything. She must discover these things on her own."

Fiona twirled in a lazy spiral, leaving the comforting shadow of his wings. "I can *guide* her toward discovery. I can make sure she's looking in the right direction when—" She laughed. "Here comes our handsome knight. How disappointed he'll be to find the damsel has managed her own rescue."

Dominic vaulted from his destrier's back before the beast even stopped completely. Fiona drifted closer.

Oh, this mortal was tempting. All brawn and passionate energy. Made her tingle all over.

"Lady Rowena?" He rushed toward the young woman.

Rowena raised her face, her features twisted with horror and shock. She held her hands before her, staring at their crimson stain. Had she just noticed the blood?

"My God, woman. Are you injured?" He knelt beside her, carefully checking her limbs and her exposed skin for the source of the blood. "What happened? Is this your blood?"

A harsh sob tore from the lady, and Fiona glanced at her guardian. She longed to soothe Rowena, to calm her, but even taking her Fairy form was pushing the boundaries of her exile. She was forbidden to interfere.

"Leave it be," the dragon warned. "Let the knight comfort her."

Fiona whirled, laughing uproariously. "Knights kill and maim and conquer. Knights do not comfort."

But even as she spoke, this knight sat in the autumn leaves and cradled Rowena in his arms. He smoothed her hair back from her brow and spoke in a calm, clear voice.

"Talk to me, my lady. What has befallen you?"

"I had to stab him," she cried.

He continued to stroke Rowena's hair, to whisper soothingly into her ear. Fiona was fascinated by his gentleness, amazed by the change in his harsh features. Could he be the one? Could he be more than just a vehicle by which to thwart Edwin?

Could he be…?

She looped Fearsome Dragon and dove toward the knight's massive steed.

"What are you doing?" the dragon demanded.

"Guiding her toward discovery."

* * * * *

Knowing the blood wasn't hers did little to ease Dominic's alarm. Her slender body trembled in his arms. His pulse leapt with each shuddering breath. From what sort of attack had she been forced to defend herself? How far had the assault progressed? And where was her assailant now?

"There's a stream…" Her voice broke, so she pointed, and tried to rise.

Dominic stood, still cradling her against his chest, and strode in the direction she indicated.

She shifted in his embrace, restless and anxious. "The blood." She shuddered. "I can feel it drying in my hair, sinking into my skin."

At the water's edge, he set her on her feet, but she waded into the stream and sank to her knees. "Get it off me! I want it off!" Scooping sand from the streambed, she scoured her skin and scrubbed her clothing. The water turned pink all around her.

He tugged off his boots, placed his sword within reach, and joined her in the water. "Rowena." He used her name intentionally, calling her back from the brink of hysteria. "Rowena, we need to take off your bliaud. Your skin will come clean if we dispense with the garment."

Expecting her to argue, he stumbled back a step when she tugged the sodden outer garment off and tossed it to the grassy bank.

"Now try the sand," he suggested softly.

Calling upon all the powers of Chivalry, he dragged his gaze away from her lissome body and focused solely on her battered face. The corner of her mouth was caked with blood, and a purple bruise shadowed the crest of her cheek. His fists clenched at his sides.

"Rowena, who did this to you?"

Her wide, haunted gaze lifted to his face. "My hair. It's in my hair."

Fortifying himself for the prospect of touching her, he pulled off his tunic and surcoat together, and tossed them near his boots. His loose woolen leggings were meager protection against the cold stream, but he knelt beside her.

He gathered the thick mass of her dark red hair as she bent forward, inadvertently offering him a magnificent view of her high, round breasts.

Damn William and his confounded vow! This woman was ripe for the plucking.

Snapping his wayward attention back to the task at hand, he fanned her hair out in the current, using the natural flow of the water to rinse the blood from the long strands.

"Better?" he asked.

She had begun to shiver. He stood and helped her to her feet. The thin material of her shift was virtually transparent. Her nipples had beaded in the cold, and even the shadow of her areolas was visible beneath the cloth. God's wounds, he ached for her.

Pushing her hair away from her face, Rowena noticed the direction of his gaze. She glanced down at herself and gasped. Her arms flew to cover her breasts, and her gaze rounded comically when she spotted the conspicuous bulge in his leggings.

He grinned sheepishly. "I beg your pardon, but I cannot control the way my body responds to such a display."

Her eyes clouded with the most confounding combination of emotions. He recognized curiosity and uncertainty, but what had caused the flicker of hope?

"My clothing is dry. I propose we share." Retaining the velvet surcoat for himself, he handed his tunic to her. "You can don it over your shift, if you like. But I will turn my back, if you wish to shed your shift."

"That would be my preference."

Dressed in their odd combination of garments, they set out across the orchard.

"How did you know where to find me?" Rowena asked.

"Thora told me. What information did this man have that you did not already know?"

"None. This was all for naught."

She sounded so forlorn that he couldn't help but believe her. "Was the man you agreed to meet the man who attacked you?"

Pausing she raised her gaze to his and stiffly explained, "A second man came unexpectedly. I was forced to stab him or submit to his unwanted attentions. The first man threatened my life if the second dies because of his wound, but they don't know who I am."

The urge to berate her for her foolishness nearly overwhelmed him, but tears shone behind her long eyelashes and her lips trembled. "You are safe, my lady," was all he said.

Trepidation suddenly gripped Dominic. He stepped in front of Rowena and drew his sword.

"Majesty." Keeping her behind him, he advanced. "I left him there. Where is my horse?"

"Your horse is gone?"

"Could these men still be about?" Agitation made his voice terse.

"I don't believe so. Could your horse have wondered off?"

Dominic snorted. "Majesty does not wander. Something foul is afoot." An odd sound escaped her. He glanced at her, amazed to find she had smothered a laugh. "What is so amusing?"

"It would seem that *we* are afoot."

He shook his head and sheathed his sword, but his senses remained alert. "We have nearly lost the light, and it will take several hours to reach your castle on foot. Your steward spoke of a monastery built for defense. That would be an acceptable location to protect you for the night. Is it nearby?"

"I cannot…" She averted her face.

"We can't stay here."

After a long pause, she admitted, "It's just beyond the meadow. Not far at all."

* * * * *

Rowena tossed upon the fur, unconsciously searching for warmth. Wiggling beneath the blanket separating her body from Sir Dominic's, she snuggled close against his back.

For a long time she did nothing more than press against him. He had been the perfect gentleman the entire evening. He provided what comforts he could with the meager provisions kept stashed in the monastery for emergencies such as this, but he had treated her with kindness and complete deference.

Even when she suggested they spread the fur pelt before the hearth and conserve their body heat, he had insisted on a blanket barrier. You would think *he* was the virgin!

Dominic turned in his sleep, rolling onto his back, and pulled her tight against his side. Her breath caught in her throat. Heavens above, heat emanated from him like rays off the sun. It felt wonderful.

Her shift tangled about her hips, and one of her legs lay across his thigh. Her naked pelvis was flush against the hard contour of his hip. Rowena knew she should pull away, disentangle their bodies and go back to sleep. But she couldn't bring herself to move, to deprive herself of the warmth of his hard, muscular body.

Afraid to disturb his sleep with her restlessness, she tried to relax against him, but her body wouldn't cooperate. Her hand rested lightly in the center of his chest. The lacings of his surcoat gaped, offering her bare skin. Slowly, she stroked her palm across his chest, absorbing the texture of his flesh, the contour and the heat.

He mumbled groggily, but she didn't stop her brazen exploration. His skin was intoxicating. She suddenly wished they were naked. Drawing nearer, Rowena pressed her parted lips to the side of his neck. His strong, steady pulse pounded against her mouth, and she sighed.

She felt so odd, hot yet shivery.

His large palm found her leg, and Rowena gasped softly against his throat. Sweeping up along her thigh, his hand cupped her bottom and squeezed, drawing her more tightly against him. He encircled her in his arms, sweeping her beneath him. His weight pressed her down into the fur. His knee wedged her legs apart and his hips settled between her thighs.

Tangling his hands in her hair, his mouth covered hers. His lips brushed back and forth until Rowena moaned and clung to his thick upper arms. He coaxed her lips apart, tracing the soft crease between with the tip of his tongue. She hesitantly opened her mouth. He licked and nipped, driving her mad with the fluttering caresses.

Was this what it was like to kiss? She never imagined there was so much…motion, so many different sensations.

His mouth finally sealed over hers and he eased his tongue just barely between her lips. She responded tentatively at first, touching his tongue with hers. Warm and wet, firm yet incredibly soft, his mouth intrigued and fascinated her. A hot ache flared within her. She arched against him, kissing him wildly.

He wanted her!

The realization astounded Rowena. His body was hard and throbbing against her, undeniable proof that he wanted her. Her senses soared. Tingling triumph heightened her excitement. She'd finally understand. He'd show her what it meant to be a woman, all the pleasures Thora enjoyed, and wives...

Dominic pulled back suddenly, extending his arms to put distance between their heated bodies. Rowena groaned in ragged protest and reached out blindly for him.

"Damn you," he muttered. "I cannot do this. I gave my word."

"I need this, Dominic. Please, I need you to do this." She whispered the words against his throat, but he disentangled her arms and rolled to her side.

Rowena felt cold air assail her as he flipped back the covers and moved away. She could hear him fumbling in the darkness, and she quickly sat, yanking the shift down around her. She turned her back to him, drawing up her legs and resting her forehead against her knees. Twice now she had failed to seduce this man. She closed her eyes. At least this time he had shown some interest. He had wanted her—just not enough.

"Rowena."

She raised her head and glanced over her shoulder. He set the burning candle on the stone mantel and moved toward her, his expression grim.

"Please explain this to me."

This was not a man used to requesting information. "I cannot." She turned back to the darkness.

"Why?" He eased down beside her.

"I don't trust you," she admitted honestly. "I don't know you. How can I trust you?"

"I will not hurt you, Rowena. I have no reason to betray you."

"You have no reason to be loyal to me either."

"I need to know what frightens you. I cannot protect you from an enemy I don't understand. I give you my word that I'll not betray your confidence. The word of a knight is a sacred vow. I will not break it."

He had vowed not to touch her, and they were sitting side by side instead of thrashing about on the fur. Surely that was proof enough that she could trust his word. "To whom did you promise you would not bed me?"

"William Marshal. He wouldn't explain the request, and I thought it odd at the time, but apparently the stipulation was justified. Why were you so anxious to mate with me?"

Rowena had never felt this helpless. She might well be falling into Edwin's trap, but she was too exhausted, both physically and emotionally, to fight on alone. "Edwin intends to prove that my marriage to Gaston was never consummated. Then he will seek to have the marriage annulled, thereby abolishing my claim to all Pendragon holdings."

"Edwin is your mother's husband but not your father."

He would want to know every detail, every twist and turn. Rowena steeled herself against the painful memories and prepared to indulge his curiosity. "Edwin at one time was betrothed to be *my* husband. He chose to marry my mother after my father's death rather than wait for me. I was in no way opposed to this, you understand. I have always despised the man."

"Did Edwin negotiate your betrothal to Gaston of Pendragon?"

"Aye."

"Does Edwin share kinship with Gaston?"

"Aye," she said again. "Gaston was Edwin's nephew."

"Is he the closest surviving relation?"

"Aye, except for me," she clarified.

"Is Edwin's claim valid? Was the marriage consummated?"

"Aye and nay."

"Aye, his claim is valid and, nay, the marriage was not consummated?"

Frustration and humiliation twisted inside her, making her response harsh and hurried. "Aye, I am a virgin still! My husband was so displeased with me that he brought his whore from the village and installed her in my place. I was subjected to humiliation and ridicule from them both until the day he died."

He just stared at her in incredulous silence. "I do not understand," he said finally.

"Then you are daft. I explained far more than you need to know." She scrambled to her feet, hating the weakness blinding her with tears. Dominic caught her around the waist and pulled her back against his chest.

She struggled against the tenderness, needing anger to drive away the pain. Spinning within his arms, she shoved against his chest, arching away from his embrace.

"Calm, Rowena, be calm. We are not finished yet."

"Let me go," she said. "I find your touch repulsive."

He laughed. "Do you now? It did not seem so a few moments ago."

"You were a means to an end. That is all."

The barb must have found its mark. He released her. She grabbed a blanket and wrapped it around her shoulders then sat and scowled into the glowing embers of the fire.

"Edwin will demand an examination," she muttered. "I cannot be a virgin when I reach William Marshal."

"And I cannot be the man to take your maidenhead," he countered heatedly.

"Then once again we are at an impasse. I will not surrender everything I hold dear because my husband failed to keep his promise! It is not fair. I did not fail as a wife. He failed as a husband."

"What promise?"

She clutched the edges of the blanket to her chest, her throat burning with surpassed tears. "I was delivered to Gaston at fifteen. Not an uncommon age for a bride, but he was supposed to have spent the summer with me before we exchanged our vows. He arrived two days before the wedding."

"But you said the marriage was never consummated."

This was plain speaking indeed. Rowena felt her face heat. He was confused and she could not blame him. The events seemed twisted to her, and she had lived through them. "Gaston came to me, drunk and abusive. I was *terrified*, but he saw only that I refused him what was his due."

"As your husband, it was his due," he pointed out quietly. "Why did he not just—take you?"

She closed her eyes. "He tried."

"What stopped him?" he persisted.

"You won't believe me."

"We will never know unless you try."

Meeting his gaze directly, she said, "Fair Fiona."

"Who is Fair Fiona?"

She hesitated. Only Thora and Brother Leland knew the details of what had transpired between Gaston and her. Did she dare entrust them to this man? She lowered her lashes, shielding her eyes. He would probably think her daft, so what difference did it make.

"An entity of golden light appeared that night and stung Gaston until he ran naked from the chamber. I believe it was the same Fairy who has placed a curse upon the Pendragon line. Her name is Fair Fiona."

His dark brows arched and he absently nodded. He didn't believe her. She hadn't expected that he would.

"I learned the following morning that he had fetched Lissette, his leman, from the village."

Again he only nodded. Why should his doubt upset her? It *was* a wild tale.

"He produced bedding, proving that we had consummated the marriage. But he announced publicly that I had failed to stir his passions, that he found pleasure only with Lissette." The closer they drew to the heart of the matter the harder she found the words.

"'Failed to stir his passions'? That is ridiculous. Was there no one you could turn to? Nowhere you could go?"

"My mother had taken to her bed, as she was great with child, so that left only Edwin."

"What kept Gaston from your bed in the following years?"

His obvious discomfort in asking the question gave Rowena the courage to answer. "I don't know. I told him I would keep my marriage vows if he would but treat me with kindness. He…preferred Lissette. Thora believes the Pendragon curse delivered me from Gaston because I was not meant for him. All I know is I'll never allow myself to be that powerless again. I'm free. I'm controlled by no one."

"And you honestly believe you can remain thus?"

"If you hadn't stopped a few moments ago, I'd be well on my way to a happy tomorrow," she muttered.

"What would have prevented me from telling Sir William I compromised you and asking for his blessing on our marriage?"

His tone was light and conversational, but Rowena's head snapped toward him and her gaze bore into his. "Pendragon is mine. Nothing and no one will take it from me."

"And how will you produce a Pendragon heir without a husband?" His brow arched, accenting the challenge.

"If I find a man willing to think of me as more than chattel, I will consider wedding again. If not, I will simply become one more Lady Pendragon to die childless, as the curse foretells."

"You honestly believe in this curse?"

She huddled beneath the blanket trying to hide her shivering. The room was frigid, but he seemed to be oblivious to the cold. "How can I doubt it? I have seen Fair Fiona with my own eyes."

"Lie down. Let me warm you."

She didn't argue. Regrettably, her virtue was perfectly safe with him. She lay on her side, and after he had snuffed the candle, he lay close behind her. One arm slipped beneath her neck, the other reached around her waist and pulled her snugly into the curve of his body.

"Tell me about the curse," he prompted.

He settled the blanket over them and stroked her hair. She started her story. "The curse was all I heard about when first I came to Pendragon. Thora speaks of the events with such vehemence you would think she experienced them. Lady Fiona is a documented Pendragon wife, but all of the other elements of the story cannot really be substantiated or refuted."

"What is the story?"

"Fiona fell hopelessly in love with the first Lord Pendragon. Tyrus, I believe was his name. She gave her love freely, but he was untrue. Do not all curses begin with betrayal?"

"Most do," he agreed. "Lord Pendragon betrayed Lady Fiona, so she put a curse on him?"

"It is more complicated than that. When Lady Fiona discovered that her husband was untrue, she summoned all of the powers of the Fairy realm and cursed not only the man but all his descendants." His long fingers glided through her unbound hair and Rowena began to lose interest in the story.

"Then Gaston was not the first Lord Pendragon to die without an heir?"

"Nay, they all have."

"What will it take to break the curse?"

"I am trying to remember her exact words. Thora sings a ballad that explains the whole story, but I cannot recall all the verses. I remember, 'Til the Lady finds the fate that once I sought, disappointment, pain and death shall be thy lot.' That's how the curse is worded."

"That is rather dire." He chuckled. "So, who is the Lady? If Fiona was, then Pendragon Castle is doomed for all time."

"Nay, it was Fiona who spoke of the Lady. She was not referring to herself."

"Do you believe you can break the curse?"

Rowena laughed and shook her head, dislodging his hand. "I don't know. Only something miraculous could have kept Gaston from hurting me that night, and then he died. I'm now in a position to choose my next husband, which is rare. If I can find a man whom I can love and who can love me in return, then according to the legend the curse will be broken."

They didn't speak for a time. Rowena allowed herself to enjoy the simple comfort of being held.

"You told me Fair Fiona appears to you," he said. "Do you sense her presence or actually see her?"

"I see her," Rowena said firmly.

"Virgin widows, golden lights and Fairy curses." His voice grew softer, his breath stirring the hair at her temple. "What do I tell William?"

"Tell him nothing. Gaston displayed proof five years ago that the marriage was consummated. I will just have to convince Sir William that Edwin's claim is the ludicrous ravings of a greedy madman."

Chapter Four

Motivated by hunger and the tension still crackling between them, Dominic and Rowena set off at dawn. She hid her near nakedness beneath his cloak but already a purple bruise had begun to darken the crest of her cheek.

They hadn't gone far when a search party from the castle found them.

"Majesty came trotting in last night without you," Ezra explained. "It didn't look like he'd been through a skirmish, but we weren't sure what to think."

"I think someone tried to steal him," Dominic said. "Lady Rowena was set upon by thieves. She was forced to defend herself and one was wounded. The other may seek retaliation."

They would have to have some idea who she was for that to happen, but Rowena wasn't about to volunteer that particular detail.

"Under no circumstances is she to leave the castle compound without me personally escorting her. Is that understood?"

Her jaw dropped. Ludlow, the captain of *her* castle guard, obediently nodded. Adding insult to injury, Dominic swept her into his arms and placed her on Majesty's back, immediately mounting behind her.

"Have you lost your mind?" she sneered for his ears alone.

"You may not take your safety seriously, but I do. Until I set you at the feet of William Marshal, consider yourself my prisoner."

His tyrannical mood continued when they arrived at the castle. He lifted Rowena from Majesty's back and directed one of the stable boys to find Ephraim. Apparently, Milton's skills weren't acceptable to the mighty Undaunted.

The door to the keep banged open and Farrell swooped down the stairs as Rowena reached the inner bailey. A flush darkened his cheeks and his dark eyes shone with relief and tenderness. "Lady Rowena," he called then restrained his enthusiasm. "We have all been sick with worry."

Word must have been sent on ahead when they crossed the drawbridge, Rowena realized. Farrell was obviously expecting her. "I am well. Thanks to Sir Dominic."

"What do you require?" Farrell began. His smile became strained at the mention of the knight. "Food? Drink? A hot bath? How may I serve you?"

"Please have a tray brought to my solar and water for a bath."

"Oh my lady, your face. Sir Dominic didn't—"

"I have never struck a woman, Farrell. Impudent stewards on the other hand… Be about your duties."

Farrell stood his ground, addressing his question to Rowena. "Shall I send Thora to you in your solar?"

"Aye," she and Dominic answered in unison.

"If I am not mistaken, I am still the lady of this castle," she protested angrily. "Who are you to order my steward about?"

"You are my prisoner until I have fulfilled my pledge to Sir William. Like it or not, my lady, you will do what I tell you until you are released from my care."

She glared at him in mutinous silence.

Dominic followed her up the stairs and into the solar. Crossing the room, she sat on the wooden chair facing the small stone hearth. Benches flanked the chair and rich tapestries warmed the walls. Though numerous candles had been scattered about, none burned. What little light filtered in through the narrow slit windows left the room rather gloomy.

"You cannot stay here," Rowena said. "I wish to bathe."

"I will not stop you from bathing, but I will not leave your side. The dilemma is entirely of your own making."

Before the argument could get fully underway, Thora arrived with a large tray of food. A procession of other servants followed in her wake. A wooden bathing tub was dragged up the stairs and placed to one side of the fire then a veritable bucket brigade began to fill the tub. Rowena nibbled from the tray and watched the servants work. Thora moved about the room, lighting candles and stealing long appreciative glances at Sir Dominic.

Thora did not speak, which was tantamount to miraculous. Rowena watched Dominic fill his belly with considerably more appetite than she.

"Do you really intend to watch me bathe?" she asked when the servants had finished and he still made no move to vacate the room.

"Aye."

Realization dawned. He intended to punish her for intruding upon his bath two nights before. More significantly, she recognized challenge in his dark blue eyes. He didn't think she'd do it.

Forcing her eyes away from his insolent gaze, Rowena looked instead at Thora. Her waiting woman stood beside the doorway to the wardrobe, silently watching them. She held a tall taper in one hand and her lips battled a smile.

"Thora, attend me."

"Of course."

Rowena rose and headed for the curtained entrance to her wardrobe, but Dominic got there before her. He flipped back the curtain and stepped into the small antechamber. Satisfied that there was no means of escape, he nodded his silent permission and went back to the bench and his food.

With an angry jerk, Rowena pulled the heavy curtain across the doorway, enclosing Thora and her inside the wardrobe. "That man is insufferable," she hissed.

Thora quickly lit the candles secured in the iron wall sconce. "Did he find you before or after? Are you out of danger?"

"Nay, damn the man. I failed completely."

"And last night?" Thora persisted, her blue eyes wide with curiosity. "Where did you spend last night?"

"It is a long, tiresome story."

"Then speak quickly. He will not leave us in here indefinitely."

"Everything went as planned until Thom's brother arrived. He was horrible."

"His brother? Milton said nothing of a brother."

"Thom seemed genuinely surprised. I don't think he intended for Jack to follow him." Crossing her arms, Rowena tried to keep the memories distanced from the telling. "The brother was a beast. He turned my horse loose and then came after me. I had to stab him with my dirk to fend him off."

"Oh, good heavens." Thora gave her a quick hug. "I knew I should have gone with you."

Rowena cleared her throat, hesitant to finish the tale. "I think I may have killed him, Thora. What if they learn who I am?"

"I'll have Milton make inquiries. If this brother is dead, it's no more than he deserves. Oh you poor dear."

Shuddering, Rowena explained all that had transpired in the monastery. "Sir Dominic made some ridiculous vow to Sir William that he would not touch me," she concluded.

"Of course." Thora sounded relieved. "I knew there must be something holding him back. Was he tempted, do you think? Did he respond to you?"

"Aye, but his honor demands that he leave me alone. He will not bed me, Thora. We are wasting our time."

"Honor can be worn down. Even the strongest of vows can be eroded. He will not let you out of his sight. He has promised as much. So he is your only hope."

"I have tried, Thora. He will not be seduced."

Thora laughed, a deep mischievous sound. "Any man can be seduced. I will help you. He will have given in by the time we reach William Marshal, or I will give up men."

"That is a very serious proposition. I know how much you enjoy men." Rowena's smile vanished as she thought of another complication. "He said something to me at the monastery that I found troubling."

"What did he say?"

"He inferred that he would demand my holdings if I compromised his honor."

"How would that be possible?" Thora asked.

"He would tell his liege he had dishonored me and ask Sir William to bless our union, regardless of my feelings on the matter."

"He cannot do that. Can he do that?"

Rowena's head was pounding. She wanted to curl up in bed and cry herself to sleep, but her battles were far from over. "If I can solidify the fact that I'm a widow, I cannot be forced to wed again."

"Then we have returned to the beginning. You must seduce Sir Dominic. We will start right now. If that arrogant fool refuses to give you privacy for your bath, then we will provide him with a display to tempt the saints."

Rowena hesitated. She was not comfortable with her nudity as Thora was. She generally wore a shift to bathe. She didn't know how to be alluring and sensual. If she had Thora's skill, Dominic would have lost the battle with his determination the night before. "I don't think I can, Thora. I would only embarrass—"

"All you have to do is disrobe and ignore him completely. Take a very slow, leisurely bath. Water and candlelight are the only weapons you need. Trust me, Rowena. You can make him regret his vow, and risk his soul, without so much as glancing his way."

"He will know what I am doing," she objected. "I confessed the whole sordid tale."

Thora was silent for a moment then she shrugged. "That may work to our advantage. He'll have no doubt you want him in your bed."

Rowena didn't comment. How could she purposely bare her entire body before Sir Dominic? "It is not my custom to disrobe entirely when I bathe."

"Sir Dominic doesn't know that."

It would be humiliating to be rejected yet again. "I'm not sure I can make myself do that with him looking on."

"How did he react to the tale?" Thora asked. "Was it only his vow to Sir William that kept him from you? I know he is not wed. Sir Ezra told me that his friend has no wife or steady consort. They say he was betrothed years ago, but it ended badly."

As usual, Thora had been busy. Nothing transpired within the walls of Pendragon Castle without Thora finding out every detail. Before Rowena could respond to Thora's information, Dominic's deep voice penetrated the curtain barrier. "Enough, my lady. Your bath is getting cold."

Rowena's eyes shot to Thora and silent encouragement returned to her from her servant's bright blue gaze.

Dominic moved slowly back to the wooden bench after growling his warning to the two women inside the wardrobe. He hadn't been able to make out their words, but it didn't take a great deal of imagination to figure out what held their interest.

The curtain opened and Thora entered the solar, Rowena one step behind. The lady had abandoned her borrowed tunic and an ankle-length dressing gown enveloped her slender form. Carefully keeping her eyes averted, she moved toward the wooden tub.

Would she actually drop the dressing gown, knowing he was watching, and climb naked into the bath?

He didn't have long to wait for the answer. She paused beside the tub, her back to him. He could almost picture her expression as she summoned her determination and then, the dressing gown slipped off her shoulders and pooled at her feet.

Dominic had seen naked women before, had seen her all but naked in the stream, but never had his body responded so violently. His fingers tingled to caress the perfection of her skin, to see if she was as soft and silky as she appeared. She stood there, firelight dancing across her alabaster body. Thora leisurely secured Rowena's thick auburn hair atop her head. He wanted to loose the heavy mass, bury his face in the thick strands and spread it across his chest.

After torturous moments, Rowena carefully stepped over the rim of the tub. The sleek muscles in her long legs reflected an active life. Dominic watched the taut splendor of her bottom and supple hips until they disappeared behind the wooden protection.

He could only see her head, her shoulders, and her slender arms now, but his body ached with burgeoning interest. Narrowing his gaze, he imagined sending Thora away and disregarding his vow to William. He'd kneel beside the tub and drag her to her feet. Cupping her bottom with both hands, he'd bury his face against the apex of her thighs. She'd cry out and wiggle as he stroked that secret knot with the tip of his tongue.

The waiting woman handed Rowena bathing implements as Dominic continued his fantasy. Dazed from the pleasure he'd given her with his mouth, she'd watch as he stripped and joined her in the bath. He'd move her feet to either side of his hips so he could see her rosy folds, trace that delicate slit until she trembled. She'd clutch the edge of the tub, her head thrown back, while he prepared her with his fingers. Finally, he'd arrange her astride his lap and lick the water from her nipples as he sank into her hot, tight core.

Pressure built inside Dominic, his abdomen tense to the point of spasm. Why was he doing this to himself? He couldn't have her. No matter how desperately he wanted her.

Thora set about washing Rowena's long hair, and Dominic tried not to watch them. But his rebellious gaze gravitated toward the tub again and again. Thora spoke softly to Rowena. Dominic couldn't hear what she said, but Rowena's reply sounded argumentative. Another hushed demand came from the servant and then a long pause. What were they about?

Like a nymph rising from a forest pool, Rowena eased her legs beneath her and stood. Rivulets of water rolled off her body, glistening colorfully in the candlelight. Without sparing him so much as a glance, she bent at the waist and drew her hair down in front of her. The position fueled his imagination all over again.

He stood behind her in the tub as she bent forward, bracing herself against the rim. He cupped her breasts as he eased between her thighs then held her hips firmly when he began to move. Desire slammed into his gut, driving a strangled groan from his throat.

Damn her! Damn them both! His chest heaved and his nostrils flared.

Thora was slowly pouring a bucket of clean water over her lady's bent head. Dominic didn't even realize he'd moved until Thora's gaze shot to him. She didn't speak but her expression taunted him.

"Leave us!" he growled out in English, and immediately Thora obeyed.

Rowena straightened. Backing as far away as the tub would allow, she shoved her sodden hair off her face. "Thora," she protested as the other woman deserted her, but she couldn't drag her gaze away from Dominic. She didn't attempt to hide her nudity. This was what she wanted, what she needed from him.

"The dilemma is entirely of your own making." She repeated his words back to him.

He didn't speak. The expression on his face should have terrified Rowena, but she needed to provoke him beyond endurance, to inflame him to a point where nothing mattered but the urgent demands of his body. The intensity in his dark blue eyes showed her just how close she was to her goal. She had pitted herself against his will, and she could not back down.

Their eyes locked and held. She could almost see the conflict raging within him. His physical desire was in direct opposition to the vow he'd made to his liege lord. It wasn't fair for her to manipulate him in this way, but Rowena was desperate. All her other efforts had failed and she was running out of time.

Slowly he raised his hand. Would he hit her? Fear fluttered through her belly. Would his frustration manifest itself in violence?

But he didn't strike her. He clasped her upper arm and yanked her across the tub until their faces were only inches apart. "It will not work," he insisted. "I will not lie with you no matter how you tempt me. Do you really imagine that I have no more control over myself than that?"

Yanking her arm out of his restraining grasp, Rowena stepped out of the tub and reached for her dressing gown. Dominic's temper was not yet appeased. He snatched the gown away and advanced on her menacingly.

"Have you ever felt it, Rowena?" He stalked toward her. "Do you understand what it's like to burn with desire but know you'll not be appeased? Nay, you could not, or you would not continue to flirt with the flame."

He grabbed her wrist and drew her gradually toward him, his eyes devouring her. Rowena tugged against his hold, but he didn't seem to notice her resistance. Fury burned within his eyes, not passion, and Rowena was afraid.

"I'm sorry," she whispered.

"Not yet, but you will be."

Tossing her over his shoulder, Dominic stomped across the solar and ducked into her bedchamber. Her breath had been driven from her lungs as his shoulder connected forcefully with her midsection, so Rowena didn't make a sound. He flung her onto her back in the middle of the bed. Before Rowena could roll over or scramble from the bed he came down on top of her.

"That's the trouble with fires, Rowena. If you don't know what you're doing, you're almost certain to get burned."

His mouth covered hers then, and Rowena could do nothing but endure his cruel touch. Where his kiss had been tender and patient before, it was savage and hurtful now. He thrust his tongue into her mouth boldly, shocking her with the sudden invasion. When she tugged at his hair, trying to force him away, he simply drew her arms over her head and pinned them to the bed with one large hand.

He left her mouth, his lips moving down her neck, exploring, lightly sucking and licking. Rowena gasped. Her body came alive, suddenly humming with awareness and sensation. She felt the coarse fabric of his tunic rub against her breasts and belly. The apex of her thighs began to ache with a longing she didn't fully understand.

She squirmed beneath him, no longer trying to escape, just anxious, restless. His hand swept down across her breast, and she gasped. He cupped her firmly, his fingers framing her nipple. His face hovered over her breasts. She felt the hot brush of his breath and then the moisture of his tongue as he traced the outer edge of her nipple. It hardened, puckered and tingled. Rowena had never felt anything like it.

He closed his teeth carefully on her nipple and tugged until she moaned, arching her back, pressing herself more firmly against his touch. His lips parted, and he drew her deeply into his mouth. Rowena cried out. Hot sensation shot from her breast to the juncture of her thighs to intensify the burning there.

"Please, Dominic," she mumbled, her head tossing from one side to the other.

The warm flutter of his lips moved down onto her abdomen, making her quiver and start. She needed him there, deep inside her, where the ache was the most acute. Why did he seem content to taste and stroke her skin, to memorize the feel of her, the texture and the heat?

His palm pressed down over her mound, and Rowena gasped. Her entire body shuddered. He chuckled against the satin-smooth flesh of her stomach. "Are you burning yet? Do you feel the fire?"

"Aye," she cried without hesitation.

Rearing up, he stared into her face. His expression was contorted with tension and suppressed desire. Would he take her now? Would he end this torment for both of them and secure her future? She trembled as she waited for his next move.

With a harsh growl, he flipped her over onto her stomach. What was he doing? Could it be done in this position? Her confusion evaporated as his hands began to stroke. Once he began to touch her, all rational thought was driven from her mind. He ran his fingers along her spine. Tingles trailed in their wake and intensified the heat pulsing in her core. She felt empty and achy.

Then his hands were in her hair, brushing it aside to bare the nape of her neck. He pressed his lips against the sensitive skin there, warming her flesh with his breath. Rowena clutched at the coverlet beneath her. This was madness. Her senses were on fire.

She felt his weight lift then his hands were at her knees, guiding her legs apart and raising her hips. A sharp cry tore from her throat at the first stroke of his fingers against her swollen folds. His hoarse, tormented groan filled her ears as he touched her. His fingers slid smoothly, triggering tingles and spasms of pleasure.

"God's blood, Rowena. You are so hot. So wet. Are you truly a virgin?"

She wasn't insulted by his doubt, didn't care what he thought as long as he continued to touch her. His finger found a spot so exquisitely sensitive it made her jerk and moan. He circled the little nub with a smooth, steady rhythm. She sobbed, overwhelmed by the need for something she didn't understand. More, faster, *more*.

He slid away from the wonderful bud and focused on the opening to her passage. "Hell," he whispered the curse as his fingers encountered her maidenhead.

Rowena sobbed again. "Dominic, please!" She arched her back, willing him to continue, but he pulled away and slipped his hand from between her thighs, leaving her empty and alone.

The bed shifted subtly and she knew he had left her. Rowena pressed her face into the pillow and cried. Her flesh still tingled, throbbing with unfulfilled desire, which was exactly what he'd wanted. He'd wanted her to understand the power of passion.

He'd been a masterful teacher.

* * * * *

Frigid water rapidly saturated Dominic's braies as he stomped into the river. He didn't stop until he was submerged to the waist, but it did no good. With an exasperated growl, he plunged his head beneath the current, but that didn't cool his anger — or his desire.

He stood up and pushed his sodden hair out of his face. *God save me from irrational females!*

He should have known better. Women were seldom what they seemed. They lied and deceived. Honor was alien to them. Rowena was determined to make him her accomplice despite his solemn vow.

What had or had not happened between the lady and her husband was none of his concern.

Poor William, Dominic thought with a gruff laugh. It would be the regent's responsibility to sort through this entire mess and award the Pendragon holdings. Dominic didn't envy his liege the task.

He waded back to shore and welcomed the cool night air. He tried to release the tension in his muscles and defuse the heat still simmering in his blood, but he could still see her satin skin and feel the incredibly soft texture beneath his fingers and lips. The fantasies he'd entertained while watching her couldn't begin to compare with the reality of touching her.

A groan escaped him before he could completely squelch the image of his fingers sinking into her dusky core. He wouldn't think about her. He wouldn't think about how perfectly she fit in his embrace, how ready she'd been to abandon everything to their passion. He wouldn't even consider how profoundly his body reacted to her inviting display.

Light, musical laughter dragged him from his memories. He searched the trees along the river, listening with the finely tuned senses of a warrior.

A flickering golden glow bounced among the branches then disappeared. Something brushed his cheek and he spun around. "Who goes there?"

Carefully creeping toward his sword, Dominic visually explored the shadows. He could feel a gaze upon him. He had felt something touch his cheek!

A hushed, husky voice reached his ears. He couldn't understand the language, couldn't determine if he heard words or singing.

Warm tingles spread across his chest and down his arms. But the night air was chill.

"Who are you? Where are you?" he whispered. "Show yourself."

He heard laughter again. It surrounded him, like the swirling current of a summer breeze. He couldn't move, didn't want to move. It caressed his exposed skin and threaded through his hair, soothing him, relaxing him. The sound and the sensation drifted away, and Dominic knew he was alone.

Stunned for a moment, he shook his head, clearing the haze from his mind. "This accursed place has me talking to the shadows," he muttered.

He tugged his tunic on over his soggy braies and strapped on his sword, comforted by the familiar weight.

Ludlow, the captain of the guards, was in the lower bailey when Dominic passed through the west tower. Ludlow was speaking with several of his men, so Dominic chose not to interrupt. He stood back for a moment and assessed the other man's competency.

Tall and lanky, Ludlow possessed the craggy sort of face that made it hard to determine his age. Keen intelligence shone in his hazel eyes and put some of Dominic's uncertainty to rest.

When Ludlow had finished giving instructions to his men, Dominic approached him with a casual greeting.

"How may I be of service, milord?" Ludlow's gaze was just as assessing as Dominic's had been.

Dominic came right to the point. "Is the threat from Edwin of Llangly real, or has Lady Rowena simply used it be contrary?"

Ludlow laughed, apparently amused by Dominic's candor. "Lady Rowena needs no excuse for her contrariness. She can be quite difficult when she chooses. But the answer to your question is not a simple one. Edwin of Llangly is more of a threat to Lady Rowena than to the Pendragon Castle, but she has not invented the threat."

"I must take her to my liege. She could be gone a fortnight, perhaps more. Will this increase the threat? Is it possible that Sir Edwin will use the opportunity to lay siege to the castle?"

Ludlow shook his head. "Sir Edwin would only consider taking Pendragon by force if all of his other options have been exhausted. He is trying to prove a legal claim to the holdings, not wrest them from Lady Rowena."

Nodding thoughtfully, Dominic considered the other man's explanation.

"Besides, Sir Edwin is on his way to Windsor Castle. He left this morning." Ludlow provided the information with an enigmatic smile.

"Are you certain? William told me nothing about summoning Edwin."

"I don't know that he was summoned. I only know he went. Nearly everyone in Llangly is kin to someone in Pendragon. Movement of the nobility never goes unnoticed."

Dominic accepted the information with a nod.

Ludlow headed for the battlements then paused. "Sir Dominic, Lady Rowena is still very young. Her life has not been easy."

"Meaning?"

"She is in dire need of a champion."

Dominic smiled at the odd comment. "Why do you tell me this?"

"I have seen the way she looks at you. If you treat her kindly, you would be welcomed by the people of Pendragon." Ludlow bowed and walked away.

It amazed Dominic that the people of Pendragon spoke of Rowena with such affection. To listen to the lady herself, one would think she was despised and feared, yet her people revered her. Her steward was unwavering in his loyalty. Thora supported her lady with uncommon protectiveness. And now Ludlow asked for understanding on her behalf.

Ezra sat on the bottom stair leading to the solar wing, idly scraping a whetstone along the edge of his sword.

"Has she come down or attempted to leave?" Dominic asked.

"Have not seen hide nor hair of the lady or her waiting woman. They're up there. I've heard their voices from time to time, but there has been no trouble."

"Good. Hopefully she's realized the futility of running away. Are the men ready for the journey?"

"The men are always ready, Dominic, as you have made them."

"Then we leave with the dawn."

Chapter Five

Windsor Castle wasn't at all what Rowena expected. Knowing it was a royal residence, she thought to find a grand, luxurious palace. The compound dominating the horizon was a stark, stone fortress, and Rowena couldn't disguise her disappointment.

"It may not seem impressive at a glance, but when William of Normandy came to England, he ordered the construction of eleven castles. Each stronghold was within one day's ride of the others. This allowed forces to reach any of the other locations with little notice," Dominic explained.

Rowena felt her cheeks heat. She hadn't realized her expression revealed her thoughts. "Then Windsor Castle is one of these fortresses?"

He nodded.

They had hardly spoken since they left the monastery. He remained polite and courteous, faithfully seeing to her needs and what little comfort he could supply, but he made certain they were never alone. Last night he'd insisted they sleep in a ring surrounding the fire pit, allowing no one any privacy.

She studied the thick curtain walls for a long moment. "Why are some of the towers round while others are square?" She didn't care about castle construction. She simply wanted to prolong their conversation.

"It was learned in the Holy Land that round towers are stronger and offer a wider field of fire, so the wall will be completed with round towers."

Before she could think of another question to retain his attention, he urged his horse forward to catch Ezra, who was riding in the lead.

Rowena sighed. At least he hadn't demanded she stay cooped up in a "lady's wagon". Knowing the customary wagon would only slow them down, Dominic easily agreed when she insisted that she be allowed to ride her palfrey.

Ignoring her disappointment at his inattentiveness, Rowena lifted her face and enjoyed the warm caress of the late afternoon sun. The soft fabric of her wimple fluttered about her neck and shoulders, disturbed by a gentle breeze.

They arrived a short time later, but again Rowena found herself unimpressed. William Marshal was closeted with a group of advisors and couldn't be disturbed. Dominic knew many of the servants by name and responded to the entire situation with casual familiarity.

He is the ward of William Marshal. Why would he not be comfortable at court?

Their horses were led off to the stables, and they were taken directly to the apartments they would occupy during their stay.

Though the outward appearance of Windsor Castle had been a disappointment for Rowena, the interior exceeded her expectations. The room designated for her use appeared slightly smaller than her bedchamber at home, but the furnishings were opulent. Rich brocades in red and gold dressed the high box bed. A large, fringed tapestry covered the wall opposite the fireplace.

Rowena moved toward the tall, narrow windows cut into the wall across from the door. Greenish glass panes had been installed to keep the chilly winds at bay. Fascinated by the luxury, Rowena reverently touched the cool glass. Pendragon Castle had stout, well-fitted shutters that could be secured with iron bars, but only a king could afford this extravagance.

"Lady Rowena."

An odd hesitation in Thora's tone drew Rowena's attention. "What is it?"

"He arrived yesterday," Thora announced.

"Who arrived yesterday?"

"Edwin." She spoke the name as if it tasted foul. "He has already made his case to the regent. Thank God you can prove him wrong. Just think what would happened if Sir Dominic had not…"

Rowena didn't hear the rest of Thora's sentence. Fear and desperation leached the strength from her legs as she turned back to the window. She grasped the window frame, faint and unsteady.

It was not supposed to be like this.

She was supposed to expose Edwin's evil before the regent heard his case.

If Edwin had already persuaded William Marshal, then what hope was left for her?

* * * * *

The boy king had left Windsor Castle three days before. Dominic was not at all disappointed to learn this fact. The frivolous life of a court follower had never appealed to him. He didn't understand how Sir William survived in the midst of such turmoil and treachery. So many courtiers harbored hidden motivations and deceitful ambitions that Dominic made it a point to stay away.

Edwin of Llangly had arrived the day before, Dominic learned from a servant, but Edwin had not yet been granted an audience with the regent.

Dominic was sure William knew of their arrival, but Dominic was waiting for an invitation as well.

Glancing indifferently around the small room, he wondered what Rowena thought of Windsor Castle. The stark, defensible exterior had taken her by surprise. Did she find the rich luxuries distributed so freely within the chambers more to her liking?

A deep chuckle rumbled through his chest. Why the lady's opinion should matter to him, Dominic could not fathom. Her dilemma had nothing to do with him. He had fulfilled his obligation to William Marshal the moment he passed beyond the walls of Windsor Castle. What the regent did with her now was entirely up to him.

Dominic was still attempting to convince himself of this when he clasped arms with his liege lord some time later.

"You look well," William said, sincerity clear in his intelligent eyes. "Come. Sit by the fire and tell me everything."

Dominic smiled at the regent. His affection for William was complex. He had never thought of William as a father, but even as a child, Dominic had admired and respected him. The passing years had brought depth and maturity to their friendship. "My thanks, but I *should* look haggard and exasperated." He took the chair William offered.

"Why is that? Was the lady troublesome?"

The questions seemed innocent enough, but something in William's expression made Dominic suspicious. "You knew she would give me hell, did you not?"

"I have heard tales of her obstinate nature, but I never doubted that you were equal to the task." William sat across from Dominic and stared into the leaping flames.

Dominic took the silent moment to study his friend. William didn't look well. He was still an imposing figure for a man in his seventies, but fatigue had deepened the grooves in his weathered face and stooped his once broad shoulders. Knowing that Sir William was far too proud to admit it even if he were ailing, Dominic said, "Well, she is finally here, as is her nemesis. Have you spoken with Sir Edwin, yet?"

"Nay. I wanted to talk with you first. What is your impression of Lady Pendragon?"

"In what respect?"

William snorted impatiently and shifted his weight in the tall-backed chair. His penetrating gaze came back to Dominic. "I've never known you to be evasive. Was she that disruptive? Is she truly the Shrew of Pendragon Castle?"

Dominic had heard the title bandied about before their departure. "I didn't find Lady Rowena shrewish, and her people seem to like and respect her. I wonder if the title is part of Edwin's campaign to take her holdings?"

"It's possible. His strategy is strange at best." Their gazes locked. "Is she comely?"

Dominic's gut twisted as his passing suspicions were confirmed. William knew he desired holdings of his own and set before him a temptation beyond imagining. It was almost painful to hope that such a thing could come to pass. "She seems almost unaware of it, but aye. She is lovely."

"Her husband has been dead since autumn. How did you find the castle?"

"Impressive. The manor was well run, the keep clean, the people hearty."

"All of that can be attributed to a well-trained steward," William said.

"Perhaps."

"Was her reception of you gracious? Why did it take you so long to return? I had nearly given up on you and headed back to London."

"Well, the lady wouldn't admit me to the castle, so I had to take matters into my own hands."

"You announced yourself?" Dominic only nodded, so William persisted. "You presented *my* missive and she would not let you in?" When Dominic nodded again, William's eyes widened and his jaw dropped.

The unflattering expression made Dominic laugh. "Edwin has been causing all manner of mischief, so Lady Rowena feared I had been sent by him."

"What sort of mischief?"

"According to her steward, Edwin has pilfered livestock and started fires, he has harassed her tenants and spread malicious rumors. Anything that would cast suspicion upon her competency."

"I see." William was silent for a moment. "How did you finally get inside? I've heard Pendragon Castle is very well designed."

"I sent Ephraim up the chute of the latrine." Dominic laughed, watching the expected grimace materialize on William's face.

"And Lady Rowena is still intact? I've seen that temper of yours unleashed a time or two."

"I was very angry, but she's very young. If a man had greeted me in the bailey that day, my reaction would have been quite different, but Lady Rowena is little more than a child."

One of William's brows shot up at this description, but he didn't argue. "I'm anxious to meet this precocious *child*. I have invited Sir Edwin to dine with me. I will extend the invitation to Lady Rowena as well. Much can be learned from observing the interaction of enemies."

"May I also attend?"

The old man smiled. "You are always welcome."

* * * * *

Rowena wrapped both hands around her cup and stared down into the murky contents, too angry to raise the beverage to her lips.

"You're not eating," Dominic commented.

He sat to her left. William Marshal occupied the head of the small table, and Edwin of Llangly sat directly across from her. Rowena felt betrayed by Edwin's presence. She wasn't prepared to face him. Her feelings were still too volatile. Besides, she couldn't fabricate a story with him seated across from her, ready to point out any inconsistency. Likewise she would be able to object to any falsehood presented.

"I'm no longer hungry," she responded automatically to Dominic's observation, not lifting her eyes from her wine.

"As agreeable as ever, I see," Edwin muttered. "You need not be so hostile, Rowena. I've no doubt we can come to an agreement, if you'll only be reasonable."

She scoffed and placed the wineglass on the table. "By reasonable I'm sure you mean surrender my holdings to you."

William intervened before the argument could escalate. "I had not anticipated this level of hostility when I suggested a more casual setting for this discussion."

Rowena had to force back a laugh. He had to know they were at odds or he wouldn't be involved. Edwin was trying to steal everything from her! How could she possibly feel anything but hostility? This setting was strategic. "Sir William, it may well be more productive to interview us separately."

"It would be more comfortable, I have no doubt, but one tends to be more truthful when faced with the one you are accusing."

Rowena had been thinking nearly the same thing, so she merely nodded.

"Why is he here?" Edwin motioned toward Dominic with his chin.

"Sir Dominic is my vassal and trusted friend. I requested that he bear witness to any decision I might make."

"Then let's proceed. The sooner we have this argument settled, the sooner I can return to my responsibilities."

Again Rowena wanted to laugh. If Edwin didn't win this argument, he would have very few responsibilities. Llangly manor was a small fiefdom, easily managed.

"You wrote to me requesting that I recommend the annulment of the marriage of Lady Rowena and Gaston of Pendragon," William began. "Do you understand that my influence only extends so far? Ultimately the Church will have to grant the annulment."

Edwin nodded. "I am aware of that, but my dealings with certain members of the Church have been less than successful. I hoped to find justice in the Royal Court where I was disappointed in the Church."

"This sort of request is unusual coming from a third party. Did Gaston have a Last Will and Testament?"

"Aye, and it bequeathed his holdings in their entirety to me," Rowena explained. The question hadn't been specifically directed toward Edwin. Still, she felt uncomfortable, as if she were overstepping the bounds of propriety.

"Do you concur?" William asked Edwin.

"The estate is bequeathed to Gaston's widow. I contend that to qualify as a widow, one must have first been a wife."

"I understand the grounds on which you base your request, Sir Edwin. You didn't answer my question."

"I do not dispute Gaston's Last Will and Testament."

Rowena wasn't sure why that fact was important, but Edwin seemed uncomfortable relenting even to this small degree. She shifted her gaze back to Sir William. He was much older than she had expected. Dominic spoke of him with such deference. She'd pictured the regent larger and more robust.

"To judge this issue fairly, I need more information. Explain to me the connection between your two families."

Rowena would have loved to explain exactly what Edwin had done, but William wasn't looking at her. His gaze remained on Edwin.

"Gaston of Pendragon was my nephew," Edwin began. "I'm his closest living relative."

"Except for his widow of course," Dominic said.

Up to that point, he had shown only mild interest in the conversation. Rowena looked at him and hope fluttered within her breast. Had she won an ally after all?

"That is the crux of the issue," Edwin muttered. "Is my claim more valid than hers?"

"Lady Rowena," William spoke directly to her for the first time. "Is it your desire that your marriage to Gaston of Pendragon be annulled?"

"Nay, my lord, it is not. Sir Edwin has been unscrupulous in his dealings with me for longer than I can remember."

"Explain."

"We were betrothed when I was still a child, yet Edwin broke that betrothal and married my own mother shortly after my father died."

"Is this true?" The regent's penetrating gaze settled once more on Edwin.

"I had known Yvonne for years when her husband died. Our love had actually sparked before Gilbert's death."

"You lie! My mother loved my father until the last breath left her body. She married you out of desperation and insecurity."

"How old were you when Sir Edwin wed your mother?" William asked.

"I was ten, sir. 'Twas our broken betrothal that set him at odds with the Church. Brother Leland made it clear that to set aside the daughter to marry the mother was unseemly at best."

The regent didn't comment, but the shrewdness in his gaze assured Rowena that he took in everything. "At what age did you wed Gaston?"

"Fifteen." She spat out the number like a curse.

William turned back to Edwin. "Did you personally agree to the original betrothal or was it arranged by your parents?"

"The betrothal was arranged by our fathers, both of whom had died when the contract was broken. I was three years younger than Yvonne, yet I am fourteen years older than Rowena. And as painful as it is to the lady, Yvonne and I were lovers for several years before her husband died."

Rowena bit back her angry denial. She had already objected to his ridiculous lie. She would not give him the satisfaction of knowing how infuriating she found his slander.

"How long were you married to Lady Yvonne?" William continued.

"We had been wed five years when God granted us our fondest wish and allowed her to conceive. But neither Yvonne nor my son survived the birth."

William offered a solemn nod. "Who arranged for Rowena to marry Gaston?"

"As I have stated, we were kinsmen. I arranged the marriage to make the bond between Llangly and Pendragon all the stronger."

Rowena laughed at this boast. "You speak of the two as if they are equal. Llangly is a tiny village struggling in the shadow of Pendragon Castle."

William didn't comment. He seemed to make mental note of the fact and then changed the subject entirely. "I have heard tell that there is a Pendragon curse. Was Gaston the only Pendragon heir to live to manhood?"

Again he hadn't addressed the question to a specific person, so Rowena answered. "Gaston was not *born* of the Pendragon line. Edwin's older brother Edgar married Constance of Pendragon when Gaston was eight. Gaston was born of Edgar's first wife. There were no children of the second marriage."

"Fascinating," William said softly. He leaned forward, absently stroking his chin. "And Gaston was killed without issue, leaving Pendragon without an heir once again."

"As is foretold by the curse. No Pendragon male will find happiness until they stop forcing their will upon Pendragon females."

Dominic and William both laughed at her passionate declaration, but Edwin's expression was anything but amused. After shooting Rowena a scathing glower, he turned back to the regent. "My claim to Pendragon Castle is one of blood ties," Edwin reiterated. "While Rowena's only claim is through a marriage that was never consummated. She did not produce a Pendragon heir because Gaston of Pendragon never touched her."

"Is this true?" William once again met Rowena's gaze.

She thought about Edwin's statement and realized that she could honestly answer the charge. "Nay, Gaston touched me, he just preferred the company of his whore Lissette. The same woman who now shares Edwin's bed."

William leaned back against his chair, studying Rowena and then Edwin. "I begin to see the nature of this conflict. Tell me about this other woman."

"Lissette has nothing to do with this," Edwin insisted hotly.

"What led you to believe Rowena and Gaston never consummated their marriage?" William calmly pushed his trencher aside and folded his hands on top of the table.

"It can be proven quite easily." Edwin ignored William's question entirely. "Call for a midwife and—"

"Explain to me why I should have the lady subjected to such an offensive examination," William charged, growing impatient with Edwin's evasions.

"Gaston confided to me that a battle wound had left him incapable of the act," he answered stiffly, his expression rather strained.

"And yet he had not only a wife, but a leman? I find that rather odd."

"All of this rhetoric is needless," Edwin sneered. "I insist that Rowena be examined and the truth of my claim be proven. I will settle for nothing less."

"Ask anyone at Pendragon Castle. The bed linens were displayed to prove the consummation," Rowena said, and every word she said was true. "I also have a statement from Brother Leland, who officiated over the wedding. This petition is rubbish."

"If I have a midwife examine Lady Rowena, will you accept the results as fact?" William asked suddenly.

Rowena panicked at the question. He couldn't mean to give in to Edwin's demand! The entire conversation had led her to believe that Dominic's faith was well placed. Sir William hadn't seemed to believe Edwin until now. "My lord," she protested. "This is absurd. I—"

"She can choose a midwife, and I will do the same," Edwin suggested, interrupting Rowena's objection. "Then neither can lie about the findings."

"I will do no such thing!"

"Sir William." Dominic drew everyone's attention with the sharpness of his tone. "My lord, there is no need for an examination."

"How so?" Edwin demanded.

Rowena unconsciously held her breath. He had sworn he wouldn't help her. He'd resisted her every advance for the sake of his honor and yet...

Their eyes met, and Rowena could hardly think. His beautiful blue eyes stared back at her coldly, expressionless, impenetrable. Would he defend her—or betray her?

"By your leave, my lady." She could only manage one stiff nod. "Lady Rowena and I spent the night together in the old monastery."

"I don't believe you!" Edwin rose out of his chair. "Rowena wouldn't lie with you. Lissette told me she is terrified of men. He is lying. I demand that she be examined—"

William raised his right hand, cutting off Edwin's impassioned protest. "I have heard enough. Your request for an annulment is denied, Sir Edwin. Lady Rowena will remain in control of all Pendragon holdings. Dominic, I would speak with you in private."

Rowena was so elated by the regent's pronouncement that it took her a moment to recognize the fury in William Marshal's eyes. Dominic rose and followed Sir William from the room, inadvertently leaving her alone with Edwin.

"Do not, for one instant, let yourself imagine that this is over," Edwin threatened through clenched teeth.

"You've lost." She leaned across the table and whispered, "Go back to Lissette. You deserve each other."

He stood there glaring at her for a long moment as if he meant to continue the argument. Then he abruptly uttered an extremely profane word and strode from the room.

Finally, Rowena allowed herself a long, shuddering sigh. What should she do now? Would Dominic return? Was Sir William finished with his questioning? Why had he wanted to speak with Dominic, and why had he looked so angry?

The vow.

He believed Dominic broke his vow.

Why had Dominic done it? Why had he perjured himself to protect her? He hadn't actually lied, but the insinuation had been clear. He made Edwin believe they were lovers. Why would he do such a thing?

Rowena was far too upset to sit idly by in the empty room. On shaky legs, she made her way toward the door.

How would she ever repay him?

Nay, what would he expect in return? It made no sense. No one was so selfless. What was he hoping to gain?

The answer came with staggering clarity and Rowena stumbled to a stop. She turned and gazed at the door through which Dominic had followed the regent. Suspicion reared its ugly head. He wanted the same thing as Edwin. How masterfully this had been played. She hadn't been rescued—she'd been ambushed!

Chapter Six

"Why are you lying to me, Dominic?"

Few people could match the incredible persuasion of William Marshal's unwavering stare. When others ranted and raved, flailing their arms and cursing, Sir William would quietly request the truth. He had avoided wars and secured international treaties with the power of his personality.

As a child Dominic found his calm approach intimidating and often bowed to Sir William's demands without argument. As a young man he attempted to manipulate his liege, needing to try the limits of his own power. But now Dominic found himself shamed by Sir William's relentless integrity.

"Not one word I uttered was false," Dominic defended.

"You've not bedded Lady Rowena," William calmly argued. "I specifically asked you not to touch her, and you would not disobey a direct order. Not you, Dominic. Besides, the lady seemed more surprised by your confession than Edwin of Llangly."

"I didn't say I'd bedded her. I said we spent the night together in the monastery, and that is true."

"You also said that an examination was not necessary, which implies that Lady Rowena is no longer a maiden."

Dominic didn't reply to the charge, instead he asked, "Would you really have allowed the examination?"

"That is not the issue, Dominic. You purposely gave Edwin the impression that you are Rowena's lover."

All formality had fallen away. They were simply two men attempting to solve a problem, an old man and his beloved ward. "I didn't know what else to do. Rowena doesn't deserve to be betrayed, again."

"Betrayed by whom?" When Dominic did not answer, William said, "Tell me now, truthfully. Is Rowena a virgin?"

"Aye," he grumbled. "What really constitutes a marriage? Is it only the physical act? What about devotion and loyalty?"

"Was Lady Rowena devoted and loyal to Pendragon?"

"Not the man, but the manor. She has worked hard to earn her people's respect, and she has shown far more dedication to Pendragon Castle than Gaston ever pretended. And Edwin! Edwin is vile. Can you not see that?"

Heaving a heavy sigh, William sank into his favorite chair. It was a huge throne-like affair with padded cushions at the seat and back. They had returned to the small room that adjoined William's bedchamber. It was where Dominic had spoken with him earlier.

"You seem to have developed quite an opinion of Lady Rowena in your short acquaintance. Tell me about her."

Dominic recognized an order when he heard one. "She was fifteen when she was given to Gaston. He had promised to spend the summer with her, but he arrived mere days before he took her to wife. He came to her bed a stranger."

"It happens all the time, Dominic. My wife came to me at thirteen, and I barely knew her on our wedding night. I see no betrayal here."

"He came to her drunk and abusive. She was frightened and she fought him off. He humiliated her, degraded her, and then brought this Lissette person to Pendragon Castle."

"And in the five years that followed he never once attempted to bed her again?"

Dominic snickered. "That may have been Edwin's only true statement. I know it would take impotence to keep me from Rowena's bed for five years."

William watched him intently. "Then how do you explain the leman? Something here does not make sense." He shook his head, his expression distant, thoughtful.

Having no intention of repeating Rowena's tale of Fairy lights and magic powers, Dominic tried to refocus

William's attention. "Edwin played an enormous part in placing Rowena in that deplorable situation and now he has the gall to demand that she relinquish her claim to the estate. She suffered five years of hell. I think that entitles her to something."

"What is *just* and what is *lawful* is not always the same."

Dominic tried not to panic. He paused to see if William would say more before he offered a comment. "If I had to choose between what is just and what is lawful, I would always choose what is just."

William Marshal nodded, the faintest of smiles playing about his mouth. "If I base my decision on what I have learned in an official capacity as opposed to what I have been told by my friend, I would send you back to Pendragon Castle. I would request that you remain with Lady Rowena until it can be determined whether or not she is carrying your child."

This was not at all what Dominic had expected to hear. "And when it is determined that she is not with child?"

"Then I would request that she choose her next husband as quickly as possible. The Pendragon holdings are vast. Edwin will not give up. Lady Rowena needs a strong husband to stand by her side."

"She will not be forced to wed. She was quoting Magna Carta as we traveled. She knows her rights as a widow, and you have just ensured her standing as such."

"I didn't say I'd require her to marry. I said I'd request that she marry."

"Then why send me back with her?"

"So that you can convince the lady that *you* are the best choice for her new husband."

Dominic was torn between elation and dread. "I'm not ready to marry, William."

"Few men are ready to marry when the time comes. You need to put Monica behind you once and for all. This is an extraordinary opportunity. You are attracted to this girl. I see it in your eyes."

"There is much about Rowena that appeals to me, but she can sting like a hornet when she's a mind to be difficult." Dominic smiled as his mind happily supplied several instances to support his claim. Then he sighed. "She wouldn't have me in any event. When it comes right down to it, I'm not her equal."

"That is Monica's ghost speaking, Dominic. You are my vassal. If King John had not seized your family holdings, you would be an earl. Your lineage is as noble as mine. What is really bothering you?"

Again Dominic found William's insight amazing. "You see too much, my lord. I *want* Pendragon Castle."

"Wherein lies the problem?"

"I am attracted to Rowena, but the Pendragon holdings are everything I have ever dreamt and more. I knew when I first beheld the castle that I would do anything to claim it as my own."

William's deep chuckle drew Dominic's attention to his weathered face. "I still do not see the dilemma."

"What if I cannot love her?" He stared deeply into his liege lord's eyes, looking for answers, hoping for reassurance. "What if she senses that my real passion is for her holdings? She will think me no better than Edwin. I will be no better than Edwin."

"You are not Edwin. No one in Christendom would confuse you with that self-serving bastard."

Rowena's innocent face materialized within Dominic's mind and he felt his chest constrict. She was so vulnerable and yet so brave. Every protective instinct he possessed surged to the surface whenever he was near her, but she would resent his interference and reject his protection. She was free, independent, and she had sacrificed much to become so. How could he take that away from her? "She doesn't trust anyone, much less any man. I wouldn't know how to woo her."

"Patiently. That's how you will woo her."

Dominic was not known for his patience. He could be stubborn to the point of obsession. Loyalty, ambition, strength were all characteristics Dominic claimed, but patience...

"I will not require your cooperation," William said with a grin. "But if you managed to win this particular lady, I would be well pleased."

"You have always been more adept at cajoling than intimidation." Dominic chuckled. "I will think on it."

A bright smile softened the old man's face, peeling years off his weathered features and making his eyes sparkle. "Good."

"You realize, of course, that you are asking me to risk my very life."

"Surely you are not afraid of Edwin."

Again Dominic laughed. "Nay. I was referring to the Pendragon curse."

"If I rolled over every time someone threatened me with a curse, I'd be spinning like a top. The bishop of Ferns has been threatening me with all the furies of hell since I seized two manors that belonged to his church. He has threatened me with excommunication and eternal damnation and sworn that my line will die with me. Yet I have lived long past my prime, I have five thriving sons and two daughters, so I find his threats somewhat hard to believe."

"But this curse was not applied by a meager bishop, but by an enraged Fairy *female*!"

William laughed softly and patted Dominic's brawny shoulder. "A fierce, war-seasoned knight against an obstinate girl and a vengeful Fairy, this is a battle I would love to watch."

* * * * *

Titania was shocked from sleep by a stinging slap. The pain cleared her mind in time for her to restrain the instinctive gathering of Fairy energy about to burst with lethal intensity. She covered her cheek with her hand and cowered against the wall.

"What… Why did you —"

"I should kill you!" Edwin screamed, raising his hand to strike again. She sent a calming pulse through him and he lowered his arm. "She was no virgin, Lissette. You were wrong."

"That's impossible. I would sense —" She caught the slip just in time. "Rowena is lying."

He glared at her, his hands balled into fists. "Dominic of Chapstow himself plowed her belly."

"I don't believe it."

With an angry hiss, Edwin explained, "I arrived before them so William Marshal would hear my petition first."

She slipped into a dressing gown and crawled out of bed. Why would this fool accept their word? She had instructed him to demand an examination. "And?"

"I was ignored. Then Rowena rode into Windsor Castle like a queen. At her side was Dominic of Chapstow."

"The man Rowena claims to have bedded?"

"Rowena claimed nothing. Dominic volunteered the information. He said they spent the night in the old monastery just before leaving for Windsor Castle."

"It doesn't make sense." She tossed her thick braid over her shoulder. Damn it! Edwin was supposed to return victorious. Fiona would be thwarted for another generation, and Titania could go home to the Fairy realm.

"It makes perfect sense. They were stranded alone and he spent the night on top of her. What is there to understand?"

She longed to loose her power and punish this obnoxious human. She was queen of the Fairies. How dare he treat her— Focus! She was a sniveling lightskirt named Lissette. "You don't know Rowena as I do. You didn't see her after Gaston had finished with her."

"Do you not mean after *you* and Gaston had finished with her? From all accounts, my dear Lissette, you were quite the spiteful viper when it came to your competition."

She didn't dignify the comment with a reply.

"Dominic had no reason to lie, and judging from William's reaction, there will be hell to pay because of what he did. William prides himself on his honesty, and his ward compromised his ability to make a just decision."

"What will he do?"

"I'm not sure."

"What if he forces this Dominic to wed with Rowena?" *What if Dominic was the man destined to break the curse?* She couldn't allow that to happen. Fiona must remain in exile until she convinced Oberon to name another his heir. Many of his children didn't resent her, many could be controlled. He must choose one of the others.

"Rowena will not allow it, and as a widow, she can prevent a forced marriage."

"Then what should we do?"

Edwin shrugged. "I have another plan already in motion, so for now, we wait. We wait and see what the others do."

* * * * *

The following morning, a written summons from William Marshal arrived with the breakfast tray. Sir William had already ruled that Rowena would remain in control of the Pendragon holdings, so she couldn't guess the purpose for the summons. Would Dominic be there? She hadn't seen him since the night before, but she had thought of little else.

"Put this on," Thora suggested from behind Rowena. "It will show the regent how pleased you are by his judgment."

Rowena turned around and smiled. The servant was holding an elaborate surcoat, constructed from rich velvets. It was primarily blue, but the front had been emblazoned with the colorful standard of Pendragon Castle. The dragon sat on its muscular hind legs, the long, serpent-like tail curving around to rest in front of the creature. A golden crown encircled its head and both its claws clasped the hilt of a long sword. To either side of its green body spread wings, which were brightly hued with every imaginable color.

Rowena had always loved the standard. A less elaborate version decorated the uniforms of her castle guards and the long banners that accompanied her knights into battle.

"Very well." All she really wanted was to be surrounded by the walls of Pendragon Castle.

She'd donned a simple linen chemise and soft, butter-colored gown earlier that morning. Thora moved up behind her and lifted the surcoat over her head then pulled it down into place. Rowena smoothed the soft fabric along her sides and over her hips. "Does it look all right?"

"It looks beautiful and so do you. What do you suppose Sir William wants?"

"I don't know. He was very angry with Dominic last night, but I have no idea what transpired once they left the room. Hopefully, he just wants to formalize his judgment and send me on my way."

William Marshal was alone when Rowena was escorted into the stateroom. The regent sat in a large wooden chair with thick cushions attached to the seat and back. The chair angled toward the hearth yet allowed him to view anyone entering the room. A crackling fire embraced the room with warmth and hospitality, but Rowena could not seem to move from her place by the door. She'd not been this intimidated last night and Edwin had been there, but so had Dominic, the only man who had ever defended her.

"Come," Sir William bid. "Sit beside me. Let us talk."

He was trying to put her at ease, so Rowena wrestled her uncertainty further back in her mind and moved forward. She sat in the chair he indicated, smaller and less elaborate than his.

"I like to believe that honesty is as important to others as it is to me," he began, "but time and time again I find this is not the case."

She'd witnessed how effortlessly he could control a conversation the night before, and she'd yet to guess his purpose for the meeting, so she said only, "How unfortunate."

"Edwin of Llangly has departed. Will he cause you trouble, do you think?"

"He will try. I will be ready for him."

"How?"

She refused to take offense. Squaring her shoulders, Rowena explained her position. "Foreknowledge of an enemy's intention is often the greatest weapon. I know that Edwin will not rest until he has found a way to claim Pendragon, so I'll be ready for anything."

"Dominic got past your defenses," he pointed out. "Were you ready for him?"

"I had never dreamed anyone could imagine something so vile. Do you know how he managed to gain entrance to my castle?"

"He told me. I was impressed by his resourcefulness." The regent smiled. "You cannot expect Edwin to fight fairly. Do you realize that?"

"Aye. He will employ any number of unscrupulous tactics in his quest for what is mine."

"And you alone are equal to the task of fending him off?"

She hesitated. Honesty. He had said honesty was vitally important to him. What should she say? Responsibility weighed heavy upon her heart. She thought of Peter, the young guard who had lost his life when she refused to admit Dominic to the castle. How much worse would it get? How many more would die before her future was secure and all the people of Pendragon along with her?

"Nay, my lord. I have the courage and determination, but I lack the experience and the skill to fight this battle."

"I agree."

He gazed into the fire for a moment, leaving Rowena to battle her dread. He couldn't force a husband on her, but what else could he mean by his questions?

"As distasteful as the prospect is to you, my dear, you need another husband. A strong, competent man will be able to protect and shelter you from this conflict.

Your claim to Pendragon will never be completely solidified until you have an heir. A legitimate heir is not possible without a husband. Is there no one in your life who you find suitable as a spouse?"

"My first marriage was an abomination. I have not even considered any man since Gaston died. I would have to give the idea some thought."

"What of Dominic? He is a good man. *I* trust him. If his child grows in your belly, he will not be willing to watch another man raise his offspring."

She knew his concern was misplaced, but she couldn't explain this to Sir William. "We only spent one night together. I doubt there will be a child."

"Still, Dominic has the right to know. And if it comes to pass that you do carry his babe, I will request that you accept him as your husband."

"Request?" Challenge rang in her voice.

"You have no father to guide you in this area. You are still very young. Your entire life lies ahead of you. Do you not want children?"

"I did not want Gaston's children."

"Edwin will not relent. He may become so desperate that he'll attempt to take your life. I'll do what I can to see that doesn't happen, but a husband would protect you."

"I know," she muttered. Everything he said was true, but she couldn't marry for protection. Her next husband must love her, and she must love him. How could she hope to make William Marshal understand?

"I have instructed Dominic to escort you back to Pendragon Castle. More than that I will not decree. I would be pleased if you would invite him to stay until you have determined whether or not you carry his child."

"And when that determination is made?"

"Then I request that you either accept Dominic as your husband or name another. I want this thing settled quickly. Are we in agreement?"

He would be *pleased* if she remarried. He *encouraged* her to accept Dominic as her husband. Under all the pleasant phrasing, Rowena recognized his authority.

Her hands crumpled the soft material of her surcoat. The beautiful standard felt oppressive now. She had been such a fool! She had honestly believed that it would end here, that she would be allowed to control her own destiny. "I have a fortnight, perhaps the passing of a moon, to choose the man with whom I will share the rest of my life?"

"I didn't mention a specific period of time. I only said quickly. But Dominic is the *only* man I will accept if you are carrying his child."

"I understand."

"And you agree?"

"What choice do I have?" she flared. "You have made your preferences quite clear, my lord."

"Rowena," he said gently. "I'm thinking of your safety and hoping for your happiness whether you believe it or not."

She swallowed and forced herself to speak. "My lord, you mentioned the Pendragon curse yestereve. When Gaston died, I allowed myself to believe that I might be the Lady destined to end this cycle of unhappiness."

His thin lips pressed into a grim line. Rowena feared she'd angered him until she realized he was trying not to laugh.

"Laugh if you like," she muttered. "I have seen Fair Fiona with my own eyes."

One silvery brow arched at her claim. "So what must you do to break the Pendragon curse?"

"I must marry for love and love alone."

"Is the order specified?"

She scooted to the edge of her chair. "The order of what?"

"Must you love this man before you marry him or is it permissible for love to come after the wedding? And what if he loves you, but you do not love him? Love can also prove false, dear child. If you are in love and the curse is broken, will it be reinstated should you be betrayed?"

He was mocking her. Gently and deftly, but mocking her all the same. "There is no detailed charter to be agreed upon and then disregarded."

William guffawed at her bold rejoinder. "King John might have taken offense to that, young lady, but I am not King John. Besides, we have strayed far off course. Your belief in this curse does not change the reality of your situation. You need a husband."

"I need a husband I can love," she insisted.

"Then I suggest you fall in love with all due haste."

* * * * *

They departed Windsor Castle the following morning. The distance between Windsor and Pendragon could be covered in a single day, but the leisurely pace set by the large procession would require a night in the forest.

Rowena relaxed into the rhythm of her horse and tried not to think, but she was unable to hide her frustration from anyone. Even Thora's persistent attempts at humor failed to draw her from her angry silence.

Dominic found a clearing for their camp as deepening shadows claimed the forest. Rowena slid down from her palfrey's back and groaned softly as her muscles cramped in protest. One of the men led her horse away toward a rope pen while another bent to build a fire. Dominic and Ezra disappeared into the trees in search of game. A small tournament tent was quickly erected for the women, and Rowena found herself feeling rather useless.

"Rather impressive, aren't they?" Thora asked cheerfully.

"Very efficient." Rowena arched her back and rolled her shoulders.

"Are you still simmering?"

"He expects me to find a husband as soon as I possibly can. Why would I be angry?"

Rowena regretted her biting tone when Thora turned around and walked away. Thora went to help with the meal's preparations, but Rowena loitered by the edge of the campsite.

She should follow Thora and apologize, but what Rowena really needed was a moment alone in the trees. There would be time later to make amends.

Finding a secluded spot, Rowena answered nature's call. She could hear voices and the muted shuffle of restless horses, so she wasted no time. After straightening her clothing, Rowena tried to appear casual as she picked her way back to camp.

"Do ye think she realizes what they've done?"

The question brought Rowena up short. She didn't recognize the man's voice, wasn't certain why she'd stopped, but she waited for the voice to speak again.

"What *you* think they've done, more like it," a different man replied.

Rowena crept toward the sound of their voices. They spoke English, a language most noblewomen couldn't understand.

Were they speaking of her?

"There's no thinking about it, man," the tall one said. "Dominic makes no secret of his ambition. He intended to secure a holding and now he has one."

The trees offered some protection, but Rowena kept to the shadows, moving slowly, deliberately, placing each foot carefully as not to make a sound. They were tending the horses. She'd heard Ezra call the taller one Hubert, but she didn't know the other man's name.

Hubert continued. "No year-long siege, no bloody battle, just a wedding. What could be easier?"

The other man turned suddenly, and Rowena ducked behind a clump of bushes. Her heart pounded as anxiety stole her breath. Had he seen her?

"If a woman's involved nothing's easy." Both men laughed at the comment and Rowena began to relax. She moved a leafy branch aside to better her view.

"Besides, if she proves to be too difficult, Dominic knows how to deal with unwanted women," Hubert said.

His companion laughed. "Aye, snap their necks and toss them down the stairs."

Shifting her weight onto her knees, Rowena slowly exhaled. They were laughing again. How could they find humor in such violence, even in jest?

"Don't let him hear you talk like that. He's still prickly about what happened," Hubert cautioned.

"I'm not a woman, so what do I care? He only kills men on the battlefield, and I fight at his side."

Hubert cuffed his companion playfully on the shoulder. "Just keep your wagging tongue between your teeth when Dominic is around."

A lump formed in the pit of her stomach. These men honestly believed Dominic had murdered someone. Their conversation moved on, and Rowena carefully backed away into the darkness.

She had been the victim of vicious lies, so she tried not to pay heed to whispered rumors. Still, their words echoed through her mind. What did she really know about Dominic? He had William Marshal's ear. If he wanted something he could persuade the regent to act on his behalf.

Her steps sped as her anxiety escalated. William Marshal told her Dominic was the only man he would accept if she were carrying his child. Had the regent offered Dominic a secret encouragement? Had he approved Dominic's plan to…to what?

She collided with something huge and solid and screamed. Large hands clasped her upper arms and she screamed again.

"My lady." Ezra's voice cut through her fear. "What is amiss?"

A ragged sigh escaped Rowena and Ezra released her arms. "I…I lost my way." Dominic and one of his men came crashing through the underbrush, swords drawn, expressions fierce.

"What? Who screamed?" Dominic demanded.

"Lady Rowena lost her bearings. She is well." Ezra took a step back, his gaze narrowed with speculation. "Why were you running?"

Rowena felt like a fool. She glanced from Ezra's concerned face to Dominic's dark visage and swallowed the lump in her throat. "I thought I saw something. As you said, I am well."

Dominic sheathed his sword and came closer, his penetrating gaze searching her face. "Why did you leave camp?"

"It was a rather long ride."

It took a moment for him to understand the meaning in her expression, but then he nodded. "Are you hungry?"

He reached for her arm, and Rowena shrank away.

"What is wrong with you?" His tone was hushed and confused.

Rowena glanced beyond him. The other two had departed. She was alone with Dominic. "I want to go back to camp."

He raised his hand slowly, as if to soothe a spooked horse or a frightened child. "What frightened you so? You've never pulled away from me before."

"It's just the darkness. Please, take me back to camp."

With a resigned sigh, his hand left her skin, and he motioned her in the direction the others had gone.

The camp was bustling when they returned. Several rabbits had been spitted and were roasting over the fire. Thora chatted away as she helped Ezra rotate the meat. Rowena found a log near the tournament tent and sat. She stared off into the darkened forest, gradually becoming oblivious to the activity around her. Shock and disappointment kept her from feeling anything stronger.

"Are you sure you are well?"

Rowena looked up and found Dominic standing directly in front of her. Warm awareness melded with a tingle of uncertainty. For one sparkling moment she had believed there was good in the world, that a man could be brave and true. But now the moment was past and she must protect herself again.

"There's no reason to fret." She forced calm into her voice. "I'm tired, but it's nothing a good night's sleep will not heal."

"Good."

She wasn't sure he believed her, but it no longer mattered.

"I find myself once again entrusted with your safekeeping. Are you going to be as difficult to protect as you were before?"

"Do you believe I need protecting? Could Edwin be nearby, waiting to ambush us?" She tried to sound lighthearted, but the thought had crossed her mind.

"I believe Edwin scurried home. You should be perfectly safe unless you wander off into the woods alone." He offered her a challenging smile.

"I will behave."

His smile disappeared, and he leaned toward her, his voice soft and low. "But I will not."

Feeling vulnerable with him towering over her, Rowena stood. "You will not, what?"

"Behave." He reached out and stroked her cheek. She managed not to shrink away this time. "I vowed not to touch you before, Rowena. No such vow binds me now."

The wind caught the filmy fabric of her wimple and tangled it around his hand, trapping his fingers against her skin. "Is that a warning?" She tried to ignore the irrational ache low in her belly. She couldn't still want this man!

"Warning. Promise. Solemn vow. It is whichever you prefer."

Before she could respond, he withdrew his hand and walked away.

Chapter Seven

"It looks like Sir Dominic won that round." Thora returned to Rowena's side.

"It wasn't a verbal joust, Thora, just a confusing exchange."

Thora handed her the hindquarters of a rabbit, and they sat on the log, side by side. Rowena nibbled absently, licking the grease from her fingers and her bottom lip. Ezra handed her a leather pouch of nuts and dried fruit. She poured a small pile onto her lap and passed the pouch to Thora. A wineskin followed. Rowena did her best to pretend nothing was wrong.

Hubert and his uncouth friend sat directly across the fire from Rowena. She couldn't look at them without feeling her skin crawl. When she raised the rabbit to her lips, her stomach heaved. With a pang of guilt, she tossed the half-eaten leg into the fire and brushed the last of the nuts into the dirt. Food was precious, but her appetite had deserted her. Hubert wolfed down his portion, conversing casually, as if he hadn't disrupted her entire world.

Thora prattled on about the Pendragon curse, and Rowena glanced at Dominic. His strong, harsh features captivated her. Why was she drawn to this man? How could she still find him attractive? He tore off a chunk of meat and raised it to his mouth. His hands were large and capable. *Capable of breaking a woman's neck?* Rowena shuddered and looked into the fire. It was a rumor, nothing more.

"So, if Lady Rowena can produce a male child, the curse will be broken?" Ezra asked Thora.

"Nay, the barrenness of Pendragon ladies is a result of the curse, but not the curse itself. It's the Lady's happiness that must be won for the curse to be truly lifted."

"'Til the Lady finds the fate that once I sought," Rowena quoted ominously. "Disappointment, pain and death shall be thy lot!"

"What fate was Fiona seeking?" Hubert asked.

"Happiness," Ezra echoed Thora's sentiments.

"Nay, 'tis more than that," Rowena said. "Fair Fiona was searching for a heart true and honorable enough to deserve her love. I think the Lady, whomever she may be, will have to find true love."

"And if true love doesn't exist?" Dominic challenged.

"Then Pendragon Castle is doomed." Rowena glanced off into the darkness.

"Even if the Lady can manage to find true love, she will still have the riddle to contend with," Thora reminded, drawing the men's attention back to her.

"Riddle?" Ezra asked.

"Of course." Thora's gaze glistened in the firelight. "My...er, Grandmother said that it's a vital part of freeing us from the curse. To vanquish the curse, the Lady will have to unravel the riddle."

Rowena laughed. "It's odd that this riddle is not part of the original ballad. No one remembers when or how the riddle became part of lifting the curse."

"How does it go? Can you recite the riddle?" Ezra encouraged, obviously captivated.

"What is always lonely but never alone? Possesses nothing but has riches untold? Speaks only silence but shares tales far and wide? Remains hidden forever in the shadows of night?"

A long silence followed Thora's oration. Rowena watched their expressions turn distant as they struggled through the questions, trying to find some common element.

"What does it mean?" Hubert asked.

"No one really knows." Thora was in her element with every eye fixed upon her. "Only the Lady will be able to find the meaning."

Another hush followed and Rowena chuckled, deciding to amuse herself just a bit. "I think it is referring to Fearsome Dragon."

"Really?" Hubert's gaze shifted to Rowena's face. "Explain, milady."

"Well, if you are a dragon, you cannot be seen by most mortals, so that would make you lonely. You would own nothing, yet even the dragon on the Pendragon standard has jewel-encrusted wings. A dragon cannot speak, but tales about dragons are known far and wide. And like many other mythical creatures they are hidden from our world like a shadow."

"She doesn't believe a word of it." Thora glared at her across the fire. "This is the fourth solution milady has concocted since first she heard the riddle. Our present Lady Pendragon does not believe in the legend."

Rowena shook her head. "Not so. I know that powerful forces are at work over Pendragon Castle. Fairies are real. I have seen Fair Fiona. But the legend has evolved over the years, becoming more complex and darker. The riddle was not part of the ballad, and the ballad does not mention the treasure. I think the legend has been twisted 'til it is hard to know what is real and what is—"

"Real?" Sir Ezra interrupted. "You believe that fairies are real?"

"Treasure?" Hubert asked before she could respond. "There be a treasure promised to the Lady?"

Ignoring Hubert, Rowena answered Ezra. "I *know* that fairies are real. Whether they have the power to control the lives of men, I can only suppose. But generation after generation has fallen to the curse. What other explanation could there be?"

"Ill fortune, war, treachery, disease," Dominic listed. "These seem a bit more feasible than a Fairy curse. Gaston was killed in a tournament, was he not? There is nothing mystical in that."

Thora looked at her expectantly, but Rowena held her peace. She should be used to others mocking her belief in the legend, but somehow it still stung.

The conversation turned to the tournaments recently held in the North of France, and Rowena stopped listening. She had no patience for men and their foolish games.

Without thinking to explain her actions, she stood and slipped away into the darkness. A narrow trail led to the brook, which wound its way down through the forest. She could still see the fire in the distance and hear an occasional voice.

With a frustrated sigh, Rowena sat on a flat rock near the water's edge and drew her legs up under her tunic. She wrapped her arms around her knees and stared out over the rippling water.

What in the world was she going to do? Her world had shifted from agony to bliss and back all in a matter of days.

Moonlight danced on the surface of the brook and the crisp scent of pine gently perfumed the air. She should be soothed by the tranquil night, but she wasn't. Half of her wanted to close the gates to Pendragon Castle and never allow another male within the curtain walls. The other half wanted to pretend she had never heard the hateful things Hubert and his friend had said. To believe Dominic was noble and true. That his only motivation for misleading William had been to protect her from Edwin.

"Am I intruding?"

Dominic.

She unfolded her legs and slipped to the ground on the far side of the rock. She couldn't let him touch her. Rational thought abandoned her whenever he touched her.

"Will you leave if I say you are?" She slowly turned to face him.

"Nay." He smiled. "I think you want me here."

"Do you now?" She crossed her arms over her chest, hoping to hide their trembling. "You think I crept away into the night, hoping you'd follow?"

"I didn't say that. I know you intended to be alone with your thoughts. But thoughts are far easier to decipher if you have an objective assistant."

Her lips were suddenly dry and she found it hard to swallow. "You don't want to decipher my thoughts just now. I have no use for anyone of your gender."

He moved toward the rock. Rowena wasn't foolish enough to feel protected by the barrier.

"Then don't think of me as a man but as a friend."

There it was again, the false gentleness, the counterfeit caring that made her want to trust him. She drew in a deep breath and nervously licked her lips. "You're far too much a man to ever be my friend."

"Then let me be your lover."

It was a velvet temptation, a honeyed lure. She dug her fingernails into her palms as she struggled to resist. "I cannot."

"Aye, you can." He reached across the rock and took her wrist. "You should." He pulled her around to stand before him. "You will." He wrapped his arms around her.

Rowena felt as if he cast a spell. Her rational mind was screaming *Beware!*, but her body went willingly into his embrace. Heat radiated off him, beckoning her, attracting her. "I will not lie down with you." She turned her face aside.

"Then we will not lie down."

He lowered his face, but she twisted away, shoving against his broad chest. "I will not be your lover. Not tonight, not ever!"

Slipping under her wimple, he grasped the back of her hair. His eyes burned into hers, and his expression promised no mercy. "We will be lovers, Rowena. If not tonight, then soon."

Before she could argue, he kissed her. His lips pressed against hers, moved over hers, molded and contoured until she finally opened to him. His tongue sank slowly into her mouth. It was an act of possession, a deliberate penetration that clearly staked his claim.

Rowena trembled, overwhelmed by the sudden onslaught. Her hands clutched against his shoulders, neither pushing him away nor drawing him near. Every nerve in her body hummed with awareness and anticipation.

His face shifted, his lips angling so he could stroke her tongue with his, dance along her teeth and taste every surface of her mouth. Rowena allowed his intimate exploration for a time, but soon she was returning each caress, stroking and curling and learning his taste.

He wouldn't let her breathe except from his breath. Her head spun and her legs wobbled. He threaded his fingers through hers and pushed her arms behind her, pressing their joined hands down against the rock.

Rowena couldn't think. She needed more of him. She needed all of him.

She arched her back and murmured his name.

"I could take you now, Rowena," he whispered against her moist lips. "But I want more than a frantic moment, stolen in the shadows. I want to see you and touch you and taste you. I want to take you over and over until we are both too weak to move."

His words cut through the haze and Rowena opened her eyes. He was right. She would have wrapped her legs around his waist and allowed him anything.

Shame and fear intertwined. Rowena dragged great gulps of air into her burning lungs. He still held her hands interlaced with his. "Let go of me."

"Not yet." He moved in closer, crossing her arms behind her back. "I would have your word first."

"My word?" she echoed, shaken and confused.

"Tell me I am welcome in your bed."

She glared at him. Why was he pushing her like this? "Release me."

"Nay. I would have this settled between us. We are meant to be lovers. You feel the fire, I know you do. Can you deny it?"

She stared at him in mutinous silence. "Why did you defend me to Sir William?"

Even in the darkness she could see confusion in his eyes. "Would you rather I didn't?"

"Nay. You rescued me from Edwin, and for that you have my gratitude, but I'll not allow you to take his place."

He made a harsh, scoffing sound, and Rowena arched away.

He leaned in closer, pressing her against the rock. "I am not Edwin. Do not *ever* compare me to him again." His grip eased and his expression changed. "This is not about your holdings. It's about the fire you ignited the first time you touched me."

His mouth hovered above hers, part promise, part threat.

"You know why I behaved that way," she objected.

"And you know why I cannot stop thinking about you. Why you torment my dreams and burn in my blood. We *will* be lovers, Rowena."

Her body stiffened. She refused to be bullied.

His expression softened, and Rowena saw her opportunity. She raised her knee into his groin with just enough force to startle him. He groaned and staggered back a step, immediately releasing her hands.

She didn't pause or look behind her. She ran back to camp and ducked into the tournament tent. With an exasperated curse, Rowena tore off her wimple and threw it across the tent.

"Now that is not a nice word at all. You should be ashamed of yourself."

Rowena turned on Thora with all of the emotional combustibility building within her all day. "I will not do it! I will not bow and scrape every time a man tells me to. I will not sacrifice my freedom and surrender the only power I have ever known!" Each declaration brought her closer to tears. "I do not care if I must remain cursed. Men cannot be trusted. They lie. They manipulate. They cheat and…seduce." The last word ended on a sob.

Thora's arms closed around her as Rowena surrendered to the tears.

* * * * *

Brother Leland no longer feared the dark. It had become part of him. Not like the bleak, empty blackness of an evil man's soul, but the velvet tranquility of a starless night.

The long, mournful moan of rusty hinges disturbed the silence, drawing his head toward the door. A cool draft curled around him and he inhaled the blissful scent of untainted air. But the fetid stench of his barren cell quickly corrupted the breeze, making it rank and putrid.

"You look rather peaked, Leland. I thought you *brothers* were used to confinement and want."

He recognized the voice, yet the features had faded to shadows, lost forever in the mist of his memory. "Edwin," Brother Leland rasped, turning his sightless eyes in the direction of the voice. "Why do you persist in this foolishness?"

"Because you persist in your denials. You need only open your mouth and I will set you free."

From somewhere deep within his frail form, spirit bubbled to life. Brother Leland parted his lips and defiantly opened his mouth.

A silence as absolute as death fell upon the room. Would Edwin beat him? Would he finally release him from this purgatory? Leland was not afraid to die, but he was weary of hunger and waiting. How long had he been imprisoned here with little to drink and less to eat?

"Solve the riddle and I will feed you. Tell me how to find the treasure and I will let you go." Edwin's voice finally cut through the tension.

Leland sighed. So, it would go on. "The riddle, like the legend, is nothing more than superstitious nonsense. I'm a man of God. I'd be foolish indeed to believe in those blasphemous tales. I told you this before you departed for Windsor Castle. If I were hiding some great secret, would I not have told you by now?"

"How do you account for what Gaston told me?" Edwin demanded.

He heard the scuffle of Edwin's boots, could picture his physical advance. But visual intimidation was wasted on him. "Gaston was dying when he insisted that I understood the riddle. You told me yourself he was nearly mad with the pain. He was babbling nonsense. You must accept the fact and make things right or God Himself will judge you."

"I'm not afraid of your god," Edwin stated. "Nor do I believe in a fiery hell where evil men shall suffer for all eternity."

"Yet you accept this legend as fact?" Brother Leland challenged. "It's harder to believe in a Benevolent Maker than in a Fairy curse?"

"Why would a benevolent maker allow his servant to rot away in a cage? Why has your god not smote me dead and set you free?"

"Who am I to question the ways of God? I yet live, and if you slay me I'll go on to my eternal reward. Do as you please and I'll pray for your soul."

"The world has had its share of martyrs, Brother Leland. I'm not yet ready to deprive myself of your company."

Leland snorted and shook his shaggy head. "I cannot solve the riddle, so set me free or end it now. I have no preference."

Edwin was silent for a long time. "I have misjudged you."

Leland's bony hand moved to the simple wooden cross that hung around his neck. "How so, my lord?"

There was no reply.

Heavy footfalls announced his captor's departure, but Leland didn't hear the door close. His heartbeat became painful and he scrambled to get his legs beneath him. Straw abraded his knees and one foot caught against an uneven stone. Was he intended to escape?

Heaving with all his might, Leland pushed himself upright on trembling legs. How would he ever get away when he could hardly stand?

There was no specific sound, no shift in the air, but suddenly he knew he was no longer alone. "Is someone there?" He extended his hands in front of him.

Warm fingers encircled his upper arm and Leland gasped.

"Come with me," a stranger's voice said softly. "I will not hurt you."

Fear uncurled with brutal intensity. *Have I always been a coward?*

"Where are you taking me?" The stranger helped him toward the door.

"I'm to clean you up and find something to fill your belly."

The voice belonged to either a lad or a young woman, but Leland wasn't certain which. The hand on his arm was gentle yet strong. "What's your name, child?" He was too exhausted to puzzle it out.

The stranger navigated him out of the cell and turned him toward the right. "Nan, Brother Leland. I've not seen you in many years, but I remember you."

A dark-haired child with large brown eyes and rosy checks flickered to life within Leland's mind, and he smiled. "Nan. You have a sister named Bess and a brother too if memory serves me."

"There be four brothers now. As I said, it's been many years." She paused then took several steps farther down the stone corridor. "I cannot believe the evil done in this house. I sometimes fear for my very soul just setting foot in this place."

He didn't respond. They climbed to a landing. "Now what?" He was embarrassed that his legs were trembling from the strain of so simple a task.

"Rest a spell then I'll take you to the kitchen." Nan rested a comforting hand on his narrow shoulder.

Leland took a long, deep breath, trying in vain to convince himself that his ordeal was nearly over.

* * * * *

Submerged to her chin in warm, scented water, Rowena did her best to relax, but as Thora had suspected, she was still simmering. She had hoped to return with her future secured forever, but William Marshal had spoiled her plans. How did one fall in love with all due haste? The regent scowled at her from one side while Fair Fiona pressured her from the other.

"What are you brooding about?" Thora asked. She held a pitcher of clean water for Rowena's hair.

"There has to be some way to thwart that man. I must have time to make a love match."

Thora paused beside the bathing tub, the pitcher resting against her hip. "Which man are we thwarting now?"

"William Marshal." Rowena looked up at Thora as she began to laugh. "Why are you laughing?"

"You've grown so bored tormenting knights and barons that you'll now provoke King Henry's regent? He is an old man. You might well kill him with your antics."

Rowena sat up straight in the wooden tub, abandoning all pretence at relaxation. "He insists I need a husband *immediately* to protect myself and my holdings." Rowena began to scrub herself vigorously. "Could not those same protections be provided by mercenaries and a personal guard?"

Thora's amusement faded away. "I thought we had this settled last night. If William Marshal bid you marry, you had best get yourself a husband."

"But think about it, Thora. If I reinforce my household guards and hire someone to see to my personal safety, then there would be no need for an immediate wedding. I must marry for love this time or the curse will continue to the next generation."

Thora set the pitcher down beside the tub and sank to her knees. Rowena looked up into her face when Thora laid a gentle hand on her shoulder. "You know I believe in the curse, Rowena, but that is not what troubles you. I think you're frightened. You're hiding behind the curse to avoid marriage altogether."

"I will wed again. But I must have time to find a man—"

"You cannot fight William Marshal."

"I will not fight him, exactly. I will only find a less conventional way of fulfilling his expectations."

The compassion in Thora's bright blue eyes made Rowena fidget. She needed an ally to support her scheme, not the voice of reason.

"It might put him off for a time, but eventually you will need an heir. You have no siblings, no male relatives. The closest you can come to kin is Edwin, and I thought we were trying to keep Pendragon out of his hands."

Rowena threw a wet chunk of soap as hard as she could. It bounced off the wall and went skidding across the floor, leaving a slimy trail in its wake.

"Feel better?" Thora gently mocked her tantrum.

"I cannot do it, Thora." Her bottom lip trembled and she drew her knees up to her chest. Indulging her temper had only robbed her of anger's strength. "I cannot pledge my troth and promise to obey."

"You could find some sniveling fool who will scramble to do your bidding. Or at least a man who is easily intimidated. Of course that's not the sort of man I'd want in my bed, but it might pacify Sir William."

"I don't know many timid knights," Rowena grumbled. "Besides, he made it clear that he expects to approve my choice."

"And what sort of man will he approve?"

Glancing at her handmaiden, Rowena said, "Sir Dominic's sort."

She stood and bent forward so Thora could rinse her hair. This was the pose that had sent Dominic over the edge. Or nearly over the edge. Goose flesh broke out on her arms, but Rowena blamed it on a nonexistent draft.

"Have you spoken with him?" Thora apparently guessed her thoughts.

"Nay. I'm not sure there is anything left to say."

Thora handed her a drying cloth and Rowena stepped from the tub. She wrapped herself in the soft cloth and accepted the second, smaller cloth meant for her long hair.

"Are you in love with him?" Thora gaze studied her intently.

Rowena bit off an immediate denial. "I don't know. He affects me as no man ever has, but I cannot trust him."

"Do you believe what you heard those men say? Is he capable of murder?"

Rowena started to defend him, when doubt held the words at bay. She had glimpsed the dark, ruthless side to Dominic's nature only the night before. Undaunted. He would have what he desired and *nothing* would stand in his way.

"I don't know." The admission tore at Rowena's heart.

"Then stay away from him."

Rowena accepted the advice with a stiff nod. "Have you seen Milton?"

"That's where I'm bound as soon as you've finished with me."

"Then be gone." Rowena dismissed her with a halfhearted smile.

Thora didn't hesitate.

She left the solar and quietly closed the door. Pausing in the stairwell, she transformed, dissolving her human glamour and returning to her Fairy shape. She'd sent Fearsome Dragon to spy on Dominic, hoping a male could garner a clearer perspective of the enigmatic knight.

The dragon drifted out of the soldier barracks, his hulking form only visible to her. "What did you hear? Does the knight have Sir William's permission to seduce Rowena?" Her voice melded with the wind, blended with the night sounds until no human could discern her words.

"Despite his men's continual encouragement, the knight did not speak of private matters."

She harrumphed, twirling rapidly with the exhalation. "Just what we need. A secretive man."

Fearsome Dragon chuckled. "Leave them alone, Fiona. If it's meant to be, they'll come together on their own." He drifted out into the night.

"Where are you going?"

"Away from these cursed walls. Summon me if I'm needed."

Fearsome Dragon was right. This was best left alone. The human couple felt desire for each other, but attraction wasn't enough. They must love each other. Love couldn't be forced. And unfortunately, it couldn't be rushed.

Fiona searched the bailey for a secluded place to transform. Milton was waiting for her. He was amusing for a mortal, good-natured and kind. Still her lack of progress frustrated her. She was ready to go home. She missed the Fairy realm. Even missed her obnoxious father.

Dominic strode out of the barracks, moonlight glistening in his freshly washed hair. Quickly masking her presence, Fair Fiona studied him. Strength and purpose emanated from his posture and movements. Here was a man who knew what he wanted and was not afraid to pursue a goal.

But murder?

She flew backward in front of him, perusing his face. There was no cruelty in his eyes, no barbarism.

This was not a murderer.

Where was he bound?

His present course would take him... Surely, he wasn't headed where he appeared to be headed.

Taking the stairs two at a time, he climbed to Rowena's solar. Fiona flew in his wake, knowing she couldn't interfere. The outer room was empty, as was the bedchamber. Rowena must be in the wardrobe.

He unfastened his sword and placed it within reach.

The curtain leading to the wardrobe slid open and Rowena stood framed in the opening, a candle clasped in one hand. Her eyes widened as they focused on him.

Fiona watched desire ignite in the lady's gaze, a soul-deep longing that made Fiona ache just looking at it. This was more than physical attraction. The air was sweet with deeper, richer emotions.

"What are you doing here?"

"You knew I would come. We have unfinished business, you and I."

Encouraged by the unexpected progress, Fiona flew from the room.

Chapter Eight

Dominic stood beside the bed, his gaze fixed on Rowena. Her hand trembled so badly he feared she'd drop the candle. Her face appeared fresh and rosy in the soft candlelight, and his suspicion that she wore nothing beneath the dressing gown fueled his imagination.

He'd frightened her the night before. He'd moved too quickly and she panicked. His determination to have her had not lessened, so he spent most of the day praying for patience.

"I shall scream."

"Perhaps." Her brow furrowed at his taunt and he smiled. "The guard at the foot of your stairs is my man. He has orders to keep anyone and everyone at bay. For this one night, Rowena, you are mine."

"I belong to no man!"

"This isn't about possession. It's about passion. This moment became inevitable when you first touched me." He moved toward her slowly, commanding her attention with his gaze. "Tell me honestly that you don't want me and I'll leave."

"I don't *trust* you."

He took the candle from her hand. "I can accept that."

She crossed her arms over her chest, lifting her chin. "I know what you're doing."

"I'm seducing you."

"You're seducing Pendragon Castle."

Dominic shook his head. "Not tonight. Tonight we are only a man and a woman. There is no past and no tomorrow, just this room, and you and I."

She turned around. He could see her shoulders tremble. "I cannot pretend, Dominic, not even for one night. Too many people depend upon me. If I make a wrong decision it affects the lives of —"

"I know what William asked of you," he interrupted. "When you're ready to marry again, your husband will expect a widow not a virgin."

She whirled around. A strand of her damp hair whipped his face. "How do you know what William Marshal said to me?"

Dominic took a deep breath and chose his next words more carefully. "There is no other resolution to your dilemma. You must find a husband. What else could he have said to you?"

"And what did he tell *you*?"

He didn't want to lie to her, but he wouldn't allow her suspicions to compromise his purpose. She would sleep in his arms this night. The rest they could negotiate on the morrow. "He told me to stay long enough to find out whether or not you carry my child."

"I do not, you may go."

He laughed. He couldn't help himself. She looked so adorably affronted. "Rowena, you're making this much too complicated. I want to make love to you. That's all I want."

"Rubbish. You want it all. Just like Edwin, you want everything."

Her words stung. He had expected them, perhaps even deserved them, but they made him angry all the same. "Not tonight. Tonight is for us. Dominic and Rowena. Nothing else."

"Unless you plant your child in my womb, then William Marshal will make sure you get more than just one night."

"There are ways to prevent conception, Rowena." She stared back at him in silent confusion, obviously unaware of what he meant. "I will not spill my seed inside your body then there can be no child. But we will have this night."

She said nothing, so he turned and walked back to the bed. Setting the candle on the stone shelf, he sat and took off his boots. She stood where he'd left her, silent and uncertain. He drew off his tunic and tossed it aside. Her eyes followed his every move.

Standing again, he shed his braies. Dominic waited for her to emerge from her stupor. Her eyes widened as her gaze moved over his naked body. He knew that his body was a testament to his life, hard and honed by battle. She seemed pleased, he supposed, interested certainly.

"I cannot do this." He could barely hear her words.

He strode back across the chamber and stood before her. "Touch me," he whispered.

She shook her head.

He took her hand and splayed it across the middle of his chest. "Feel how my heart pounds." Rowena curved her fingers into the flesh of his powerful chest. She had dreamed of this, longed for this, and he knew it. His heart hammered against her palm, and she felt her own heart take on the same rhythm.

He took her other hand and guided it to his erection. She gasped. He groaned. Giddy excitement raced through her and she had to fight back a giggle. He was so hot, so hard. She looked down at the thick column of flesh cradled in her palm, and her inner muscles clenched. Her body knew how they would join, understood she was meant for this. Her fingers looked pale against his dusky skin. She passed her thumb over his flared tip. A bead of moisture welled from the tiny opening. She glanced up, but his eyes were closed, his chest shuddering with ragged breaths. Fascinated, she smoothed the liquid over his skin. She licked her lips, filled with the urge to taste this secret elixir. Was such a thing allowed? If she slipped to her knees, would he let her —

Suddenly, almost violently, he brushed her hand away and swept her up into his arms. He strode across the room and placed her in the middle of the bed. He quickly settled himself beside her, his breath harsh and heavy. Instinctively, she tried to stop him as he reached for the cord holding her garment together.

"I want to see you," he whispered.

Rowena stared up at him. He was the most amazing man she'd ever seen. Fully dressed and scowling, she found him attractive. Naked and seductive, she couldn't resist.

He moved her hands to her sides and parted the dressing gown, exposing her entire body to his heated gaze. She bit her lip and steeled herself for the rejection. She was skinny, her breasts small, her hips narrow. He'd scorn her and leave her.

She held her breath, waiting...

"God's blood, Rowena. I could spend a lifetime just looking at you."

His voice was so husky, so strangled, she looked into his eyes. "You find me pleasing?"

"Pleasing? You're perfect." He covered her breast with his palm. "See how well we fit. It's as if you were fashioned for me alone."

Her heart leapt in response to his praise, but she was still afraid. How could she surrender her body to a man she didn't trust?

What was she doing?

For this one night, Rowena, you are mine.

You are perfect.

It is as if you were fashioned for me alone.

She could give him one night. She could give it to herself. They would be lovers—for this one night.

His hand gently squeezed her breast. "Kiss me, Dominic. Don't stop kissing me."

He slipped one arm beneath her neck and settled his mouth over hers. She parted her lips and met the intimate thrust of his tongue. Her fingers found his hair and tangled there, preventing his withdrawal.

He touched her, patiently stroking her breasts and only her breasts. She wanted his hands everywhere and she wanted to touch him too. Her free hand found his back, absorbing the texture and the heat with greedy abandon. His fingers plucked her nipple and Rowena quivered. There were so many sensations, each of them new.

His fingers drifted down along her torso and she automatically brought up her leg, bending her knee and angling her leg to protect the apex of her thighs. He deepened the kiss, drugging her mind, distracting her while his hand insinuated itself between her legs.

Her head spun, but shock brought everything he did into sharp focus. Fear and excitement alternated, tugging her in opposite directions. His long fingers combed through her tight curls. He kept kissing her. His middle finger sank between her folds. He kept kissing her. He found that sensitive spot that made her whole body jump, but he kept right on kissing her.

She clutched his shoulders and held perfectly still as he rubbed her and slid the length of his finger against that special spot. Tension built within her. She couldn't seem to catch her breath.

"Relax, love," he whispered against her mouth. "Let me touch you."

He nudged her legs apart, making more room for his hand. "You are touching me."

He'd done this once before, but he'd left her aching then. He wouldn't stop tonight. There was no reason for him to stop. His fingers slid over and around, and the pleasure built inside her. Rowena grabbed his face and abandoned herself to their kisses. Kissing was safe, kissing was familiar.

He stroked her, desire making her body slick and hot. Rotating his wrist, he caressed her from different angles. She gasped and pushed up with her heels, rocking her pelvis, grinding against his hand, unable to stop the instinctive motion.

Rowena cried out. Her inner muscles squeezed as pleasure showered her body like tingling rain. Dominic moved between her legs, pushing her knees up and back. He spread her thighs with his knees and rubbed against her with something more substantial than his fingertips. She arched her back, the emptiness within her painful. He found her entrance with his shaft and stroked her nub with his thumb, maintaining her staggering arousal.

One of his hands slipped beneath her, tilting her pelvis upward as he drove his hips down. She felt her body stretch and burn, accepting his penetration. Rowena couldn't suppress a ragged sob. Uncertainty surged through her desire, and she clasped her thighs against his hips, trying to stave him off.

He murmured her name, part plea and part prayer, then thrust hard, burying himself fully within her. Rowena cried out. The pain faded quickly, but it had robbed her of breath. She dragged air into her burning lungs and tried not to panic.

He didn't move. Dominic held her close, stroking her hair away from her face and kissing her lightly. "The worst is over," he promised. "Just relax. Feel me inside you."

She could feel nothing else. He was huge and hot, and her body gripped him in fluttering spasms. He was kissing her again, and Rowena felt her fear dissipate. His fingers feathered caresses over her breasts.

He pulled back slowly, dragging himself nearly out of her. It stung and Rowena stiffened. She waited for him to thrust back inside, but he did something unexpected. He slipped his hand between their bodies and found that special knot just above where their bodies were joined. His fingers began a circular dance that made her whimper and tremble. A hot rush of liquid flowed through her core as if her body had melted beneath a midsummer sun.

"Oh aye," he whispered. "That's what we needed."

He rocked his hips forward, filling her in one long, steady thrust. Her fingers clutched his shoulders as he tried a second stroke. Over and over he pulled nearly out then drove deep again. Each movement was slow and tantalizing. She lay beneath him, passively accepting the fullness at first. Once she understood the rhythm, she started to move. Burying her face against his throat, she muffled her cries. Dominic increased the speed and strength of each thrust.

The urgent heat started deep in her belly, curling outward in a maelstrom of sensation. Each stroke of his body against hers and inside hers intensified the burning. Rowena dug her nails into his back as her body tightened around him, caressing him with her release.

He groaned and strained against her, burying himself to the hilt. Rowena held him tightly, her legs wrapped around his waist, the pleasure too overwhelming for her to comprehend that he spilled his seed against the mouth of her womb.

He rolled them to their sides, their bodies still entwined.

"I never dreamed it would be like this," she murmured, and Dominic chuckled. She felt liberated, enlightened. She wanted to shout and dance and — do it again!

"I'll take that to mean you approve."

She smiled, snuggling closer to him. "I was told mating was something to be endured quietly. It was a duty that you were required to submit to because your husband fed and clothed you." Gaston's ghost shriveled and shrank until it disappeared entirely from her heart.

Dominic laughed, gently separating their bodies. "I think the clergy concocted that tale to keep our young women from becoming promiscuous." Rowena stretched like a lazy cat, her hands skimming along her body. Dominic groaned. "Lie still or you will find out how many other lies the clergy told you."

She rolled to her side and propped her head on her hand, glancing down at his burgeoning erection. Feminine power unfurled within her, making her bold. "But he's begging for attention." She purred playfully.

"And you are begging for trouble."

"I never beg." She flashed a challenging grin.

"Would you care to wager on that?"

* * * * *

"Milady, you must get up. This is a disaster!"

Thora's frantic words jarred Rowena from her delightful dreams. She sat up in bed and looked around to see what crisis had befallen the castle. Sunlight flooded the chamber, piercing her eyes and pounding through her brain.

Dominic was gone.

She indulged in a loud groan and plopped down onto her back, covering her eyes with her forearm.

"Leave me be." She rolled over onto her stomach and buried her face in the thick feather mattress. Her body ached in places it had no business aching, but the contented lethargy was with her still. It could not be morning yet. Morning meant the night had ended, and Rowena didn't want the night to end.

"Rowena. You must get up!"

Knowing her servant couldn't see her face, Rowena grinned. She hadn't really expected Dominic to be here when she woke up, but the bed felt huge and empty without him.

"I asked Milton if he had heard any tales since Sir Dominic arrived, and he verified everything you told me and more."

Rowena sat up and pulled the bedding to her chin. The lingering remnants of her perfect, peaceful night were well and truly shattered. "What are you talking about?"

"After I left you yestereve, I went to Milton. He confirmed what you overheard in the forest. We have made a terrible mistake."

"What *exactly* did Milton say?"

"Dominic was betrothed to a woman named Monica. Monica was the spoiled, only daughter of a wealthy earl. When Dominic discovered the family wasn't as prosperous as they led everyone to believe, he killed her."

"That's ridiculous." Rowena shoved her arms into the dressing gown Thora handed her and crawled out of bed.

Thora gasped. "Did that beast hurt you? Oh milady, are you all right?"

Confused by Thora's concern, Rowena turned back and saw the smears of dried blood on the bed linen. She could claim that her courses had come unexpectedly, but she was weary of lies. "Nothing happened when we returned from the monastery, Thora. He stopped before my maidenhead was breached. If Dominic had not purposely led Sir William to the wrong conclusion, Edwin would have been able to prove his claim. When I was at Windsor Castle, I was still a virgin."

For a moment Thora just stared at her. She glanced at the evidence on the bed and then back at Rowena. "Then why...he admitted to something he had not done." She sounded incredulous.

Rowena shook her head. How could she explain something she didn't understand? Had the gesture been noble and selfless, or had Dominic seen an opportunity he couldn't resist? "It doesn't matter now. I'm safe from Edwin once and for all."

"Are you still bent on ignoring William Marshal, or should we start planning a wedding feast?" Happiness sparkled in Thora's eyes.

"I have no intention of wedding with Dominic or anyone else until my heart is fully engaged." Rowena gave the cord around her waist an exaggerated tug.

Thora began to strip the bed. She paused and looked at Rowena. "Then what were you doing last night? You told me William Marshal will see you wed to Dominic if you're with child."

"There are ways of preventing..." A wave of icy dread washed over Rowena. Her hands grew numb, and she could hardly think past the ringing in her ears.

"How many times?" Thora's gaze took on a knowing glint. "How many times did he take you?"

"Three," Rowena whispered.

"And each time he finished inside you?"

Rowena nodded. "Oh Thora, what have I done?"

* * * * *

"Distracted?" Ezra asked with a mocking smile.

Dominic lay flat on his back in the dirt, glaring up at his friend. "She does seem to have that effect on me."

Ezra extended a mail-covered hand and Dominic levered himself to his feet. "I believe I'll go find Ephraim. This is obviously a waste of time."

Shoving his sword into the sheath secured to his waist, Dominic stomped from the exercise yard and toward the source of his distraction.

Rowena had appeared a short time before. She made no overt attempt to draw his attention, but she had done so implicitly. A mild breeze caught her skirt, fluttering it against her legs. Dominic groaned as he pictured those long, supple legs wrapped around his waist.

Why was she here? This was a soldier's domain.

As he drew near, her expression confused him even further. Her sleek, dark brows drew together in a frown. The lush fullness of her mouth pressed into a grim line and fury blazed in her wide green eyes.

"I would speak with you." She waited only long enough for her voice to reach him at a calm, conversational level.

"So I gathered. It is not often that ladies are interested in the routines of fighting men."

"I have no interest in your routines."

"Then how may I serve you?"

She drew a slow, deep breath, her delicate nostrils flaring. Her hands had tangled in the long, trailing sleeves of her bliaud so forcefully that her knuckles were white. What in God's name had made her so angry?

"You served me quite well last night, did you not?"

A virgin often had regrets the morning after, but this was ridiculous. "I'll not apologize for last night. You were an active participant in the festivities, not a victim."

She looked around suddenly. Was she afraid of being overheard?

"You made me a promise. You told me that you were not trying to… I will not marry you!"

"I don't remember asking for your hand."

"You said you would take measures to ensure that a child did not result from our 'festivities'. Why did you break your vow?"

Dominic planted his fists on his hips. Sweat trailed into his eyes, and blinking repeatedly only made them sting more. He fidgeted beneath the weight of his hauberk, but he had no weapon to use against her anger. "It wasn't intentional."

"Rubbish."

He took off his mail gantlets and tossed them onto his shoulder. "Rowena." He reached toward her with his bare hand. "I don't think either of us were—"

"I will not share the blame with you." She avoided his fingers and took a quick step backward. "You made me a promise. You failed to do what you said you would do."

How many "you"s could she squeeze into one sentence? He crossed his arms over his chest and set his jaw. "I apologize."

The flush rose onto her cheeks and her eyes narrowed. "You apologize?"

Her hand flew fast and hard, connecting with his cheek and snapping his face to the side.

"You bastard! You'll never know if I conceive. I'll do anything and everything to ensure you never know!"

She started to stomp past him, but he caught her arm and brought her up hard against his chest. "I did not make love to you last night to get you with child!"

"Make love?" She spat the phrase into his face. "There was no love in what transpired last night. You used me. You seduced me to win my castle."

She jerked her arm out of his grasp and ran toward the keep. Dominic had to keep himself from running after her. They were both too angry to make sense of this now.

"What is God's name was that about?"

Dominic dragged his eyes away from Rowena and felt his anger deescalate. Ezra stood at the edge of the exercise yard, his sword in hand. Two steps behind him stood nine of Dominic's men, each armed and ready for battle.

Dominic chuckled, forcing his emotions into submission. "Rushing to my defense? Am I not capable of managing a woman?"

"She struck you, milord," Hubert said.

"So, you were going to lop off her head?" He nodded toward the sword in Hubert's hand.

"Only if you did not."

His men laughed. Dominic waved them away. "Back to work, you lazy dogs. I'm safe for now."

Ezra remained as the others returned to their practice. "Why did she hit you?"

Dominic absently rubbed his stinging cheek. She was surprisingly strong for such a little thing. "Because I deserved it."

Ezra's brows drew together, his face scrunching into an expression of disbelief. "You deserved to be slapped?"

"Aye."

Dominic offered no explanation. He made his way toward the keep, frustrated and angry. He hadn't even realized he'd not kept his word until she confronted him just now.

Had he been so carried away last night that he'd forgotten his vow? Or was he really a bastard?

* * * * *

Rowena paced her solar like a caged animal. Nothing she did released her frustration. She'd thrown herself on the bed and wept, but she was still angry. She'd smashed an earthen pitcher, but she still fumed. The pacing wasn't any more effective than her other strategies, so Rowena crossed to the window and threw the shutters wide.

Cold autumn wind assailed her face, fanning her hair out behind her like a banner. She leaned into nature's bluster and inhaled deeply. Pine, wood smoke, freshly cut hay and rain. She loved the smells of harvest time.

"Where is your veil? Close those shutters. You'll catch your death."

Thora bustled up beside her and tried to reach the shutters, but Rowena spun to face her. "I like the wind!" Her hair danced wildly about her face.

"Oh, you're in quite a state. Milton told me what you did out there."

Rowena leaned back against the stone sill and closed her eyes. "It was no more than he deserved."

"You're fortunate he didn't beat you senseless. You must know when and how to challenge a man. *In front of his men*? What were you thinking?"

Opening her eyes, Rowena released a deep, shuddering breath. "What was I thinking? I was thinking that he used me. I was thinking only an utter fool would allow herself to trust a man. I was thinking…" Her voice trailed away as emotion clogged her throat.

Thora wrapped her arms loosely around her and Rowena rested her forehead against Thora's shoulder.

"He told me he wanted me," she murmured. "I know he wants my holdings, he hasn't pretended otherwise, but he made me believe he wanted *me*."

"Men are very good at saying what we want to hear."

Rowena eased away and met Thora's gaze. "The worst part is I want him still. Even in the exercise yard it was more than anger making my heart pound. He attracts me, and it's irrational. How can I feel anything for him, knowing he's deceitful?"

Thora raised her hands in a helpless gesture. "I'm not the one to ask about such things. My heart leads me where it will, and my mind is never involved."

"Last night was his victory, but this war is far from over." She pushed the hair out of her eyes and straightened her dress. "There has to be a way to show him I'll not bow and scrape simply because he's a man."

"A devastatingly attractive man," Thora added, one corner of her mouth quirked.

"His physical appeal is irrelevant. I must separate my desire from my ambition." Rowena liked the sound of that. "Men have done so since time began."

Thora's brow furrowed and she crossed her arms beneath her breasts. "Your ambition? Whatever does that mean?"

"I intend to retain control of Pendragon Castle for as long as I possibly can. I'll not allow Dominic to use my desire against me."

"You see!" Thora pointing her finger at Rowena. "You are being just as dishonest as Sir Dominic."

She felt her jaw drop. "That's preposterous. How am I being dishonest?"

"You claim to champion the legend, that you've dedicated your life to breaking the curse, but you're simply avoiding another marriage. You're hiding, just as I said."

Shooting Thora a glare to illustrate her displeasure, Rowena bent and began to gather the broken pieces of the clay pitcher. "What would you suggest I do?"

"I'm not your conscience. This you must figure out for yourself."

Rowena glanced over her shoulder in time to see Thora slip from the room.

Thora, who voiced her opinion about everything, had nothing to say? Rowena shook her head and knelt, placing the fragments in her lap. Was Thora right? Was she using the legend as an emotional shield?

Dominic's handsome features appeared within her mind, mocking her, attracting her. There had to be a way to show him that wanting her was not enough. She wouldn't surrender her holdings because she found him desirable. She would marry for love. She *must* marry for love. So, until he loved her, she wouldn't accept him as her husband.

A golden light flickered to life in the corner of the room. Rowena looked at it and laughed. "You come to me *now*? The damage is done, Fair Fiona. His trap has snapped around my foolish neck."

Tinkling laughter drifted on the breeze and the light danced around her in a lazy circle.

"At least I can amuse you."

For just a moment Fiona hovered before Rowena's face. Their eyes met and Fiona's ethereal beauty held Rowena transfixed. She could see Fiona's smile through the golden nimbus, and calming warmth soothed Rowena's ravaged nerves.

"Is he the one?" Rowena whispered. "Could he come to love me? Do I dare love him?"

Just like Thora, Fiona offered no opinion. She circled Rowena one last time and flew out the window.

Chapter Nine

Brother Leland sat on the edge of a soft bed, adorned in a sweet-smelling tunic, his belly full of food.

I have misjudged you.

Edwin's ominous comment still echoed through his mind. What had Edwin in store for him now? Isolation and starvation had been ineffective. What form would his next torture take?

He heard a key grating in a lock and realized the answers were at hand.

"So, how have you found your quarters?" Edwin's voice intruded.

"I'm quite comfortable. You have my thanks."

Footfall. One step, two, three.

"Has a good night's sleep and a full belly improved your willingness to cooperate?"

He was much closer now. Brother Leland turned his face toward the sound. "I have never refused to cooperate with you. I cannot solve the riddle because there is no answer. The legend is superstition, nothing more."

Edwin laughed.

Trepidation spread its dark wings. Brother Leland began to pray.

"I expected this. You see, Leland, I realized something crucial about you yesterday. You have been conditioned by your faith to be selfless. But your faith has also conditioned you to be caring of others."

"My lord, I cannot give you what you want regardless of the punishment you have imagined."

Edwin continued on as if he hadn't spoken. "I watched as Nan tended to your needs. You felt compassion for the girl; almost immediately you were devoted. Did you know her before yesterday, or do you react this way to each person you meet?"

Brother Leland didn't answer. Fear welled up within him with sickening intensity. What was this evil creature threatening? "I have told you everything. There is no need to involve anyone else."

"Well, I must disagree."

The footsteps retreated, and then Leland heard muffled, urgent sounds as if someone were gagged.

"My lord? What is that?" He turned his head from side to side, searching the darkness with blind eyes.

"*That* would be little Nan."

Fabric rent and the muffled sounds became louder, more distressed.

"My lord, please!" Leland rose to his feet and took a step forward, but he tripped over something and went sprawling. His knees struck the wood plank floor and pain spiked up his legs.

"Oh, she is a bit younger than I realized, but she has lovely skin, so white and smooth."

"Do not do this evil thing," he pleaded. "There is no reason."

Leland tried to reach her. Scrambling about with frantic determination, he clawed at empty air. His left knee throbbed intensely, but he ignored the pain. He crawled toward the sound of the struggle, only to be kicked away. Searing pain shot through his shoulder as the boot propelled him backward.

She screamed, the sound tearing through Leland with physical force.

"Our Father Who art in heaven…" The words fell from his lips in an unconscious litany as the struggle went on. He charged in again, a pathetic charge on hands and knees. A vicious kick slammed him against the wall and his head connected with the stones. He was conscious but dazed, unable to move. Each scream, each moan, each whimper killed a piece of his soul. He could not reach her.

God forgive me. This is my fault!

When there were no sounds except ragged breathing and the inhuman keening of a wounded animal. Brother Leland wept.

"Well, enough of that," Edwin muttered. "Be gone."

He heard a shuffle, the frantic scramble of feet against wood, and then no sounds at all.

Brother Leland sat against a wall, numb and desolate.

"You really don't know, do you?"

Brother Leland shook his head. Tears trailed down his cheeks, but he was silent.

"Damn you!" Something crashed and splintered. "Damn her! God damn her!"

The first blow caught Leland by surprise. After that he welcomed the pain.

* * * * *

Rowena sat at the head table, waiting for Dominic to answer her summons. She'd changed her clothing, selected the location for the conversation and rehearsed what she'd say. Her position must be perfectly clear.

The doors at the far end of the hall opened with a loud groaning, and Rowena held her breath. She schooled her expression and sat up straight in the "master's" chair.

Farrell entered the hall, and Rowena slumped forward with a sigh, resting her forearms atop of the table. What was taking so long?

"Good eventide, milady," the steward said with a smile. "I've not seen you all day."

He was cheerful and pleasant as was Farrell's way, but Rowena found it hard not to scowl. "How have you been?"

"Very well."

"Have you seen Sir Dominic?"

Immediately his expression changed. His carefree demeanor evaporated and open hostility flared within his dark eyes. "Nay. Why do you ask?"

"Why are you scowling, Farrell? Has Sir Dominic offended you?"

He squared his shoulders and met her gaze. "He offended you and that offends me."

So, he'd heard about their little row. By now *everyone* would have heard that she dared to strike the Undaunted. "That was the reason for my question. I need to speak with him."

Rowena saw Dominic enter the hall.

"If he has insulted you, I'll have him thrown beyond the curtain wall," Farrell promised.

"That would —"

"I've never known you to be provoked to violence," Farrell went on. "He should be taught a lesson."

He was so impassioned that she could not rescue him. "Thank —"

"You need only speak the word and I will —"

"She need only speak the word and find a man big enough to enforce the threat," Dominic corrected.

Farrell spun to face him and the contrast shocked Rowena. She'd never thought of Farrell as a small man, but his head barely reached Dominic's chin.

"I don't know the nature of Lady Rowena's grievance —"

"The grievance is between Lady Rowena and me. I assure you, steward, I *have* on many occasions been provoked to violence."

Farrell looked at Rowena.

"It's best if you go. I asked Dominic to join me." She'd forgotten the "Sir" and his name sounded intimate, caressing. This would never do. She must garner her authority and prepare to put him in his place.

Farrell stiffly inclined his head and walked back across the hall.

Dominic stood before her, legs planted firmly apart, hands clasped behind his back. His armor was gone, but he was no less intimidating in tunic and chausses. He hadn't bound his hair. The thick length curled slightly against his neck and shoulders. Rowena remembered its softness crushed within her fists as he drove himself into the depths of her body. She felt heat climb up her throat and blossom across her cheeks.

She couldn't afford to indulge such thoughts.

"Was there a reason for the summons, or did you just want to look at me?"

The silken question snapped her from her reverie. She scooted to the edge of the chair and folded her hands upon the tabletop. "I've decided what to do with you."

He laughed. Not a good start.

"Have you now? What shall you do with me?"

He used a deep, sensual tone for the last question, but Rowena ignored the tingles racing down her arms. "I offer you a choice. You may become the captain of my personal guard or you may leave my lands immediately."

"That doesn't sound like a choice, it sounds like an ultimatum."

"It is whichever you prefer."

"Why do you need a personal guard?" He sounded only mildly interested.

"Because I intend to marry for *love* or remain a widow." She watched his reaction carefully.

His eyes narrowed and darkened. "You would ignore the request of William Marshal?" He folded his arms over his chest, his expression insolent. "It's better to risk political suicide than to find a husband?"

"That depends on the husband."

With two long strides he faced her across the table. Her palms were suddenly clammy and beads of perspiration dotted her upper lip, but she clung to her calm façade.

"Your husband must be strong enough to hold your land, capable of protecting your people and willing to treat you kindly. If you harbor expectations beyond those, my lady, you are being childish."

"Then I am surely childish, for my expectations rise far above that dismal list."

He smiled, a slow mocking smile that made Rowena's heart lurch within her breast. "You shall marry your true love, solve the riddle, break the Fairy curse and find the buried treasure?"

Her chin shot up a notch. "Aye, and you shall protect me until I have accomplished each of those goals."

He didn't bother to step onto the dais. Resting his hands on the tabletop, he leaned toward her and whispered, "You're only postponing the inevitable."

"Nay," she asserted, staring directly into his smoldering gaze. "I'm preventing the intolerable."

One dark brow arched, mocking her defiance. "Feel safe in the illusion, if you can. But know this, Rowena, you're mine already."

He grasped her upper arms, pulling her out of her chair and halfway across the table. Rowena gasped, and his mouth claimed hers. She shoved against his chest, but he devoured her, possessed her, and demanded a response. Light danced behind her eyelids. Heat and tension gathered in her abdomen as well as a faint tingling of fear. Why couldn't she resist this man?

Just as abruptly as he kissed her, he pushed her away.

Rowena slumped back against the chair, panting and muddled. He was walking away. This was to have been *his* reprimand, but he was walking away! "I belong to no man!" she shouted at his back.

"I belong to no man," she whispered as he slammed the massive door.

* * * * *

"I don't understand," Rowena said sharply. "Brother Leland hasn't left the village since he lost his sight."

Brother Samuel fidgeted, nervously clearing his throat before he elaborated. "One of the Carthusian monks came to get him. They said he was needed at the

Charterhouse. The monk came in a wagon, so Brother Leland agreed to go."

Rowena shifted her basket from one hand to the other. Was it only her selfish need to see her friend that churned within her belly, or was something really wrong?

"Did Brother Leland know this man? Did you?"

"I have had no interaction with any of the monks. You know how reclusive they are. I'm not certain if Brother Leland knew the man or not. His concerns seemed to be centered around the means of travel."

The tension in her stomach tightened. "When was this? How long has he been gone?"

"About the time you left for Windsor Castle. Brother Leland was upset that he wasn't able to see you before you departed, and he insisted that the message for William Marshal be delivered instead."

"I received it. Do you know when he will return?"

"I'm sorry, I do not. May I be of some assistance?"

She forced a smile. "I just brought some more of Cook's tea. It's nothing you want to consume unless it is necessary."

He took the basket from her with a chuckle. "I'll send a message when he returns. I know he treasures your visits."

Rowena fought her troubled thoughts all the way back to the castle. This entire day had been a disaster. Was she being punished for the immoral pleasure she'd shared with Dominic? Was her one moment of weakness to ruin the rest of her life?

The overly dramatic thoughts made Rowena smile. Her emotions were raw and sensitized. A nice long conversation with Brother Leland would have done her a world of good.

"Milady! There you are. We've been looking everywhere for you." Thora came racing across the inner bailey, her voice almost shrill with anxiety.

"What's amiss?"

Panting for breath, Thora clutched her throat with one trembling hand and grasped Rowena's wrist with the other. Fear twisted her expression, and Rowena felt her own respiration speed.

"Nan's in the bakery. She's hysterical and no one can calm her enough to find out the cause of her distress. She's asked to speak with you."

"Who is Nan?" Rowena searched her memory as they hurried along.

"My cousin. She works in Edwin's household."

Spurred on by the name of her enemy, Rowena ran for the bakery.

The girl's headrail was missing, and her long dark hair had become a tangled mass, which hung over one shoulder. Tear trails smeared her dirty face, and her hard sobs could be heard long before Rowena entered the bakery. Rowena knelt before the girl and gently took her grimy hands between her own. Squeezing her fingers, Rowena tried to draw her attention. "Nan, what's happened? Tell me how I can help."

The authority in Rowena's tone seemed to penetrate the girl's hysteria. She dragged the back of her hand across her eyes and let out a long, ragged sob.

"They made the poor friar think he was forcing himself on me, but it weren't me, it was all a trick."

"I don't understand, Nan. Who are they? Which friar?"

"He needs your help. He's hurt real bad."

Nan began to sob. Before the girl slipped back into hysteria, Rowena asked, "Who needs me? Where is he?"

"Brother Leland. We took him up to the old monastery. We didn't know where else to go."

Rowena told Thora to have Milton saddle her horse before she turned back to the frightened girl. She took Nan's face and tilted it until their gazes met. "Nan. You need to explain what happened, quickly. Who hurt Brother Leland? How badly is he injured?"

After taking several long breaths, Nan said, "Sir Edwin. Will he come after me now? Bert already ran, but someone had to tell you where the friar is. We didn't know where else to come. I'm so scared. Did we do good?"

"You did very good, Nan. Just relax. You're safe now. I'll take care of everything."

Rowena rose, but Nan caught her sleeve. "It was a trick. Make sure he knows it was a trick."

As she rushed from the bakery, her limbs wobbled and tears threatened to reveal her torment. She wouldn't break down in front of the servants. She couldn't. They depended on her strength, her ability to act with calm and reason.

But guilt swept in on the heels of her anger and her steps faltered. Edwin hadn't given up. He'd found a different path to his obsession.

Brother Leland had been tortured because of his connection to her. Covering her mouth with her hand to stave off her anguished cry, Rowena ran for the stables. She couldn't let him die. She wouldn't!

Edwin must be stopped.

No matter the cost, Edwin must be stopped.

* * * * *

Dominic held the sword to eye level and admired the fine straight edge of the blade. It was some of the finest ironwork he'd ever seen. Lowering the sword, Dominic turned it over to look more closely at the subtle watermark pattern that ran the entire length of the blade. "Remarkable," he pronounced.

"Liam is our best blacksmith. His father spent four years in Damascus learning from their sword makers." Ludlow took the sword from Dominic and passing him a second, equally impressive blade. "Varying amounts of carbon cause the pattern you see in both blades. When Liam has finished honing the swords, the handles will be inlaid with gold and silver, and patterns etched along the blade."

Dominic had seen many elaborately decorated swords, but he had always preferred his simple and very sharp. "Are the swords commissioned, or does Lady Rowena hoard these treasures for herself?"

Ludlow smiled. "She's generous with Liam's talent and expertise, and he's grown both rich and renowned under her sponsorship. Lady Rowena has encouraged Liam to experiment, and she's given him a freedom he never had before."

"Before? You mean while Gaston was alive."

"Gaston, and Edgar before him. The lords of Pendragon have not been as reasonable as the ladies, and Lady Rowena is no exception. She has won the respect of many, whether she realizes it or not."

Ludlow led Dominic through the rest of the spacious armory. The more he learned about Pendragon Castle, the more impressed he became — and the more determined.

He thanked Ludlow for the tour and walked off across the lower bailey. A sudden gust of wind blew his hair across his face, but Dominic hardly noticed.

He could still taste her and smell her. Rowena. It didn't seem to matter what he did to fill his head with other things, he couldn't get her out of his mind.

Captain of her private guard! How ridiculous. Did she really think she could put him off so easily? Her accusation in the exercise yard upset him more than her ultimatum. He hadn't made love to her with the intention of getting her with child — at least not consciously. But she seemed determined to think the worst of him.

He'd play her game. She could call him whatever she liked. He'd guard her and protect her as she searched for her *true love*, but all the while he'd touch her and kiss her and make her burn. He'd help her see that he possessed all of the qualities she would ever need in a husband.

Ezra sat with a small group of foot soldiers at one of the tables in the great hall. Dominic stood back and listened to their debate on strategy for a few moments before he called Ezra aside.

"There is nothing more entertaining than discussing strategy with puppies who have never tasted battle," Ezra commented as he joined Dominic.

"They'll lose their innocence soon enough. Everyone does."

Ezra shook his head and gave Dominic a firm slap on the back. "Why don't you marry the girl and be done with it? You've been surly as a bear ever since you laid eyes on her. Must be love."

Dominic sighed. Ezra knew him too well not to realize the source of his mood. "If only life were so simple."

"Life is that simple."

"Not when women are involved. She's decided that I will be the captain of her private guard."

Ezra laughed. "I know where you spent last night. Do you need more practice?"

Dominic scowled darkly and then smiled. His best glowers were wasted on Ezra. "She's frightened. She's seen her destiny, but she's yet to accept it."

"And how do you intend to make her accept it?"

"That is between the lady and me. You need only know that I don't intend to leave Pendragon Castle anytime soon. Talk to the men. See who would stay and who would prefer to accompany you to Granville Cross. I know you've been anxious to examine your new fief."

"Are you certain you can make do without us? What about Edwin?"

"I alone can handle Edwin."

Ezra didn't seem convinced, but he didn't argue. "I'll speak with the men."

Dominic had meant to say more, but Thora caught his attention. She entered the hall and started to approach him, only to shake her head and walk away. "Excuse me." He hurried to catch Thora before she escaped entirely. "What is amiss?"

"Probably nothing, but it's getting dark."

"As it does each night," Dominic pointed out drolly. "Has the setting sun always troubled you?"

"Aye, when my lady has not yet returned to the castle, the setting sun always troubles me."

Not again!

"*Returned* to the castle? Where has Rowena gone? Did she take an escort? How long has she been away?"

When Thora didn't immediately produce the answers, Dominic turned and headed toward the stables. "Damn her! Come, Thora. You'll explain while I saddle Majesty."

Chapter Ten

Rowena managed to keep her tears at bay while she struggled to bring some measure of comfort to her patient. She washed the blood carefully from around Brother Leland's numerous gashes and applied cool compresses to his swollen right eye. She had little doubt that at least one of his ribs had been cracked by Edwin's brutal treatment, but without assistance she couldn't bind his torso. Mercifully, the friar remained unconscious during her ministrations. She trickled one of Cook's potions down his throat before pity and fury overcame her.

Grabbing one of the thick tapers, Rowena rushed into the outer chamber. Tears streamed down her face and sobs gathered in her chest. She set the candle on the wooden mantel, no longer trusting herself to hold it.

A large hand came down on her shoulder, and Rowena cried out. She spun and released a ragged sigh. Dominic stood there looking tall and ominous. Still, she flung herself against him. Wrapping her arms tightly around his back, she buried her face against his neck. Never before had she been this angry, never had humanity seemed so craven. She needed comfort. She needed reassurance. She needed — Dominic.

Hard, shuddering sobs shook her body. She was beyond words. Fury and guilt crashed over her in alternating waves. Her hands mangled the fabric covering his chest as her grief drove the breath from her lungs.

How could anyone be so cruel?

This was all her doing. How could she ever make it right?

Dominic stroked her hair and whispered soothing words against her ear. The deep timbre of his voice gradually penetrated her anguish.

"Why did God allow this to happen? Brother Leland is a kind and gentle soul." She couldn't bring herself to move. The solid strength of his arms and chest made her feel safe. She could hide within the shelter of his embrace and he'd keep the world away.

Dominic eased her back, taking his body just out of reach. "How is the friar?"

Rowena heard anger in his voice and stiffened. He was obviously not here to comfort her. "He's sleeping." She dragged her sleeve across her wet face. "I don't think the beating is the worst of his afflictions. Edwin has been starving him. He is miserably malnourished and I fear…he is too weak to recover." She had to force the words past her raw throat, but for the moment, Rowena had mastered the tears.

"Is Edwin aware that his prisoner escaped?"

Rowena shook her head and took a deep breath, strengthening her composure another degree. "Not yet, but it's only a matter of time. Nan is terrified. It was all we could do to piece together the gist of what happened."

"If Edwin valued this man enough to take him prisoner, do you believe he'll simply let him slip away?"

"Should I have let him die alone?" She crossed her arms, burying her hands in the opposite sleeve.

"You should have summoned an escort or sent a healer to tend the friar."

Her temper flared at his insensitivity. "The nearest leech is in Llangly, and sending for him would have alerted Edwin."

"And the escort?"

"There was no time." Rowena snatched up the candle and pushed past him. "I'm overwhelmed by your compassion."

The friar hadn't moved since she left him. Regardless of Dominic's objections, Brother Leland's recovery was her first priority. Setting the candle aside, she lifted the compress from his face and laid the back of her hand across his forehead.

"Have you done all you can for him?" Dominic stood in the doorway.

"I need to bind his ribs."

Without a word, he helped her wrap a long strip of sheeting around the friar's emaciated torso. Brother Leland moaned as Dominic gently manipulated his position. She pulled the bandage snug, and he cried out. "It's all right. You're safe now."

"God's blood, I have never seen such an assortment of bruises on one body."

"Edwin can be quite creative when he decides to inflict pain." She settled a blanket over the friar and rewet the compress.

"Did he ever...hurt you?"

"Nay, but he frequently used force to motivate my mother."

"Is this all that can be done for the friar?"

She glanced at Dominic, noting the grim set of his jaw and the mixture of anger and compassion in his gaze. "His recovery is in God's hands now."

"Then you'll return with me to the safety of the castle."

"Nay, I will remain with Brother Leland until I'm certain he'll make a full recovery. I owe this man more than you could possibly understand. I will not leave his side."

"Then I will have him moved to the castle."

She stood and faced him squarely. "He is too weak to be moved, and dragging soldiers up here will draw Edwin's attention."

Dominic took her by the arm and pulled her back into the outer chamber. "You're not staying here alone."

The sudden intensity in his dark blue gaze made Rowena hesitate. He'd been angry when he arrived, probably intending to drag her back to the castle with or without her consent. But instead he'd helped her tend the friar. He'd been gentle and compassionate. Did she dare push him further?

She glanced toward the cell and saw Brother Leland's bruised and swollen face. Each blow, each vicious kick had been because of her. On this she would not bend. Yanking her arms out of Dominic's grasp, she stood her ground. "I will not leave him."

"There is good reason for my caution, Rowena. The condition of that man should show you plainly how demented your foe has become. If he would abuse a frail old man, what would he do to you?"

He was right, she admitted and her heart sank. She wanted to fling an insult into his face and storm away, but his logic was sound. "I cannot leave him. I owe him more than you will ever know."

"You cannot stay here."

She glared up into his impassive face, fighting back a smile. "You're the captain of my personal guard. It's your responsibility to protect me. I'm needed here, so you will protect me here."

The intensity in his eyes changed, melted and smoldered. He took a step toward her. A sardonic smile curved his lips. "Ask me nicely."

Rowena felt her heart flutter. With strength and intimidation at his disposal, he shouldn't be allowed to use charm. She resisted for a moment longer for the sake of her pride.

"Stay with me." His eyebrow shot up. "Please."

* * * * *

"How far could he have gotten! God's blood, the man was half dead," Edwin shouted at the four soldiers who stood fidgeting uncomfortably before the central hearth in his hall. Nearly six hours had passed since he discovered the friar was gone.

Titania stood back and watched Edwin's fury, annoyed by the unexpected turn. Her Fairy perception was greatly hampered by the human form surrounding her. She should have sensed the friar's escape.

"We've searched everywhere, milord." The oldest soldier stepped forward to speak for the group. "Someone must be hiding him."

"Search every house and barn, every stable and hut until the friar is found. Do you understand how important this is? I'll reward the person responsible for finding him. And anyone proven to have aided in his escape will die!"

"Aye, milord. We'll carry on."

The others followed the spokesman across the hall and out into the night. Edwin slammed his closed fist against the rough wooden window shutter. "I cannot believe this. You would think I was the one who had been cursed."

Titania came up behind him and wrapped her arms around his waist. "You're Edgar's brother. Perhaps the Pendragon curse passed to you upon his death." She kept her tone light and playful, but Edwin tensed as she knew he would. He pried her hands away from his middle and pushed her away.

"Inherit his curse but not his wealth? That would be in keeping with the pattern of my life."

"Nan is Thora's cousin. It had to be her and that halfwit Bert, which means Leland is somewhere on Pendragon lands." If she released her hold on Lissette long enough to search for the friar, the human would be dead within minutes. She had no choice but to leave the search to Edwin's men.

"Tell me something I don't know!"

She narrowed her gaze on his flushed face. If he only knew how often she restrained her violent impulses. "What is the worst that can happen because of his escape?"

"He'll spread the tale of his mistreatment to all and sundry." Edwin turned back to the open window.

"And who will believe him?"

"Rowena will believe every foul word spoken against me, be they true or nay. And Sir Dominic. What if he takes offense and comes after me? He has the ear of William Marshal!"

"You worry for nothing, my love." She didn't bother with a tender expression. He couldn't see her anyway. "The friar is dead. We should simply continue on to the next stage of our plan. Rowena is your only real obstacle. Remove her and—"

Whirling around, he grabbed both her arms and shoved her backward. "I can't kill Rowena. As much as the thought pleases you, it's impossible."

What was this? He had obediently marched down each path she pointed him toward. How dare he gainsay her now? "Why?" she demanded. If Rowena's marriage wasn't going to be annulled, then Rowena must die. Titania was beginning to fear Rowena was the Lady. "Why not kill the bitch and be done with it?

She's all that stands between you and what's rightfully yours. If Rowena dies, you'll inherit Pendragon Castle and everything that goes with it."

"You don't understand." He stomped back to the table where he had set his tankard of ale when his soldiers arrived. Picking it up, he took a deep swig, his expression lost behind the tankard.

"Explain it to me. Why can you not remove the obstacle? Tell me what holds you back."

"The damn curse!"

She laughed. She couldn't help it. The irony was overwhelming. In her determination to sabotage Fiona, she had made Edwin a believer.

"Scoff if you like, Lissette, but the riddle must be solved and the curse lifted before anyone will find happiness within the walls of that castle."

Unbelievable! "How do you know Rowena is the Lady spoken of in the legend?"

Edwin held his ground, his expression resolute. "She's the only one who has been innocent in all of this. All the other ladies were flawed, immoral, untrue."

"Rowena is either immoral or a liar. If she didn't bed a man who was not her husband, then she lied to William Marshal when she said she was no longer a virgin."

"She was forced to protect what was hers," he snapped. "Her actions will not be held against her."

Titania shook her head. How had she overlooked his obsession? "What is the answer? If you believe Rowena is protected by this curse, then how do we get what we want?"

"I'd hoped Brother Leland would answer that question."

"Brother Leland is gone. If he isn't dead already, he's beyond our reach. So, what do we do now?"

"I do not know!" he shouted, and stormed from the room.

Titania released an exasperated screech. How could it have gone so horribly wrong? If Oberon learned of her involvement… She refused to finish the thought.

Oberon wasn't going to find out anything. If Edwin was useless to her now, she would simply have to find another way.

* * * * *

"What do you owe this man?" Dominic asked. Rowena had known nothing but cruelty and tragedy. Patience. If he honestly wanted to woo her, he would have to accept William's advice.

Rowena angled her body so she could see her patient. Candlelight revealed worry and guilt in her wide green eyes. Why was she taking the blame for Edwin's depravity?

"Brother Leland lived in a Charterhouse on the border of my father's estate." She glanced at the friar and smiled, her memories obviously pleasant. "My father had an unscrupulous bailiff rob him blind, so he determined to learn the written word. I wanted to learn as well. It took some persuading on my part, but Father allowed Brother Leland to tutor me as well until…until my father died."

"And your mother wed with Edwin."

"Aye."

Dominic looked at the battered face of the friar and felt his blood run cold. He was no stranger to brutality, but this was a defenseless old man. "What does Edwin believe Brother Leland knows? Why was he mistreating the friar?"

"Because he is a sadistic pig," Rowena flared. She crossed her arms over her chest, hiding her hands in her sleeves as her gaze returning to his face. "During his years with the Carthusian monks, Brother Leland was given a detailed journal of the Pendragon household. It was nearly destroyed by mildew and he was charged with restoring the manuscript. He knows more about the history of the Pendragons than any person alive. Edwin likely believes Brother Leland is privy to all the secrets of the legend. He may even believe Leland can solve the riddle."

"I find it surprising that *you* aren't more interested in the riddle." He stroked the high curve of her cheek with his thumb, unable to keep from touching her.

"I never said I wasn't interested in the riddle. I said it's the one aspect of the legend that has no basis in fact." Turned into his caress, she lowered her lashes. A slow, churning heat washed over him. "Lady Fiona is real. Her marriage to Tyrus is well documented."

"And according to historical fact, what happened to her?"

She released her sleeves and placed her hands on his chest. It was such a simple gesture, but Dominic's entire body came alive. His heart hammered, his skin tingled, his respiration raced.

"She disappeared shortly after she found Lord Tyrus with his lover—or lovers by some accounts. His reputation for infidelity is as well documented as their marriage."

Dominic chuckled and lightly placed his hands on her hips. Slowly. Gently. "After her disappearance, what became of Tyrus?"

"He went mad. He became a recluse in this very monastery. When he took his own life in one of the cells, the other monks declared the monastery desecrated and abandoned it."

"And all this can be proven?"

"If written history is to be believed." She stared up at him, her eyes wide and luminous. "I suppose historians can record falsehoods as well as fact. But the author of the journal had no reason to lie."

Silence descended. Dominic wanted nothing more than to kiss her, to end the conversation, and avoid another conflict. But she must understand the foolishness of her actions. He must have her vow not to intentionally put herself in harm's way.

Or they could talk after…

"If you were dead, Edwin would inherit Pendragon Castle."

She averted her gaze with a stiff nod. "I know. But Edwin doesn't want me dead. Thora insists he's terrified of the curse, and I tend to believe her. Edwin could have killed me long ago if that was his want."

"The curse may have kept you alive thus far, but that could change in an instant. He wants Pendragon and he won't stop until he has it."

"Or until *he* is dead." She glanced up at him.

"Is that an invitation?"

"Would you kill Edwin if I asked it of you?" She searched his gaze, waiting for his answer.

"Not without provocation. *I'm not a murderer.* But should he be foolish enough to attempt you harm, I'll not hesitate to take his life."

"I don't think Edwin is desperate enough to kill me just yet. Besides, he's the only one to directly benefit from my death, so suspicion would immediately fall upon him."

"I agree, and William Marshal is well aware of that fact. But accidents can be arranged. The world is filled with criminals who would turn a robbery into a murder and then slink away into the night."

"You are such a comfort to me." Pushing away from him, she dislodged his hands. She snatched one of the candles from the floor in the monk's cell and moved deeper into the outer room.

"It's not my intention to frighten you." His boot heels rang against the stone floor. "But you must understand that the danger is real. Coming here alone, going anywhere alone, is a luxury you can no longer afford. You must be on your guard, and you must do as I say if I'm to protect you."

"I'm not helpless. I can protect myself."

"Nay, you cannot. Not against Edwin. And I cannot protect you from him if you continue to be reckless. Don't leave the castle unescorted. Let me know where you're going if you venture beyond the castle walls. Are we agreed?"

She set the candle on the mantel and turned to face him. "I'm tired of being afraid. I'm just beginning to feel secure, and you're asking me to become a prisoner in my own life."

"That's not what I'm asking. I'm asking that you take certain measures to ensure your safety."

She squared her shoulders and glared into his eyes. "I suppose I must do as you say. After all, you are the captain of my private guard."

He moved slowly, never breaking contact with her gaze. "I'm more than that, and we both know it."

"I know what you think you are. I know what you want to be. But there is no place in my life for you."

She faced him squarely, her expression defiant. If he pushed, she'd push back. Under the bluster he sensed her fear. She fought his authority, rebelled against control, but how would she battle tenderness?

"No place in your life for a friend, a lover?" He ran the backs of his fingers across her cheek. "That's what I want to be. You have been alone for so long, Rowena. Why—"

"You want more than that, Sir Liar." She twisted away, her voice choked and tremulous.

He caught her arm and drew her toward him. "You're not ready to give me what I want."

"I'm not *willing* to give you what you want."

Possessive desire expanded within Dominic and he smiled. "You will be."

He wrapped her in his arms, trapping her against his chest. She immediately arched her back and shoved with her hands. This only ground her pelvis against his hardening erection.

"I will not wed with you," she cried. "I will not—"

"I've not asked you to wed with me." Holding her tightly with one arm, he cupped her face with his other hand. Fierce desire clawed through his determination to go slowly. He wanted her now. He needed to be inside her so badly he shook. "I want you in my arms, Rowena. I want to feel the pleasure we shared before. Not just for one night. I want to be your lover."

She went perfectly still, her breathing the only movement in her body. Her wide green eyes spoke to him, revealing far more than she realized. He saw her desire, but it was not just passion burning within her gaze. She wanted—him.

"You want to be my *husband*." Fear flared through the passion. It was all there in her eyes. "I'm not a fool. You intend to…each time we make love it increases your chances that I will conceive."

He pressed his lips to her temple, heating her skin with his breath. He was so close to breaching her defenses, to touching her carefully guarded heart. Dominic felt a moment of doubt. Could he go through with this? Could he seduce her, knowing she expected love? Knowing how badly she would resent him if he couldn't love her in return? He wanted her. God how he wanted her, but love? He wasn't sure he was capable of the emotion. He had seen so much, done so much that required emotional detachment.

"I'll be more careful this time," he whispered.

Rearing back stubbornly, she punched him in the chest. "I haven't forgiven you for last time. Why would I trust you again?"

She argued with everything he said, so Dominic molded her body to his and shifted the back of her head into the cradle of his elbow. "Enough," he growled, and kissed her.

Rowena clung to his thick upper arms as his mouth moved over and against hers. His lips were warm and firm, and her head began to swim. She wanted this man, wanted the mind-numbing pleasure she had known in his arms. Yet uncertainty shadowed the passion. This could compromise her freedom and any chance there might be of breaking the curse.

She resisted the bold thrust of his tongue, but his mouth tasted of apple and wine, and she felt the slow melting begin deep inside her.

Maybe just a kiss.

Parting her lips, she stroked his tongue with her own and heard him groan. He dipped her farther back, forcing her to cling to him or fall. His tongue moved in and out of her mouth, stealing her breath, stealing her sanity. She wanted more. Her mouth became as aggressive as his, stroking, tasting, until they were both wild.

She dragged her mouth from his, panting and shaken. "Brother Leland," she whispered.

The heat of his lips moved to her throat. "He'll not stir 'til morning."

He shrugged out of his thick mantle and spread it atop the fur already on the floor. Yanking his tunic over his head, he stood before her bare to the waist.

Rowena felt her body clench and tingle. Candlelight played upon skin stretched smooth over sculpted muscles. She wanted to touch him, needed to touch him, and she didn't hesitate. She stroked and caressed each contour and plane. Her palms absorbed the heat and contrasting textures.

He snatched her cloak from her shoulders. She hardly noticed as she continued her exploration of his torso. His body was strong, his skin hot. She couldn't get enough of the feel of him.

His fingers jerked the cords binding the front of her gown then he tugged it off over her head. Her chemise soon followed, and Rowena shivered. Cold night air whispered across her heated flesh before he pressed them together, skin against skin.

Rowena moaned and closed her eyes. Her heart pounded within her chest. His big hands cupped her bottom, dragging her forward. She kicked off her leather slippers and buried her face against his chest, wrapping her arms around his back. "I must have your vow, Dominic. Promise you will not...."

She couldn't bring herself to say the words, but she knew he understood her expectation. The last thing she wanted was to end this here, but she couldn't compromise on this point. Easing away from him, she looked into his eyes.

His gaze was bright, his eyes dilated. Predatory.

"Promise."

"I will not spill my seed inside your body."

His mouth ground against hers, a momentary punishment. Had she angered him with her persistence?

Her concern eroded as sensations erupted all over her body. The slick heat of his mouth intoxicated, but she wasn't satisfied with the possessive press of his mouth over hers. She parted her lips and angled her head, silently beckoning a more intimate contact. She met the thrust of his tongue with a deep moan and an eager response.

She melted into his embrace, thrilled by the obvious strength in his arms. Arching her back, Rowena pressed her breasts against his naked chest, splaying her hands across the thick muscles of his shoulders. He wrapped his arm around her waist, pressing her more tightly against him. All the while their mouths played, nipped and licked, communicating in a language older than the spoken word.

They sank to their knees together. Rowena knew she was trembling. Her head spun with the sensations surging through her body. She wanted him, needed him inside her, filling her, overwhelming her.

His hands descended along her sides, settling against her hips. He pulled her forward until her belly cradled his hard length. Rowena released a shaky breath. He wanted her as much as she wanted him. An explosion of heat accompanied the thought. She felt giddy and restless. Wiggling closer, she looped her arms around his neck and hugged him tight.

"This feels like heaven," she whispered against his lips.

He chuckled, a deep rumbling sound. "Not yet, but soon. Lie back. Let me look at you."

She lay on his cloak and spread her hair out in shining waves all around her. His gaze moved slowly over her, lingering on her breasts and the dark red curls at the juncture of her thighs. Her skin tingled, anticipating a caress more tangible than his heated gaze.

Suddenly frantic, Dominic tore off his boots and discarded the remainder of his clothing. His obvious need thrilled Rowena. She felt heat roll through her, leaving her tingling and anxious.

He joined her on their makeshift bed. Lying at her side, he propped himself up on his elbow. "You are extraordinary."

Warm and firm, his palm enveloped her breast. She quivered at his touch, savoring his tense, needy expression, amazed that she had inspired it. He bent toward her, his mouth opening over her nipple. She sighed as his lips brushed her skin and his tongue teased her flesh into a hard, throbbing peak.

He moved on top of her, nudging her legs apart with his knees. She opened for him, eager for the fullness of his body inside her. Dominic held back. His practiced mouth moved from one breast to the other, suckling, licking, driving her mad.

Shifting position, he knelt between her legs. Rowena was shocked by the carnality of the arrangement. Her thighs were spread wide, her knees bent, her body brazenly offered for his pleasure. She tried to draw her legs together, but he wouldn't allow it. He stared at her feminine slit, his expression ravenous, intense. Uncertainty and anticipation warred within her, making her head spin.

The first touch of his fingers made Rowena gasp. He traced her crease with just his fingertips, forward and back, forward and back. She shuddered and caught his wrist.

"Relax," he coaxed. "You'll enjoy this. I promise."

This was Dominic. He would never hurt her. She released his wrist, and his fingers continued their sensual dance. He explored her folds and circled her opening. Rowena moaned, tossing her head, her eyes drifting shut. The sensations were somehow intensified with her eyes closed. She could feel each stroke, each caress more distinctly.

He pushed his fingers into her passage then retreated despite her murmur of protest. His hot breath wafted across her inner thigh, and his lips touched her skin. Heat radiated out from the simple contact, and she stiffened. Did he mean to kiss her—there? His lips drifted nearer, confirming her suspicion. She should be shocked, mortified by the erotic act, but she wasn't. Licking her lips, she waited for the first brush of his lips.

He parted her folds and pressed his lips against the knot of nerves at the top of her slit. The kiss was an innocent foreshadowing of what he intended to do. His tongue passed over her nub, and pleasure darted through her abdomen. She clutched the cloak beneath her as he caressed her, excited her, worshiped her. On and on he swirled his tongue against her, curled it around her, becoming ever bolder.

Rowena bit back a scream. Her body throbbed with unbearable need. She arched into his torrid kiss, not caring that she was brazen, lost completely in the sensations he unleashed within her. He pushed his tongue into her core, shocking her with the ultimate intimacy. His mouth moved, demanding all she had to give. His tongue swept back to the top of her slit. She cried out, her hands balled into fists. Her entire body trembled with the force of her release.

Tingling echoes reverberated through her body as he slid up along her body and thrust home. She cried out again, both pleasured and surprised. Her body stretched around his, grasping him, welcoming him. She hugged his back, pulling her legs up high against his sides as he pulled back and pushed in again. She moved with him, yielded to him, surrendering everything.

He drove into her forcefully. She opened her mouth against his neck, tasting the salt of his skin. The fullness of their joining thrilled her. The elemental connection forced rational thoughts away. She had been empty and he filled her. She was no longer alone.

Tingling heat quivered in time to his rhythmic movements. Each thrust, each forceful penetration intensified the burning ache. She arched, clinging to him, tightening her body around his shaft.

He pulled out suddenly and crushed her to his chest. Rowena cried out sharply at the loss. The sensations flowed on in brilliant waves, bathing her entire body in pleasure, but the pulsing in her core was somehow hollow. The warmth of his seed erupted against her belly. He had kept his vow.

As the sensual haze receded, Rowena found tears tightening her throat and burning her eyes. He'd honored his vow. So why was she so sad? Twin tears escaped the corners of her eyes as she acknowledged her own irrationality.

She could hardly move, didn't want to move, but Dominic was heavy. It felt wonderful to be wrapped around him, but she longed for the fullness he created deep inside. The realization brought more tears, and she strangled a sob.

His lips lingered on her forehead, his hair tickling her face. "Why are you crying?" he whispered against her damp skin.

"I cannot breathe."

Adjusting his position to rest his weight more fully on his knees, he looked down into her face. "Why are you crying?"

He was so beautiful in the candlelight. Rowena felt her heart clench painfully. The ragged sob escaped along with more tears. "I will not love you, Dominic. I will not love you!"

She shoved him sideways and scrambled out from underneath him. Grabbing as many of her discarded clothes as she could in her haste, she scampered into the darkened cell across the corridor from Brother Leland.

Shaken by the rush of emotions still churning within her, Rowena began to dress. She had pulled her chemise on over her head when she heard the familiar tinkle of Fair Fiona's laughter.

"I'm so glad you're amused." She tugged the chemise into place and reached for her tunic. The Fairy danced in the corner of the room, diving and spinning, creating golden patterns in the darkness. "Will you ever speak to me? I need your guidance badly."

Approaching in a slow, steady arc, the golden light hovered near Rowena's face. She felt the faint brush of wings against her cheek, and her entire face tingled. Her tears disappeared. Rowena smiled.

"All right. No more weeping. Any more sage advice?"

Laughter made the Fairy glimmer. She circled Rowena twice then darted behind her. Rowena turned — and screamed. Fair Fiona perched between the sparkling eyes of a shadowy beast.

Dominic rushed into the room, a candle in one hand, his sword in the other. "What? Why did you scream?"

She pointed to the creature now alone above the doorway. Where had the Fairy gone?

Rising his candle toward the masonry dragon, Dominic lowered his sword. Intricately carved with vicious-looking fangs and multi-faceted glass eyes, the dragon snarled at them. "He doesn't look happy, does he?"

"What is that thing doing in a monastery?"

Dominic offered a nonchalant shrug. "There are many dragons decorating your castle. I didn't realize you were frightened by them."

"I'm not. I simply didn't expect to find one staring down at me in a monastery." She was far more embarrassed than annoyed. Why did Fiona continue to tease? Why wouldn't she reveal her presence to others?

Did she want people to think she was only a figment of Lady Pendragon's imagination? It was so frustrating.

"Didn't you say the first ill-fated Lord of Pendragon lived in this monastery?"

"Lived and died here," she corrected. "Do you think he had the dragon put there?"

"Perhaps as a sort of penance, a continual reminder of his wrongdoing?"

"Then this would be the room in which he took his life." She gave a violent shudder. "Can you reach it? Is there any sort of lever or fastening? Could something be hidden within?"

Dominic handed her the candle. Stretching onto his toes, he was able to reach the sculpture. He searched it with his hands, following every contour and even pushing on its reflective eyes. "Nay. It's just a decoration."

"A rather odd decoration."

"Did you not say he'd gone mad?"

She nodded.

"Shall I smash it? It frightened you. 'Tis only right that the dragon be slain."

She smiled at his foolishness. "Nay. Leave it be. But let's sleep in the outer room."

Dominic followed her into the larger room. She returned the candle to the mantle and slipped beneath the weight of their combined cloaks. Rowena tried not to shiver, but her skin was chilled, her emotions turbulent and raw.

Dominic blew out the candle before he joined her on the fur. His strong arms slipped around her and

Rowena clung to him. He didn't mention her odd confession and Rowena was grateful. He knew her defenses were slipping. Like a lazy cat, he simply waited for her to emerge from her hiding place.

You're mine already.

The silken taunt followed her into sleep.

Chapter Eleven

A ticklish sensation drew Rowena from sleep. She stretched and shifted, arching her body against the hard warmth of Dominic's back. Sleep receded gradually like fog on a warm spring morning. He was still sleeping soundly, his fingers interlaced with hers. One of her arms nestled beneath his neck and the other circled his waist. Their interlocked hands pressed against his chest, and Rowena could feel the steady beating of his heart. A strand of his hair rested across her nose, causing the subtle irritation that had awakened her. Burying her face fully in his thick dark hair, Rowena allowed herself one long contented moment before she rose to face the day.

Dominic continued to sleep even after she disentangled her fingers and slipped from their bed. She dressed quickly, glad for the quiet moment to gather her thoughts and sort through her feelings.

Warm echoes of sensation reminded Rowena of their lovemaking. He was always tender and considerate when they touched. He overwhelmed her at times, but even at his most passionate Rowena could sense his determination to bring her pleasure.

If only she could trust his feelings as much as she trusted his touch.

Raking her fingers through her tousled hair, she tried to work some of the tangles from the long strands. She understood his agenda. He'd made no real attempt to hide his purpose. He wanted Pendragon Castle, meant to have it by whatever means necessary.

The thought made her sad and intensified the loneliness that had been part of her longer than she could remember. It was odd. Edwin wanted nearly the same thing, and it filled her with rage. Dominic's determination made her long for something more.

She looked down into his sleeping face and felt compelled by the power and nobility stamped upon his features. Sunlight gilded his night black hair and accented the healthy color of his skin. His dark eyelashes rested in dense crescents against his cheeks. She had never noticed how long they were before. One thickly muscled arm and shoulder rested on top of his cloak. Even relaxed, his shape was impressive.

He'd make a strong and competent lord, but what sort of husband? He was kind and protective now, perhaps a bit overbearing. But once he had Pendragon Castle, his motivation for treating her kindly would be gone.

Even if she decided to consider him as husband, his past still loomed between them.

I'm not a murderer.

Had he made the statement with a bit too much vehemence the night before? There had to be an explanation, but how would she ever broach the issue?

Thora confirmed that he'd been betrothed to a woman named Monica, but the rest was speculation. Rowena needed facts.

Pulling on her slippers, she shoved her troubled thoughts aside and went to check on the friar.

Brother Leland continued to sleep in blissful oblivion. His skin was cool and supple. There was no sign of fever or complicating condition.

She lit a rush torch from one of the candles and crossed into the adjacent cell. The stone dragon stared down at her. Its faceted eyes seemed to glower with menace. She'd wandered through the deserted monastery countless times and never noticed the odd decoration. Fair Fiona had drawn her attention there. Why?

"Are you certain you don't want me to slay it?"

She smiled. "I've explored the monastery on several occasions. I can't believe I never noticed it before."

"You can't see it unless you're exiting the cell, and you had no reason to enter until last night." He joined her in the tiny room. "How fares your patient?"

"Brother Leland is the same," Rowena told him. "He hasn't awakened."

Dominic took the torch from her hand and held it aloft. The dragon's eyes gleamed. "Does this concern you?"

"Not overmuch." She stepped closer, tilting her head to examine where the figure protruded from the wall.

"When do you expect he will be able to travel?"

Rowena paused and faced him. Her hands tangled in the material of her skirt. She didn't want to incite his anger but Brother Leland must be protected. "His location must remain a secret. If Edwin realizes where he is, he will try to finish what he began."

"Were you finished here?" She nodded and stepped out into the corridor. "How many know his whereabouts?"

"Thora, a few of the kitchen staff, and of course Nan and Bert."

She entered the friar's cell and knelt beside his makeshift bed. Pressing the back of her hand to his forehead, she watched his breathing and noted the color of his skin. He appeared frail and haggard. She pressed her lips firmly together, hiding the way they trembled.

Domenic reached into the cell to set the torch in the iron sconce but remained in the doorway. "The tale will have spread far beyond those few by now."

"What do you suggest?" She was almost afraid to ask. He was being uncharacteristically cooperative.

"I think we should finish what Edwin began."

Rowena gasped in horrified disbelief until Dominic laughed.

"Not literally. We should spread the word that Brother Leland didn't survive the beating. We'll have to return to the castle of course, but we could arrange for someone else to tend the friar. Many of my men will be departing in the next few days. One of them could slip up here and not be missed."

"You're leaving?" Rowena was embarrassed by the panicked quality in her voice, but the words were spoken before she could restrain them.

He crouched before her, his weight balanced on the balls of his feet. "You'll not be rid of me so easily. I'm sending some of my men with Ezra to his new fief. I'm the captain of your personal guard. I would be shirking my duties were I to leave your side."

She hadn't bothered with her veil, and his hand slipped into her hair. Rowena leaned into the comfort of his caress, resting her cheek against the cup of his open palm. "I'm frightened," she whispered. "I knew Edwin was obsessed with Pendragon Castle, but it wasn't until I saw what he had done to Brother Leland that I realized he'll do anything."

He tucked a strand of hair behind her ear with his other hand and pressed a kiss to her forehead. "I'll deal with Edwin. You concentrate on helping your friend."

She pushed to her knees and melted into his embrace. He was strong, capable of protecting her, and she was ready to be protected. She clung to him, pressing her face into the warm crevice where his throat met his shoulder.

He shifted to his knees, drawing her more tightly against his body. Stroking her hair, he rocked her gently. "I'm here. You're safe. I'm here."

She clung to him and drew his warm scent deeply into her lungs. Her body trembled, and her spirit ached to take the final step and surrender to love. Easing back just far enough to look into his face, Rowena searched his eyes. Could she trust him with her heart? Did she dare...

"We'll find our way through this together."

His mouth covered hers in a slow, sweet kiss. Rowena reveled in the warm slide of his lips and the gentle sweep of his tongue. The kiss was meant to comfort, not arouse, and she felt her anxiety melt away.

"We should return to the castle."

His warm breath brushed her lips as he spoke, and Rowena shivered.

"I'll stay with Brother Leland until you've made arrangements. I'm not comfortable leaving him unattended."

A long, loud sigh illustrated his frustration. He rose to his feet and looked down at her. "And I'm not comfortable leaving you here alone."

"I'm not unconscious." She shifted back to sit beside the friar. "Find someone we can trust with Brother Leland's care and send him to me. When he arrives, I'll return to the castle."

He was obviously displeased by her determination, but he didn't argue. He folded his arms over his chest. "You'll need to appear suitably distressed by the death of the friar. I'll spread the word when I arrive that he is not likely to survive the day. Then you'll confirm to everyone that poor Brother Leland didn't recover from the beating he suffered at the hands of Edwin."

"I understand."

"I'll not be gone long," he promised. "Don't leave the monastery until I return. I'll bring someone back to tend the friar, and I'll escort you back to the castle myself."

"As you wish, my lord." She punctuated the sentence with a smile, and he responded with a quick nod.

Rowena sat beside Brother Leland, allowing her mind to wander as she listened to the steady cadence of his breathing.

"Where am I?"

She turned her head to meet the friar's sightless eyes. Her heart leapt with hope, and she reached for his hand.

"Oh Brother Leland, thank God you're awake. It's Rowena. How are you feeling?"

"Pitiful. Where am I? What became of Nan? Oh, the poor child. That animal—"

"Nay, Brother Leland. Edwin tricked you. He didn't harm Nan. He only made you believe he had. Nan is safe, and so are you. We're in the old monastery."

"Then you must take me away. I'll not endanger you or the people of Pendragon. He will search for me. I know he will."

"Nay, he will not. Sir Dominic is going to spread the word that you have passed away. Edwin will believe you dead, so there will be no reason for him to search."

He chuckled and then groaned. Pain twisted his expression. "You were always clever."

"I'll give you something to ease your pain. Your body needs to mend." Relief did summersaults through

Rowena's stomach as she gathered another dose of Cook's mixture. She tried to concentrate on the joy, but guilt hovered in the shadows, launching hot, stinging darts into her heart.

"He has to be stopped," the friar whispered. "He has become obsessed with the legend."

Slipping one arm behind his shoulders, Rowena held a cup to his lips and helped him drink the potion. "I know what Edwin is about, and I'm so sorry you were…"

Her voice broke on a sob, and Rowena couldn't go on.

"You're not to blame, Rowena," Brother Leland whispered.

"If he didn't want my castle so badly, he would never have harmed you."

He moaned softly as she removed her arm and allowed him to settle back against the blankets. "It is more than the castle. Edwin wants it all. He wants to solve the riddle, lift the curse and find the Dragon's Tears."

"You speak of these things as if they exist." His features relaxed, his eyes drifted shut, but she doubted that the herbs could have taken effect so quickly. "Do *you* believe in the legend?"

"You would be shocked by what I believe," the friar mumbled and then slipped back into unconsciousness.

* * * * *

Storm clouds gathered on the horizon. Rowena stood in the opening of the monastery and looked out over the forest below. The original builders had cut back a wide swath of trees, making any approach to the entrance obvious, but shrubs and vegetation had reclaimed the clearing over the years. Thunder clamored in the distance, and the sweet smell of rain drifted on the breeze. If Dominic didn't hurry, they'd be caught by another storm.

He arrived a short time later with Sir Ezra.

Rowena smiled at Dominic's friend. "Thank you for coming." He was slightly taller than Dominic, but not so heavily muscled.

Ezra bowed, sunlight gleaming in the strands of his curly blond hair, before he stepped into the gloomy interior of the monastery. "Always at the service of a lady."

"I decided Ezra alone could be trusted with this secret, so he has temporarily postponed his departure for Granville Cross," Dominic explained.

"Will this not draw suspicion? It is widely known that he is anxious to claim his holdings." She glanced between the two men, each so handsome and virile yet nearly opposite in coloring. They made a striking contrast.

"The men have been long away from their homes," Dominic said. "I released them for a time and told them to await Ezra's summons."

"I'd already decided that arriving at Granville Cross with a small army would likely lead to unnecessary resistance. Even Dom's men believe we have parted ways. Only we three are aware of the deception."

"Again, I thank you. Brother Leland is very dear to me." Rowena explained what Ezra would need to do and then reluctantly followed Dominic from the ruin.

"We're racing a storm." Dominic echoed her earlier thought. "Let us away."

Rowena fell into a sullen silence as they rode. He'd not mentioned her emotional outburst the night before. Was he avoiding her embarrassment, or did he prefer not to talk about love? There was much left unsaid between them. How in creation would she ever ask him about Monica?

"What is troubling you?"

Fidgeting in the saddle, Rowena considered her options. Which issue should she broach first? Which was more important? Her feelings for Dominic would be easier to sort with Monica banished from their lives.

She took a deep breath and blurted, "Have you ever been wed before?"

Dominic chuckled, his dark blue eyes assessing her. "I wondered when we would arrive at this conversation. Tell me what you have heard, and I will tell you what is fact and what is nonsense."

She liked the idea immensely. "You were betrothed to a woman named Monica."

"Fact."

"She was wealthy."

He hesitated. "Her wealth was a fabrication, but I didn't know that when William negotiated the betrothal."

Tension gathered within her, but Rowena pushed on. "You wanted her for her wealth."

He shook his head. "Nonsense. I was in love with Monica."

His easy admission stung. Rowena snapped her face forward and fixed her eyes on the trail ahead. "I thought you didn't believe in love."

She felt the brush of his fingers against her hand and turned her face back toward him.

"I never said that, Rowena."

He smiled, and her heart fluttered madly. She quickly averted her gaze as heat spread up her neck and across her cheeks. She was much too susceptible to his charm.

"Now surely there is something more interesting than whether or not I loved the girl."

She nodded and her fingers tightened around the leather reins. "They say you killed her." She quickly looked at his face, searching his eyes for a response.

"Utter nonsense." He sounded absolute. His gaze met hers without hesitation. "I was not even present when Monica died."

Relief washed over her with staggering sweetness. "How did she die? Nay, go back farther. How did you meet? What was she like? Why do people believe you are responsible for her death?"

It was as if shutters slammed closed over his eyes. Rowena watched as the openness vanished and his expression turned tense and harsh.

"It was long ago. It has no bearing on our future."

"Our future?" she challenged softly, hurt by his withdrawal. "I trusted you with things I've told no one else, not even Thora. Everything you've wanted to know, I told you. I explained all the shameful —"

Rowena's words were suddenly cut off by her startled cry. Searing pain shot through her left shoulder as the sharp head of an arrow penetrated her flesh. She cried out again as her entire arm went numb and she could no longer control her hand. Sensing her fear, her palfrey tossed its head and pranced to an insecure stop.

Dominic vaulted from his horse's back long before the beast could stop. He caught Rowena as she slipped from her saddle with a ragged gasp. Fire shot through her breast, down her arm and up the side of her neck. She sobbed. Panic exploded within her even more powerful than the pain. Had the arrow been poisoned? Why did it hurt so badly?

"It hurts," she whimpered, unable to contain the tears. "It should not hurt this much."

Dominic sank with her to the forest floor. His hands were trembling. Rowena had never seen fear in his eyes before, but he was frightened now. *Oh God, do not let me die!*

Frantically grasping for his dagger, Dominic cut back the edge of her cloak to assess the damage. The arrow had entered her chest several inches below the shoulder, but the head appeared to be lodged against her shoulder's bone. He cursed.

"I cannot remove the shaft unless I push it through and break off the head. I don't think that's possible."

Calm! He needed to be calm. If she realized how frightened he was, it would only increase her panic.

"I cannot feel my arm." She sobbed, clutching the useless appendage against her waist with her other hand. "Oh God. The arrow must have been poisoned. My head...is spinning."

Terror spurred him into action. Dominic braced her shoulder with one hand. "Forgive me, my love." He snapped off the portion of the shaft protruding from her chest. Her harsh cry made Dominic clench his teeth. All color drained from her face until her skin appeared gray.

Dominic cried out. "Hold on, Rowena." He cupped her face with one palm and kissed her forehead. Her eyes gradually glazed over. Dominic shook with the force of his fear. "Do not leave me." Her head lulled back against his arm and she collapsed with a ragged whimper.

An anguished cry tore from his throat as he scooped her up and awkwardly mounted his horse. He urged the beast forward with the firm pressure of his heels. Clutching her against his chest, he raced through the trees. He felt wild with fear and fury. He needed to lash out, to hurt, to destroy.

"Damn you to hell!" he screamed to the forest.

They'd all believed Edwin wouldn't strike directly. He should've known better! Any animal turned vicious when it was backed into a corner.

I failed her.

The realization swept every other thought from his mind. He couldn't breathe. Guilt and remorse suffocated even his anger.

I can't let her die.

I will not let her die!

Focusing all of his energy and every fiber of his emotional being on that goal, Dominic urged his horse onward.

Blood saturated the front of her clothing by the time Dominic entered the main hall, carrying Rowena in his arms. Ignoring the startled gasps and hushed conversation that followed in his wake, Dominic went directly to the solar wing and Lady Rowena's bedchamber. He'd just laid her down across the bed when Farrell and Thora burst in upon him.

"What have you done to her?" Farrell demanded.

Shoving the angry man out of the way, Thora rushed to the bedside. "How was she injured? What needs to be done?"

Dominic spared the steward only a furious glower before he addressed Thora's questions, all the while working to unfasten Rowena's clothing. "An arrowhead is imbedded in her shoulder. How long will it take to fetch a leech?"

"Too long, she would bleed to death," Thora predicted with grim honesty.

Dominic didn't argue. "Then heat water and bring me something with which her flesh can be sewn and bound."

Thora departed without further comment, but Farrell stepped closer to the bed.

"Who did this?" the steward asked. "Where were the two of you?"

"I don't see how that is any of your concern," Dominic snapped. "The arrow came out of the woods as we rode back toward the castle. She said it might have been poisoned before she lost consciousness. Is there not an herbalist in the castle? A midwife? Anyone who knows the healing arts?" His voice became harsher, more demanding with each question.

"I'll fetch someone." Thora passed the water and clean linens to Farrell and left again.

Dominic stripped Rowena of her blood-soaked clothing and pulled the bedding up to cover her breasts. The wound had slowed its flow of blood to a gradual seepage, but Dominic knew that removing the arrowhead would reopen the wound. Could she afford to lose any more blood? She looked so pale, so still, so vulnerable.

Fear and helplessness twisted painfully inside his chest. Silently he began to pray.

He turned to Farrell. The steward stood back a step, staring silently at his mistress. His expression was as torn with emotion as Dominic felt. "You must hold her while I dig out the arrowhead."

"Should we not wait for Thora to return?" His voice squeaked just a little.

"It must come out. This much I know. The rest can wait for the healer, but why not have the worst of it finished by the time Thora returns?"

Farrell nodded, stiffly moving closer to the bed.

"Can you do it, or should I summon someone else?"

"I will do what must be done."

Dominic sat on the edge of the bed and brushed the back of his fingers across Rowena's forehead. Her skin was warm but not hot. Unconsciously, his fingers drifted down across her cheek and sank into her hair. "Rowena, hold fast. We can survive this, I promise."

He didn't realize he'd spoken the words out loud until Farrell asked, "Are you in love with her?"

The question brought him up short. He had convinced himself that Pendragon Castle was all he sought, but he found the thought of losing Rowena more painful than anything he'd ever endured. Nothing was more important than having her by his side.

"Aye," he admitted for the first time. He bounded up from the bed. "Let's have this thing done."

In a flurry of activity, Dominic drew a sharp, jeweled dagger from the sheath hidden in the top of his boot. He cleaned the blade and then passed it through the flames smoldering in the hearth. "Hold her fast."

Dominic tucked her arm under the blankets, leaving only the wound exposed. Farrell used the blankets to similarly constrain her on the other side. Lifting her slightly, Dominic slipped a folded piece of cloth beneath Rowena's shoulder and securely gripped her before he began.

Rowena was unconscious, so her shrill scream shocked him. The instant the knife blade parted her traumatized flesh she began to struggle. She thrashed beneath the covers, twisting her body madly to elude the pain. Her screams turned quickly to pathetic whimpers that were even harder for Dominic to bear.

He whispered to her, attempting to soothe her as he dug for the arrowhead.

Blood quickly filled the gaping hole created by the dagger. A crimson river flowed across Dominic's hand and spilled onto the folded cloth beneath her shoulder. Panic spread through him. His heart pounded painfully and his ears began to ring. Her blood was hot and slick. He wanted to capture it with his hand and press it back into her body, but it flowed between his fingers, slipping beyond his grasp.

"Hurry," Farrell cried.

"I have it!" He lifted a gore-covered object roughly triangular in shape.

* * * * *

Thora shot a thin golden beam into the keyhole and grinned as the latch flipped open. Rushing inside the dark apothecary, she quickly gathered the least useless of the human herbs. If only she had more time! She'd gather in the Fairy realm. Well, that wasn't possible. She must make do with what she had.

Clutching the basket to her breast she transformed and flew, riding the wind back to the castle. She paused in the solar, debating what form to choose. Farrell might question a complete stranger, so she fashioned the likeness of the castle's midwife.

"I have it!" She heard Dominic's deep voice.

He had what? What had they done?

She swept into the room with obvious intention.

"Be you the midwife?" Dominic asked.

"Aye," she affirmed. "What happened?"

"The lady and I were riding toward the castle when she was struck by an arrow. She feared the arrow was poisoned. Can you help her?"

She quickly examined the wound. "Did the shoulder bleed freely?"

"Aye, both when the arrow hit and just now when I dug out the head."

"Good, that may be our only advantage."

Without further comment, Thora went to work. She mixed a thick paste, infusing it with Fairy energy far more beneficial than the plant's healing properties. She smeared the paste generously on a piece of linen. After cleaning the blood from Rowena's shoulder, chest and arm, she pressed the linen directly over the wound.

"Should it not be sewn?" Domenic objected.

"Nay. The putridity needs to seep out of the wound. To sew it shut would encourage the foul humors to spread within her body. She will have a larger scar this way, but it is safer."

She longed to reassure him, to share her secret and put his fear to rest. But she dare not. She had risked much just tending the lady's wound. Every time she accessed Fairy energy it sent ripples through her father's realm.

"Do you think she'll survive?"

Thora paused. How to answer? They had accomplished much. What she witnessed in the monastery was very encouraging. Still, they were both so stubborn. Was it time for another nudge?

"If she survives the night she might recover, but prepare yourself, sir." She paused before meeting his gaze. "I would send for a priest. She has lost too much blood."

"Nay!" Dominic staggered back. His head pounded as if his skull would split in two. Clutching his temples, he shut his eyes. She could not die. *Please God, do not let her die!*

When he managed to open his eyes, the midwife was mixing a potion in a shallow wooden bowl. Dominic watched in a horrified stupor as she trickled it down Rowena's throat and then left the chamber.

He couldn't think. The feelings ravaging his mind were overwhelming. He wanted to wail. He wanted to find Edwin and kill him slowly — painfully. How could he lose her now? The frozen fragments of his heart had only begun to melt and mend.

She deserved happiness. She deserved to live one day of her life without fear and sorrow. She didn't deserve to die!

With a roar of anguish, Dominic swept his arm across the table. The bowl and remnants of the midwife's cure went flying. He wasn't appeased. He toppled the table and kicked it across the room. "I will kill him! If it takes the rest of my life to find that bastard, I will taste his blood!"

Farrell stood near the door, his hands clenching and releasing in front of him. Tears trailed in unabashed profusion from his eyes. "Even Edwin's death will not undo this, milord. You must marry her now."

Dominic's breath came in harsh pants and the red haze receded from his vision. "What? Your lady lies dying and you speak of weddings?"

Farrell moved toward the bed, his expression suddenly resolute. "It is *because* my lady lies dying that I speak of weddings. Do you not see? If Lady Rowena dies, Pendragon goes to Edwin." His dark eyes flashed with hatred. "All she has fought for will be lost. She will have died in vain. That cannot happen."

"He is right, milord."

Thora stood in the doorway. He couldn't say how long she'd been there, but her eyes were red-rimmed and tears streaked her face.

"I cannot wed an unconscious woman." Dominic raked both hands through his hair. "I have no right to force this upon her."

"Would this be forced upon her? You told me you love her. Has she not made a similar claim?" Farrell took two steps toward the bed.

Pressing his tightly clenched fists against his temples, Dominic growled out his exasperation. "You do not know what you ask. She will despise me!"

Thora stepped up to him and placed a tentative hand on his forearm. "It must be so. Pendragon *cannot* fall to Edwin."

Dominic began to pace. He glanced at Rowena's face so pale and helpless and then at her two closest friends. Their expressions shouted their expectations and their eyes tortured him with hope.

"There is no one who would perform such a ceremony," Dominic muttered.

"Brother Samuel would," Thora said.

Dominic paused in his pacing and looked at her. "Who is Brother Samuel?"

"Brother Leland's apprentice."

He glanced at Farrell then back at the handmaiden. "Does this friar know of Brother Leland's fate?"

"Aye. He would bless the union, and he may even say that he performed the ceremony yesterday while you two were away from the castle."

Farrell moved closer to Thora, drawing Dominic's attention. "Then you can ask William Marshal to set his seal on the union. No one in Christendom would argue with that."

It all made perfect sense, yet he knew he would be damned if he agreed. He would have his heart's desire, and it would cost him his soul. Even if Rowena survived, she would never trust him, never allow herself to love him.

"She loves you, milord. She would want this, I assure you."

Glancing into Thora's wide blue eyes, Dominic was tempted to believe.

"How could I bear to make her my wife only to watch her slip away?" His words were harsh and choked.

"Do you object to the marriage?" Farrell challenged impatiently. "Perhaps we both misjudged you. We could just as easily say that I was the one Rowena wanted. Send for Brother Samuel, Thora. I will wed Lady Rowena myself."

Dominic took an automatic step toward the other man. His possessive instincts screamed for violence. It took all his frazzled will just to keep his fists from flying.

"Nay," Dominic insisted. "She is meant for me."

Chapter Twelve

Pleased by her daring, Titania lingered in the forest. Some things could be left to chance and some things required personal attention. She kicked the bow into the bushes and brushed her hands off on her skirts. With her Fairy abilities so suppressed, she wasn't sure she could make the shot. The arrow had flown fast and true, ensuring that this generation would not see the end of the Pendragon curse.

How she missed the Fairy realm, the festive courts and glistening halls of Oberon's palace. Spreading her arms, she turned in a slow circle and inhaled the fresh autumn breeze. She only needed to stay until she sensed Rowena's death. Then she would release her hold on this human body and depart for home.

Soon. This would all be over soon.

"Sooner than you think, Titania."

She staggered to a stop and lowered her arms. How was this possible? She had been so careful.

"Since I forbade her to use her power, Fiona has done little more than shift from one form to another." His tone was conversational, but she wasn't fooled by his calm. She could smell his fury. "Today Puck asked me what had upset her."

Summoning all of her courage, Titania turned to face Oberon. Regal, ancient, ageless, he emanated power while remaining incredibly graceful. With his silky dark hair and amber eyes, no other being could match Oberon's physical beauty. His vicious expression, however, promised mayhem for his wife.

"I don't understand the significance," she evaded.

"The ripples of Fiona's emotions were so intense my *jester* sensed them. You don't find significance in that?" His eyes burned with golden fire and his lips pressed into a grim line. "Fiona is my firstborn child. That will never change. Wives can be put aside or banished utterly."

She debated her reaction. The next few moments might well determine her fate. "I will release my hold on this body and return at once."

He snorted. "That is where your penance will begin."

"I'm your wife, Oberon—"

"I'm your king!"

She sank to her knees, resentment festering along with her fear. Sometimes the wisest course was to retreat and fight another day. "I await your judgment, sire."

"Fiona. Appear to me *now*."

Titania looked up in time to see her enemy materialize.

"I'm sorry, Father." Fiona's voice was soft and contrite, with a deference Titania would never be able to muster. "I sensed the nature of the poison on the arrow and knew I was Rowena's only hope. I would never have interfered were it not for—"

"I did not summon you for reprimands. My wife has been sabotaging you in ways I can scarcely imagine. I suspect this is not the first Pendragon lady who has fallen prey to Titania's treachery."

Titania gasped. "That's not true. I have never—"

"Silence! I will deal with you when we return." He shifted his gaze back to his daughter. "You have my leave to access your power in any way you see fit. I cannot reverse your banishment, but this should make things easier."

"What? You can't let her..." Titania's objections faded away as Oberon sent her to the Fairy realm and Lissette's body crumpled to the forest floor.

Fiona held her breath. Had his decree been sincere, or was he provoking Titania?

"Will Rowena recover?" he asked.

"I'm doing what I can."

"Now you can do more." He paused, his features hardening into a fierce scowl. With a wave of his hand, he positioned Lissette's body near her horse, her booted foot hooked through the stirrup. "Titania has always been wily, but this was unacceptable. See to your human friends. I must see to my wife."

He flashed out of sight, and the horse darted off through the trees, dragging Lissette's body behind it.

* * * * *

"Are you frightened, Rowena?"

Spinning from the open window, Rowena heard her own gasp echo off the high, stone walls. Her surroundings seemed familiar yet everything was strange. The shape and structure of her bedchamber hadn't changed, but the furniture and the wall hangings were different.

Where was she? Who spoke to her?

She took a step. The room weaved and spun. Had she consumed too much wine?

Are you frightened, Rowena?

Should she be frightened?

A sudden flash caught Rowena's attention. The tiny illumination flickered and floated. She knew this light, but never before had she heard a voice. It expanded gradually, growing in size and intensity.

Rowena backed toward the window, but distinct pulses radiated from the nimbus, passing through her body like silent peals of thunder. Her heart pounded and her skin prickled.

"Who are you?" she whispered. "*What* are you?"

The light shimmered, flaring for a moment with all the colors of the rainbow, and a woman glided toward her with otherworldly grace.

Rowena wanted to run, but her body wouldn't obey the frantic urgings of her mind. This couldn't be real, yet she could see the aberration, feel the air around her stir, smell a verdant, floral scent that hadn't been there a moment before.

The diaphanous material of the woman's rich green gown floated all about her. Tall and lithe, she raised one willowy arm to brush the hair away from her face. Her hair was extraordinary, a bright true gold that fell in distinct waves to her knees, but the face now revealed stole the breath from Rowena's lungs.

She fell back a step. This creature was not human. No being of this world was so staggeringly beautiful. Rowena lowered her gaze, overcome and a bit afraid.

"Come here, Rowena. Let me look at you."

The soft, musical voice drew her, compelled her to obey. She slowly raised her face and took several tentative steps toward the apparition. Her body felt weighted, her mind dazed.

"Who are you?" she asked again.

"Why would *you* need to ask?"

The woman smiled playfully, so Rowena tried to relax.

She looked more closely at the woman's features, perfectly proportioned, elegant, fragile yet somehow fierce—*Fairy.* Her incredible eyes tilted at an exotic angle and thick dark lashes formed an accentuating frame. The pupils were not round but diamond-shaped, within irises that shone like polished amber.

"Fair Fiona?" Rowena asked.

"Aye, some have called me that."

Rowena felt almost giddy. This could not be real. "But you are a myth, a legend."

"Then what, pray tell, does that make you?" Fiona's features settled into a speculative expression. "Are you up to the test, little one? You're younger than I'd thought you'd be."

A strange tingle skittered along Rowena's nerve endings. "What test? I don't understand."

"You will, very soon."

Her liquid-amber eyes began to burn. Rowena felt their heat upon her face and her insides began to cramp and coil.

"Are you brave, little one? Are you wise?"

Rowena didn't respond. Foreboding expanded within the room. Rowena felt its cold fist grip her heart and smelled its rancid breath.

Fiona came into vivid focus, sparkling with life and vitality. She kissed Rowena on the cheek, and Rowena gasped at the heat radiated by the simple contact.

"Are you ready, Rowena? Are you worthy?"

"Ready for what? Worthy of what? I do not understand."

The light appeared again, surrounding Fiona.

"Wait!" Desperately she grabbed for Fiona's slender hand. She was leaving! She couldn't leave until Rowena understood what she must do. Beams of light penetrated Fiona's form, absorbing her shape. "Don't leave. Please don't go."

"I have protected your son, Rowena. He is safe within your womb." Fiona's voice echoed as if from a great distance.

Rowena's hands flew to her stomach. "My son?" Blood pounded through her brain, making her dizzy and weak. She sank to her knees, trembling. Was it possible? Did a tiny life nestle within her body? Her heart soared at the possibility, her joy so acute it was nearly painful. She would bear a son.

Dominic's son!

The light expanded, suddenly encompassing Rowena. She struggled against it, frightened of its relentless pull. Stinging heat kissed her skin. Her blood felt like molten lava surging through her veins.

She screamed.

She was being dragged and sucked into a fiery abyss. Blinded by the light's intensity and twisting in agony, Rowena struggled. She kicked, she hit, she writhed, and all to no avail.

Pain consumed her.

The light began to recede, but the sensations escalated until she knew nothing but agony and darkness.

* * * * *

An audible groan tore from Rowena's dry throat as she struggled to lift her eyelids. Blinding light greeted her with a merciless welcome, so she quickly closed them again.

Was she dreaming? Her thoughts were muddled and sluggish. She remembered the light and the pain that followed. Had the pain been part of the light, or was it the other way around? Perhaps it had all been a dream and she was only now returning to reality.

Nay, she realized, the pain at least was real. Her muscles felt achy and tight, as if they'd been held in a prolonged cramp. Pounding pressure beat behind her eyes and deep within her temples. Slowly, she tried to move, but weakness kept her from moving so much as her hand.

"Thora," she called, her voice raspy and hoarse.

Why was her mouth so dry?

She heard heavy footsteps on a wooden floor and then a blissfully familiar male voice. "Oh, thanks be to God!"

Rowena braved the light again, desperate for a glimpse of Dominic's face. His handsome features contorted with relief, and his gaze devoured her face.

"Dominic." It hurt to speak.

He rushed to her side and carefully pulled her into his arms. Rowena gasped as the simple movement shot pain through her shoulder and down her arm. "What happened? My arm..."

"You were injured, my love. You have been very ill."

She couldn't read the emotions converging in his expression. Were those tears in his eyes? Nay, that was not possible.

"I feel horrible." The simplest movement exhausted her. She hardly had the strength to raise her head. "I need water."

He reached for a cup on the table nearby, lifting it to her lips without releasing her from his embrace. After quenching her thirst, Rowena relaxed against him and listened to the comforting beat of his heart.

"Four days," he whispered. "You've been unconscious four days."

Rowena tried to focus her mind, but thoughts floated and fluttered just out of reach. "The arrow." Bits and pieces came back to her, terrifying fragments and images that drained her tiny store of strength.

"It was poisoned, as you feared."

"Someone tried to kill me." Rowena's voice cracked and tears burned her eyes. Never had she been this miserable. Her entire body ached, her head pounded relentlessly, and it had been done intentionally.

He rocked her against his chest, his hold amazingly gentle. "You're safe now. No one will ever hurt you again."

She tried to smile, to find comfort in his assurance, but she didn't have the strength. Closing her eyes again, she surrendered to oblivion.

*****

"Has there been any change?" Thora asked softly from the doorway.

Dominic looked up from Rowena's haggard face and nodded. "She spoke to me not long ago. She's very weak, but she was lucid for a moment."

"That's wonderful."

She filled her voice with enthusiasm, but Dominic was too drained to respond. Rowena still looked dreadful. It was too soon to tell if the poison would have any lasting effects, and hope was just too painful.

He felt dazed, almost numb. For four days he'd watched her writhe in fevered delirium, not knowing from one moment to the next if she'd live or die.

"I've never been so frightened in my life."

He found it hard to believe the crisis had actually passed. He couldn't move himself from her side, afraid that he might yet lose her to death.

"I despise being helpless."

Thora sat at the foot of the bed and smiled at him. "You look nearly as bad as she does."

"My thanks, gracious damsel. I didn't stand this vigil alone. Neither you nor Farrell have been far from this room."

"If she awakened, the crisis is past. You will need your strength to help her complete her recovery."

"And to tell her what I have done?" He took Rowena's hand and brushed his lips across her fingers, needing to touch her, to reassure himself that she was still here.

"Some things can wait until she's stronger. All she need know is that you love her and will be here to protect her."

"As I protected her four days ago?"

"Do not." Thora shook her head, her tone insistent. "We cannot give in to guilt, nor can we entertain regrets. She is alive because of you. The people of Pendragon are safe. She is recovering, and that is all that matters."

He wanted to believe it, but Dominic was not a fool. He was thrilled that Rowena would regain her health, but his greatest challenge was yet to come.

* * * * *

After enduring twelve days confined to her bedchamber, Rowena happily lifted her face to the sky.

She took in a long, deep breath, fragrant with autumn leaves and the promise of evening showers. Holding it within her lungs, she savored the cool freshness. A gentle, chilly breeze teased her cheeks, but she cuddled within the comfort of her fur-lined cloak.

"Color has returned to your cheeks," Dominic said. "You look beautiful."

They strolled along the wide aisle separating the rose bushes. Most of the blossoms had withered with the frost the night before, but one stubborn bud refused to bow to winter's brutality. Rowena gently touched the fragile blossom, admiring its deep red color and its velvety texture. "I feel completely recovered, and I have for several days." Leaving the rose intact on its thorny perch, she continued on.

"I suppose we've been a bit overprotective, but I don't think you realize how close we came to losing you."

Rowena did no more than smile in thoughtful acceptance. Dominic had taken up the odd habit of referring to himself in tandem with Thora and Farrell. Thora was almost understandable, they had both been active participants in her recovery, but why did Dominic suddenly feel a connection with Farrell?

"And when can *we* be expected to abandon this ridiculous fear that I shall wither away before our eyes?"

He chuckled, taking her hand and tucking it into the bend of his elbow. "*We* are nearly over our worry."

He'd been wonderful these past few days, utterly dedicated to her care and entertainment. Once she was strong enough to leave her bed, he'd hardly left her side. They played chess and shared nearly every meal in the peaceful seclusion of her solar. They chatted away the afternoons and in the evenings she curled up in front of the fire with her head resting on his lap as he read to her. These had been some of the best days of her life.

She could no longer ignore the obvious; Dominic of Chapstow was courting her.

"Do you think it's possible to prove that Edwin tried to kill me?" she asked quietly.

He stopped walking and looked into her eyes. "I've been to Llangly twice. Edwin has gone into hiding."

His long dark hair had been pulled away from his face and bound at the nape of his neck. Sunlight accented his strong features and the golden tone to his smooth skin. Tempered with warmth and tenderness, his eyes glowed like sapphires. Rowena felt her heart turn over and the all too familiar ache took up root deep within her belly.

"What did you intend to do if he had been there?"

"I'm not sure. If I'd found him that first day, I might have killed him, but as you say, it would be better to prove he was responsible for the attack. I've men watching his keep and the village. If he returns, I'll know."

"Once he's captured, will the danger to me be past?"

His hands came down on her shoulders and he pulled her toward him. Those sapphire eyes ignited with deep blue fire. "He'll not get near you again, Rowena. I'll find him and make sure that he can never touch you. No one will ever hurt you again."

A harsh sort of desperation rasped through his tone. It took her a moment to realize the cause. "You're not to blame, Dominic. You saved my life that day."

He moved his hands and stepped back, looking even more miserable than before. "God's blood, woman, your pity is the last thing I need."

Why was he angry? "'Tis not pity. 'Tis gratitude, but if it offends you, I withdraw it. I blame you entirely for Edwin's treachery." She smiled into his eyes, hoping to lighten his mood. "You should have anticipated his madness and had me fitted for armor or at least a shield with which I could have deflected—"

"Rowena."

She didn't understand the dread in his eyes. "Aye."

"We must speak."

"We are speaking."

"Nay." He glanced around with obvious anxiety and then motioned to the stone bench near the garden wall. "May we sit, my lady?"

His formality scared her. Why was he behaving so strangely? She sat and arranged her cloak to cover her legs.

He lowered himself beside her, each movement stiff and hesitant. His eyes studied some spot in the distance as his thumb tapped out a nervous rhythm against his thigh.

Anxiety curled around her, compounded by his obvious hesitation. "What is the matter?"

"The poison from the arrow and the massive amount of blood that you lost led us to believe that you would die."

He seemed to choose each word individually. Rowena fidgeted on the hard bench.

"If you had died that night, Edwin would have won Pendragon Castle. Not even William Marshal would have been able to deny his claim." He paused to clear his throat. "But if you had been wed before you died, your holdings would have passed to your husband not to Edwin."

"If I had been *wed?*" Her stomach cramped and she had to swallow repeatedly. He couldn't mean what he appeared to mean. It wasn't possible! "Whom did I marry?"

"I wanted to woo you gently, to allow you time to know me before I—"

"While I lay senseless and completely unable to participate, *you married me?*" She shot up from the bench and turned on him. "I have heard you called Undaunted, but it was not until this moment that I understood what that meant. You are despicable."

"I wanted you as my wife, Rowena. We both know that I did, but the decision to wed—"

"*How* was it accomplished? Who spoke my vows for me? Who presided over such an abomination?"

He reached for her hand, but she quickly backed away, burying her arms within the fullness of her cloak. "Answer my questions." A great flood of emotion trembled within her, held back by her pride alone.

"We were able to convince Brother Samuel to perform the ceremony, and William set his seal to a special license yesterday."

"Ooh!" She kicked a clump of pinecones at her—*husband.* "How could you? How could you do this to me!"

Dominic managed to frame her face with his hands before she could thwart him. "I love you, Rowena. Is that not what you have wanted all along? A husband who adores you?"

Stubbornly ignoring the leap in her pulse at his unexpected words, Rowena shoved against his chest. He didn't budge, so she grasped his wrists and dug in her fingernails. "Don't speak to me of love! I doubt you know the meaning of the word." Forcing his hands from her face, she scrambled away from him. "I will never forgive you for this. I will never forgive any of you!"

He didn't follow as she ran for the keep. He'd not spoken their names, but she didn't need to ask who his conspirators had been. Thora and Farrell.

She found Farrell in the hall. He was speaking quietly with a man she didn't recognize. With no real hint of her intentions, she stepped in between the two men and punched the steward squarely in the stomach. He doubled over with a loud grunt, and she shoved him down onto the rush-strewn floor.

"Be off my lands by nightfall, or I'll have you hanged!"

He had no breath to object, and she didn't give him the opportunity. She flew up the stairs to her solar.

Kicking a wooden stool across the room, she screamed. The sound echoed back to her, but she felt no relief. She screamed again.

Panting and lightheaded, she looked for something to smash. But even in the midst of her fury she knew that nothing could restore the hope snuffed out by what they'd done. She kicked over one of the benches.

"Is this helping?" Dominic asked from the doorway. She didn't respond well to the light mockery in his tone. She spun and flew at him, hands curved into claws.

Dominic caught her and easily trapped her arms between their bodies. She thrashed and kicked, calling him obscene names he had no idea she knew. He just restrained her and let her rage. It was only after her anger ran its course and she began to sob he attempted to speak.

Gently stroking her hair, he felt her tears against his throat. She liked to nestle there against his shoulder when she was upset. He knew she felt betrayed, how could she not? But if he let her hide behind her anger it would set the tone for the rest of their life together. He had to find a way beyond her resentment. He didn't want to live in a world where she hated him.

"You cannot stay angry forever," he said softly.

"I can try."

He heard her stubborn words and smiled. Molding her body more intimately against his, he gave thanks when she didn't resist. "May we speak about this now, or are you still too angry?"

"I will always be too angry to listen to your lies."

He eased her away, but his hands lingered on her shoulders. He needed to touch her and go right on touching her, but she raised hurt-filled eyes and he strangled a groan. If he kissed her, he knew he could ignite her passion and burn away the pain, but too much was left unsaid.

"I'll not deny this is what I've wanted all along, but I did not manipulate the situation." She started to object, but he laid his index finger across her lips. "Hush. If you had died that night, Edwin would be here right now, Lord of Pendragon Castle."

"I would have haunted him."

Dominic was unable to suppress his smile this time. "Be that as it may, there was more at stake than you or I. It was suggested to me that I go ahead and have the marriage performed. I tried to object, knowing how you would react, but—"

"Suggested by whom?"

"Farrell."

"I do not believe you. Why would Farrell offer me to someone else?"

"When he wants you for himself?" Despite his determination to win her with gentle logic, a flare of jealousy nearly ended their conversation. "He told me that he would rather burn Pendragon Castle to the ground than see it in the hands of Edwin. He also said that if I didn't wed with you, he'd marry you himself."

"I could never marry Farrell."

"He saw me as the lesser of two evils, I believe."

"I am not convinced." She shrugged off his hands.

"That I am the lesser of two evils?"

She nodded and moved back several steps. "I don't know what to think of you. I do not *know* you."

"Then get to know me. That is what I have been trying to say. Take as much time as you need and—"

"But it is irrelevant now!"

Her arm flew as if she launched something at his head. Dominic barely suppressed the urge to duck, but there was nothing in her hand.

"Do you not see? It would not matter if you were evil and perverted. What recourse is there for me now? You could have strangled your mother and snapped Monica's neck and it would make no difference. I am trapped."

His blood sank to his feet, and Dominic forgot to breathe. "I did not kill Monica." He ground out the words with all the frustration and resentment permanently attached to the name.

Rowena paused, her eyes curious and assessing. "Tell me about her, Dominic. You know all my shameful secrets. Tell me about Monica."

It was a challenge, a demand. His entire body went rigid and his heart slammed against his chest. Damn her. She knew just where to strike and how to drive him back. "I told you about Monica. I did not kill her. That is all that matters."

"I disagree. Why have people clung to the story for so long? Why is her name whispered even now? What sort of man have I married?"

He ignored her questions. She was provoking him and he knew it, but she'd chosen her weapon masterfully. "Monica is dead. The past has no place here. I do not wish to discuss it with you or anyone."

"And I did not wish to marry you," she shot back. "You owe me this at the very least."

"I had nothing to do with her death, Rowena. If you cannot accept my word on that, then we have nothing to discuss."

"Then we have nothing to discuss." She spun on the ball of her foot and strode into the bedchamber.

Damn her! Why was this so important to her? If she would not believe his claim of innocence, then why would she believe the whole sordid tale?

Kicking aside the toppled bench, Dominic headed for the stables. A good long gallop on Majesty's back might help pound the frustration from his body and offer him a new strategy.

The marshal, a lanky young man with a mischievous smile, met Dominic in the stable yard with a friendly wave and a tug on his forelock. "Evening, milord."

Dominic struggled to remember the other man's name. "Good eventide," he muttered. "I thought I'd take Majesty out."

"Very good," the marshal replied, and turned toward the stable. "The name's Milton."

Allowing the grim line of his lips to curve just a bit, Dominic followed Milton into the stable. He stood in brooding silence while Milton saddled Majesty.

"There seems to be an epidemic of accidents," Milton began offhandedly as he efficiently worked to ready Dominic's mount.

"How so?" A certain intensity in Milton's casual comment caught Dominic's attention. He moved closer to the stall where Majesty fidgeted restlessly.

"First, Lady Rowena is struck down by a stray arrow, and now I learn that Lissette was killed."

"Really? When? How?"

"The same day Lady Rowena was wounded Lissette's horse came limping into the yard. Lissette's foot was tangled in the stirrup, and her neck was broken."

"Where was Edwin?"

"He was at Llangly manor all day. I'm the last one who'd defend that bastard, but he couldn't have shot Lady Rowena."

"Such is not true of Lissette."

"Just thought you'd be interested."

Dominic nodded. "I am. Is Edwin still there?"

"Nay. He departed not long after, and no one has seen him since." Milton offered the information with a knowing smile and then took his leave.

Dominic swung onto Majesty's back and quit the stable yard. The brisk ride was invigorating, as Dominic had hoped, but when he returned to the castle, he was no closer to solving the problem with his new wife.

Was it such a sacrifice to tell Rowena about Monica, if it would allay her fears and bring peace between them?

Dominic was stunned by the thought. He was unused to compromise for any reason. As the commander of men, he expected his orders to be obeyed without hesitation or discussion.

But Rowena wasn't one of his men.

She was the most frustrating combination of headstrong pride and vulnerability. One moment he wanted to shake her until her teeth rattled and the next he wanted to wrap her in his arms and protect her from anything that had ever frightened her.

But mostly he wanted to love her, and he wanted her to open her heart to him.

If the only way to reach Rowena's heart was through the mire left behind by Monica, then he would simply have to wallow in the mire.

Chapter Thirteen

"Milady, we need your assistance. Quickly."

Rowena looked at the lanky youth for a moment before she recalled where she'd seen him. On the training field he was never far from Dominic's side. "Ephraim?" This was her husband's squire.

"Aye. Milton has readied horses. We really must go."

"Go where? What is the nature of this emergency?"

"I've been taking supplies to your *guest* in the forest, and this morning he decided that his companion was no longer necessary. Ordered him out of his *sight* at knife point."

It took her a moment to correspond the details. Brother Leland had ordered Ezra away at knife point? Why? The friar couldn't possibly stay in the monastery alone. "Let us away."

Brother Leland could be powerfully stubbornness when something contradicted his principles. And she suspected she knew the cause of his sudden surliness. His body had recovered enough to loose his fury. She could relate to the transition all too well.

Ezra lounged on a fallen tree within sight of the monastery's entrance. Thankfully he didn't look angry. Rowena dismounted and approached him as Ephraim took her palfrey's reins.

"Did you try to poison him?" She smiled, assuring the knight she was jesting.

Ezra chuckled and offered an elaborate shrug. "He awakened in the devil's own temper. No warning, no provocation. If you can make him see reason, you're a better man...er, woman than me." He laughed at his mangled words.

"Let me see if I can find out what's really bothering our guest."

Brother Leland sat in his cell, staring into nothingness. "I am not an invalid and I will not be treated thus."

"I didn't realize we were treating you like an invalid. I thought we were treating you like the victim of a brutal beating."

His weathered face turned in her direction, his sightless eyes filled with anger and pain. "I have been Edwin's victim long enough. How do I reclaim my life? I have work awaiting me, people who need me. I cannot hide in this musty prison forever."

She knelt before him, gathering his frail hands between hers. "To continue your work you must remain alive. You cannot help the people counting on you if Edwin realizes he didn't succeed in killing you the first time. These are harsh words, I know, but we must find him. And you must stay here until we do."

He said nothing for a long time. His hands gently squeezed hers and his lips trembled, but he didn't speak. "I am keeping Sir Ezra from his fief. It is not fair. Release him and let the boy tend me."

"Brother Leland, Ezra is a seasoned knight. He can protect you if — "

"If it's my time to go, I'm more than ready. Send Sir Ezra on his way, or I will stumble down those stairs and find my way back to my cozy cottage, trusting the *Lord* to protect me."

She shook her head. "Were you always this stubborn, or has it been cultivated over the years?"

He grinned, obviously pleased with himself. He'd regained some measure of control. Perhaps that was all he needed.

* * * * *

Where the hell was she!

Dominic impatiently paced the wooden floor of her bedchamber. *Their* bedchamber! They had yet to share this room as man and wife, but he had hoped to rectify that lack tonight. After he told her about Monica, he planned to make slow, sweet love to her on the softness of her fur-strewn bed. With that goal in mind, he'd arrived with food and wine, even the blasted rose she'd admired in the garden. But the chamber had been empty. Thora turned down the bed, banked the fire and shot him an encouraging smile before leaving him to his own devices.

He'd been down to the great hall twice, ventured to the guard tower, checked the chapel and the kitchens. Several horses were missing from the stables, but he refused to believe what that implied.

Fear gnawed at his belly. She wouldn't have left the castle compound. It was inconceivable that she'd be so foolish after all that had happened. Yet the church bells rang, announcing Compline, and Dominic could ignore his suspicions no longer. He strode across the solar, meaning to organize a search, but Rowena met him at the door.

"My lord," she said softly, her expression inscrutable.

"Where the hell have you been?" He snapped out the question.

Rowena's chin shot up and her eyes narrowed. "Did we have an appointment?" she asked mockingly. "I do not recall you requesting my presence."

"Where were you?" This was not a good start for their reconciliation, but damn her impetuous soul, she'd nearly died the last time she ventured beyond the curtain wall.

"I went to see an old friend who has not been feeling well."

He advanced on her steadily, but Rowena held her ground. "Who? Where?"

They stood toe-to-toe. He glared down into her upturned face.

"Can you not guess?" She pushed past him.

"Did you seek solace from a man of God?"

His convoluted question seemed to defuse her anger a bit. "Aye." Her expression turned quizzical as she unfastened her cloak. "Do you not feel free to speak his name?"

"I'll not feel free to do anything until Edwin dangles from the point of my sword!" He strode toward her. "But you don't seem to take his threat seriously. You'll not allow me to protect you."

He grasped her shoulders and yanked her up onto her toes. Their noses nearly touched.

"Did you not understand my request?"

"I...did not think..."

"Aye! God's blood, woman, you did not think. You are my wife! I will have your obedience. Do I make myself clear?"

"Aye!" She shoved herself away from him. "You make yourself perfectly clear. The wedding has taken place, so there is no need to treat me decently."

"It is indecent to want you safe? You nearly died, Rowena. And I was with you then."

Her features softened and he had to look away. He didn't want her pity. He wanted her love.

"I was not alone, my lord. Only a fool makes the same mistake twice. Ephraim accompanied me on my errand. It was he who notified me of the problem."

She swung her cloak from her shoulder while she explained what had transpired. "So you have temporarily lost your squire, and Sir Ezra is on his way to Granville Cross."

"You might have left word with someone—"

"How? No one else knows Brother Leland is still alive. Even Thora is unaware of our deception."

He crossed the room to stand before the fire.

They lapsed into silence.

"In my anger, I threatened to have Farrell hanged if he did not leave my — our lands. No one has seen him since. Do you happen to know where he went?"

Her voice came from behind him. He was unable to suppress his smile, so he continued to stare into the fire. "I didn't wish to gainsay Lady Pendragon, but Farrell is a masterful steward. I gave him leave to visit a friend until we have determined his fate."

She was closer now. He could sense her hesitation and feel her gaze upon him.

"Good," she said softly. "I'll invite him back."

He waited for her to join him, listening carefully for her movements.

"Did you hear about Lissette's accident?"

He nodded.

"If Lissette is dead and Edwin doesn't wish me harm, then am I still in danger?" Her voice was no closer. Stubborn chit.

Folding his arms over his chest, he turned to face her. "Edwin may not have launched that arrow, but he is still a danger. Never doubt it."

She stared at him.

He stared at her.

Longing pulsed between them like a beating drum.

"I'm sorry I frightened you," she whispered.

He trembled with the need to touch her, to reach beyond her defenses. "Don't do it again." Her only response was a stiff nod and his chest clenched, his heart feeling clumsy and tight. "Are you hungry?" The question sounded foolish, yet he could think of no gallant words, no romantic phrase to put her at ease. "I brought food and wine." Unwilling to tolerate the tension a moment longer, he nodded toward the tray.

"Aye." She walked to the small wooden table.

He watched the sway of her hips and the fluidity of her steps. This beautiful creature, this delicate woman, was his *wife*. The tightness in his chest released in a warm rush of sensation that settled low in his gut. He sat on the bench opposite her, but his gaze followed her slender hands as she poured watered wine into a silver cup, transfixed by the simple task.

"Do you have a confidant?"

Her softly spoken question jarred him from his thoughts and back to the reality of what they had yet to accomplish.

"Someone with whom you can share your every thought, every feeling without fear or reservation?"

"I suppose there is little about me that Ezra does not know."

"And I have Thora, but I was speaking of something else, something different."

"Like your friar?"

She chuckled and took a sip of wine. "Nay. I was quite young when my father died, but I remember many things about him. I remember his gentleness toward my mother and me."

He took the rose from the tray and twirled it between his fingers. Did she not think him capable of gentleness? He lived in a world that rewarded brutality, but he could be gentle. He longed to show her tenderness, to prove that all men were not the same. But she continued to push him away, protecting herself with mistrust and ultimatums.

"I remember their closeness, the sparkle in their eyes as if they shared a secret that the rest of the world would never understand." Her voice sounded hushed, almost reverent.

As he twirled the flower a thorn caught on his thumb. Blood beaded over the wound and he raised it to his mouth. *Typical. I focus on the flower and I'm gouged by the thorn.*

He glanced at his wife, feeling a renewed surge of determination. "My parents also enjoyed such a union. What has this to do with us?"

"My first marriage showed me all of the disadvantages of the wedded state. Deep in my heart, I knew I would have to wed again, but I wanted to find a husband with whom I could experience the sort of relationship my parents enjoyed. They knew each other, they loved each other, and they trusted each other completely."

His gaze shot to hers at the word trust. He snapped off a thorn and tossed it onto the tray. She watched him closely, speculation clear in her inquisitive eyes. He snapped off another thorn. He knew where her story led, had spent all day preparing for the conversation. "What prevents you from finding that with me?"

"Trust." She raised the cup for a quick drink. He couldn't see her expression and suspected that was the reason for her sudden thirst.

He waited until she lowered the cup and drew her attention to the rose. He snapped off the last thorn and handed her the flower. "Now you can enjoy the color, the softness and the scent with no fear of pain. It is *harmless*."

She raised the bloom to her nose, her eyes closing as she inhaled the sweet fragrance.

"It is also *defenseless*."

Her eyes flew open and a nervous chuckle escaped her throat. "Surely you need no protection from me."

"I was referring to you." He watched her gaze cloud, become guarded. "The sort of trust our parents shared made them vulnerable to each other."

"I am vulnerable regardless."

She held the flower out to him, but he folded his arms over his chest. "I will tell you about Monica, if that is what it takes to make you believe that I love you."

Her gaze dropped to the flower, and he gritted his teeth. She was still hiding from him. How could he ever hope to win her when she wouldn't let him near? The question made his entire body ache.

Patience. He must be patient.

"This isn't about Monica — well, it is, but not in the way you mean. I don't care about the woman. I don't care about the details of what transpired so long ago. I need to know that you trust me enough to share them with me. Do you understand the difference?"

"I understand." He was not sure that he agreed. The past couldn't be changed. But this was obviously important to her, so he was willing to oblige. "I met Monica at court. I never felt comfortable there, and she shared my restlessness. She seemed sweet, innocent and honest, but Monica was none of those things."

She continued to toy with the flower, glancing at him then back at the rose. "How long did you know her before you became betrothed?"

He stood suddenly and lifted the table to one side. She looked up at him, her eyes wide and uncertain. Her hands still clutched the flower, but he took that from her too, leaving nothing between them, no pretense, no barriers.

She pressed her lips together and folded her hands in her lap. He saw the way they shook and muttered a curse.

You're frightening her, you dolt.

Dominic straddled the bench and pulled her close, wrapping his arms around her waist. He needed to touch her, needed to feel her warm, supple body pressed against his. Thank God, she didn't pull away. Scooting closer, she looped her arm around his and leaned against his chest. His heart lurched and heat churned in his belly.

"Monica's family had grown wealthy during King John's reign. By the time I met her, this was no longer the case." He was uncomfortable with the tale, eager to have it told.

Rowena squirmed against him. He eased away and looked into her face. Her expression appeared strained. "What is amiss?"

An embarrassed flush colored her delicate skin and her gaze dropped to her hands. "Are you wealthy? Your interest in my holdings led me to believe..."

He chuckled and cupped her chin, turning her head to face him. Her gaze met his with obvious reluctance, so he stroked her cheek reassuringly. "I've amassed a sizeable fortune over the years, but when I knew Monica I had barely earned my spurs. I rode the best horses and wore the best armor, so many presumed I had wealth beyond my true station. I was the ward of William Marshal, nothing more."

The softness of her skin taunted him, lured him away from his purpose. He moved his hand to her shoulder and forced his thoughts again on the past.

"So, she believed you were rich."

"And I believed she was rich. The difference was my affections were genuine. I cannot say that a comfortable life didn't appeal to me. I've known no other way, but I loved Monica." He waited for the smoldering want he felt each time he thought about Monica, but he felt nothing, not even the faintest pang of longing or regret. Accepting the lack with a happy sigh, he continued. "She, on the other hand, had no interest in marriage to... Suffice it to say, when she learned of my true state, she refused to consider me as a husband."

Rowena pivoted toward him, resting her hand against his chest. His heart beat against her palm. "Then *she* broke the betrothal?"

He saw curiosity in her eyes now, but how much longer would it remain? Must he watch her gaze harden with suspicion and distain? Would he feel her stiffen and pull away? He swallowed with difficulty and pressed his hand over hers, holding it in place. How would he bear it if she…

"We'd all gathered at Longueville in Normandy. Sir William throws a Yuletide Festival each year and the events unfolded on the day of the final feast. Private bedchambers are limited, so I was sharing the room with Ezra and a man named Launce. Ezra approached me at midday and told me that he had witnessed Monica with another man."

"Did you believe him?"

Pulling her hand away from his chest, he curled her fingers around his and gently stroked her knuckles with his thumb. Tension gripped his abdomen as he realized what was left to reveal. Would Rowena think him a fool? "Nay, I'd yet to witness Monica in her full glory, so I thought Ezra misunderstood what he saw. The discussion escalated into an argument, and I ended up punching him squarely in the face."

"In her full glory?" Her gaze was luminous and tender.

"The feast was well underway when Monica began her performance." Ah, there was a pang of resentment. Even in memory Monica remained a ruthless bitch. "We shared a trencher in veritable silence. She'd already told me that she wanted to end the betrothal, and I offered no argument."

Rowena moved closer and Dominic released her hand. He slipped his arm under her knees and draped her legs over his. Her scent caressed him, distracted him. Molding her softness against his chest, he let her nearness soothe him.

"With no warning or apparent logic, she suddenly tossed her wine into my face and began shouting at me. I was too shocked to be angry—until I realized what she was about. She accused me of lying, of claiming wealth I didn't possess, of caring nothing for her. She made me appear the lecherous fool in front of my peers, my friends—Sir William."

She took his face between her palms and kissed him softly on the lips. "I'm so sorry."

Her compassion caught him off guard. Dominic froze. Reality slowly narrowed until he saw only her beautiful eyes.

She loves me.

A shocking jolt of happiness speared his heart, rocking him backward. He hadn't dared to believe it until he saw it shining in her eyes. His wife loved him. Regardless of his past, Rowena loved him. She might not realize it yet, but Rowena loved him.

"What is amiss?"

Her soft voice called him back from paradise, and Dominic laughed. "Nothing. Nothing at all."

He felt the shadow of Monica shrink and shrivel. His heart vibrated with happiness, giving him strength and confidence. "I stayed in the hall long after she marched out. Sir William asked me what had caused her outburst. He suspected that she was attempting to protect her pride, to paint me the villain, so she could continue with her quest for a rich husband."

"His logic was sound." She reached for the thong binding his hair.

A strangled groan escaped him as she freed his hair and raked her fingers through it. "Do you want to know the rest or not?"

Her hands returned to his shoulders. "I apologize."

He cupped her cheek and pressed his lips to her temple, burning to do so much more. "You need never apologize for touching me. I'm your husband. It's your right."

"Then tell me the rest quickly, so we may explore our rights."

Desire thickened her voice, and he felt blood pound in his loins. Quickly indeed! "I stayed in the hall and drowned myself in ale. Just before dawn, I staggered to the bedchamber and found Monica there with Launce and a man I didn't know. She disentangled herself from the men. I watched in silent fury as she gathered my belongings and tossed them to me. She told me I was an ignorant fool, which was true. She told me that she'd rather be a rich man's leman than a poor man's wife."

Her hands shot into his hair and she pulled his face close to hers. "Then she was the ignorant fool." Devotion shone brightly in her green eyes.

He grinned, his heart pounding. Her vehemence shot tingling warmth through his entire body, and he could restrain himself no longer. He brushed her mouth with his, not really kissing her, just feeling her lips with his.

Caressing her back with his hands, he peppered light kisses across her features as he told her the rest. "I slept in the hall, but many had seen me leave and return. Her body was discovered the following morning, naked at the foot of the stairs. Her father accused me of her murder."

She pushed him back just a bit and traced his mouth with her fingertip. "What do you believe happened?"

"She must have thought of some final insult or hateful demand and come after me. I wasn't the only one drowning in spirits that night. It's the only thing that explains her nakedness. I believe she fell shortly after I reached the hall, no mystery, no murder. Monica's death was an accident."

Dominic expelled a long ragged breath. It was finally over. No more secrets. No more ghosts. He returned his gaze to Rowena's face. Her eyes swam with unshed tears and her luscious lips trembled. What in the name of God had changed her reaction? He felt as if someone punched him in the belly.

"Why are you in such misery? This is my penance, not yours."

He reached for her tear wet cheeks, but Rowena turned her face away, too ashamed to meet his gaze. "I'm a beast."

She heard his soft laugh.

She pulled her legs back and knelt on the bench, facing him. His brows drew together and confusion shone in his gaze. She placed her hands on his shoulders and rested on her heels, putting their facing on a level.

"My demand seemed reasonable when I made it." She sniffled. "I want to be your friend, your confidant. Friends don't torture each other with unpleasant —"

"Rowena," he cut in, "Monica has lurked in my life like a specter, but today I spoke of her without anger or self-recrimination. You have shown me, *forever*, that she has no power over me." His voice rang with conviction, and she had never seen his eyes so bright.

Tears trailed down her cheeks, but Rowena smiled. "I want us to be happy. I want…I want you to love me." Her breath caught in her throat, and she feared that her heart would stop beating. Crushing his tunic with her hands, she waited for his response.

He stood, grabbed her by the waist, and swung her from the bench. His arms encircled her, pulling her snug against his body. She felt his heat and his desire, and the beating of her heart galloped wildly.

For a long moment he just molded her body to his, searching her gaze with his burning blue eyes. "How can you doubt it?" His voice was rough and tremulous. "I think I fell in love with you when I first saw you glaring daggers at me because I dared to best you."

Her laughter shuddered. The thundering of her heart was painful now, but what a glorious pain. She brushed her knuckles along the stubbly angle of his jaw, absorbing his masculine texture with greedy pleasure.

Stretching onto her toes, she kissed his mouth, drawing his breath into her lungs and pressing her wildly beating heart directly over his.

"I've fought my attraction to you for so long, I'll feel lost without the struggle." She looped her arms around his neck.

"You can continue to resist me if you like, just don't expect me to cooperate with your resistance."

277

Tingling heat erupted in her belly and spread throughout her body. His taunting words no longer frightened her. She tangled her fingers in his ink-black hair and pulled his face toward hers. "Nay, my love, I officially surrender. I can't help loving you, Lord Dominic of Pendragon, my husband, my heart."

She kissed him tenderly, exalted by the knowledge that this man belonged to her. Her lips memorized the texture of his, and she offered herself willingly to his questing tongue. She captured his groan in her open mouth, growing dizzy and hot.

Rowena pulled away with a throaty murmur. "We shall end up on the floor here in the solar if we continue like this. I want you to share my bed."

"I want you to share my life."

Joy surged through Rowena, and new tears filled her eyes. "Come, this shall be our wedding night."

Chapter Fourteen

He raised one hand to her soft cheek and allowed a gentle smile to part his lips. "We cannot have a wedding night until we have a wedding."

Her delicate brows drew together but tenderness warmed her gaze. "Are we not already wed?"

"Aye, but only one of us participated in the ceremony. I want to hear you pledge your troth and accept me as husband with your own voice."

Her lips trembled and her tongue darted out to wet them. "I'll honor and obey you, so long as your demands are reasonable."

He laughed and pressed a quick kiss to her mouth. "I don't remember that stipulation in the vows. Do you accept me as your husband? If I asked for your hand today, would you agree to wed with me?"

"I do, and I would."

He framed her lovely face with his hands. "Then let us have a wedding night."

Dominic lowered his mouth to hers. He savored the petal-soft texture of her lips as they parted in a breathless sigh. He felt her tongue venture forth, encouraging his advance as no words ever could. His heart swelled with pride and tenderness. She was beautiful, fiercely proud, intelligent—and his.

He pulled her into his arms for a long, lingering kiss. They had all night; they had the rest of their lives to explore their passion and savor the elemental connection forming between them.

A simple white wimple covered her glorious hair. She helped him remove it and unweave the braid. Combing his fingers through the thick, wavy strands, Dominic momentarily closed his eyes as the softness caressed his fingers. "So beautiful."

He unlaced her woolen gown and tugged it down along her arms. Rowena pulled the long-sleeved chemise off over her head and stepped from the gown in one fluid movement. The fair perfection of her form was revealed to his anxious eyes as she stood before him, silently waiting for direction.

Dominic pushed her hair behind her shoulders and leisurely explored her curves with appreciation and longing. Her arms remained at her sides, her firm, round breasts quivered slightly as her breathing accelerated. Raising his gaze to her mouth, he watched her tongue wet her lower lip. He wanted to touch her, to kiss and caress her, but the tension humming between them was too exciting to ignore. Anticipation heightened the pleasure, and Dominic was in no hurry.

Rowena felt her nipples tighten into achy little buds, and he had yet to touch her. Already her core ached with throbbing need. Her skin tingled as his dark blue gaze moved in leisurely assessment across her flesh. If he couldn't decide how best to begin, then she would have to help him.

She stepped forward and grabbed the hem of his sturdy tunic, tugging it up along his torso until, with a muffled chuckle, he raised his arms and allowed her to pull the garment off over his head. Before he could successfully disentangle his arms and toss the tunic aside, Rowena had moved on to his linen braies. He quickly kicked off his shoes and released his knitted leggings as she attacked the drawstring securing his remaining garment. She pushed it down over his hips, until it fell to his ankles and he kicked it aside.

Rowena gazed at his nakedness and then threw herself against him. Dominic laughed. Her obvious eagerness seemed to please him. Running her palms up along his chest, she encircled his neck and molded herself against the entire length of his hard, hot body. She needed so much more than what her hands could touch. She needed all of him, touching her, filling her, part of her. A groan escaped her throat. She tangled her hands in the thickness of his dark hair and looked up into his shining eyes. "Kiss me, Dominic, please."

He growled an unintelligible response just before his mouth sealed over hers. Rowena responded eagerly to his demand, parting her lips and seeking his tongue with hers. Pressing her breasts against his chest, she rubbed her nipples against the hair sprinkled across his skin. One of his legs eased between hers, and Rowena gasped. She clutched his shoulders and arched her pelvis, grinding her mound against his thigh.

"Easy, love," he whispered, separating their bodies.

Rowena moaned. Cool air wafted across her heated skin, compounding her loss. Did he not want her as desperately as she wanted him?

Tossing back her hair, Rowena stubbornly reached for him again. She clutched his upper arms, her fingers digging into his thick biceps. She pressed her mouth to the upper curve of his chest, trailing hot, wet kisses down to his flat nipple. The frantic pounding of his heartbeat pulsed beneath her lips, hinting at his desire. Her tongue darted out to explore the dark circle of flesh, teasing him as he had often teased her. She sucked the hardened tip into her mouth and heard his ragged sigh. If his body responded to the same sorts of stimuli he used to arouse her, then the possibilities were intriguing.

She wanted him to tremble. She needed him desperate for her.

Dropping gracefully to her knees, she nuzzled her cheek against his flat abdomen and lowered her gaze to the target of her brazen exploration.

His shaft had already hardened in anticipation of their joining. Rowena trailed teasing fingertips across his lean flanks and slowly closed her hand around his erection. A harsh gasp from Dominic rewarded her daring, and Rowena became bolder still. She couldn't doubt his desire, but he wasn't trembling — yet.

Extending her tongue, she circled the flared tip crowning his shaft and waited to see his reaction. One of his hands moved to the back of her neck, preventing her retreat. He didn't force her forward, but it was obvious he wanted her mouth on him. Parting her lips, she slowly slid him into her mouth, flicking her tongue against his tip as he sank deeper.

There was nothing tentative in his response this time. He groaned loudly and rocked his hips forward. He pulled back, and she understood the movement he needed from her. She tightened her lips around him, swirling her tongue as he moved in and out of her mouth. He held the back of her head with a steady pressure, but Rowena knew that if she tried to pull away he'd let her go. She didn't want to pull away. The tension in his body clearly sang her praises. Each gasp, each throaty moan was its own reward.

He began to tremble, and Rowena's body responded forcefully to the knowledge that this battle-hardened knight was shaking uncontrollably because of her. She felt her head spin dizzily, and her breasts ached for his attention. Closing her eyes, she concentrated on the sensations coursing through her body in response to his desire.

Finally, with a hoarse cry, Dominic stepped back, quickly pulling out of her clinging mouth.

"God's blood, Rowena," he gasped. "I can stand no more."

"Then, lie down, my lord," she purred with a smug little smile.

The hazy languor in his midnight blue eyes instantaneously flared into demand. She released a nervous chuckle as he took a menacing step toward her. The nearly euphoric power she had experienced moments before fizzled, leaving only a trembling uncertainty. He was so much bigger than she, so much stronger.

A startled gasp escaped her when he effortlessly swept her up into his arms and strode with her toward the bed. "I...I'm sorry." He tossed her onto the mattress and came down immediately on top of her.

His elbows rested to each side of her shoulders, and he levered himself up, his face hovered over hers. "Sorry? Sorry I want you so much I nearly lost control? Sorry I ache for you still? Or sorry it's my turn now to make you tremble?"

He didn't allow her to answer his string of questions. He kissed her with slow, gentle tenderness until Rowena melted into him, surrendering completely to the power of their desire.

Inhibition fell away. She felt free for the first time in her life, to express the feelings surging through her being. Her heart was so filled with love and tenderness that it was nigh unto bursting.

Her hands greedily moved across the hard contours of his back. She couldn't absorb the feeling of his warm skin fast enough.

She cried out when he tore his mouth from hers, but he moved from her face to her neck and began a thorough investigation of her sensitive skin. Chills and hot little tingles took turns racing down her spine as his mouth moved across her shoulders and on to her breasts. Her nipples had been hard and aching for so long, she moaned when his mouth finally closed over first one then the other. She needed this burning nearly as much as she hungered for the release she knew would follow.

He nipped and licked his way down her torso and across her quivering abdomen. She knew what he intended and eagerly parted her thighs. There was no need to protect herself from him. She was safe within his arms, free to abandon herself completely to the pleasure.

His mouth danced along her inner thigh, purposely avoiding the throbbing apex to skim down the other side. Rowena moaned. "Please, my love, please."

Gently he touched her with just his fingertips, lightly brushing the damp curls that concealed her feminine secrets. She shuddered and arched her back, asking and offering. Dominic leaned in close and fanned her with his warm breath. The persistent ache intensified.

He pushed two fingers into her core, and she felt her entire body convulse for a moment before resuming its rhythmic pulsing. She trembled. This was bliss, and he had barely begun. Holding her open with one hand, he slid in and out with the other, his gaze intent upon her face.

"I want to feel your pleasure and taste your cream." His head dipped, his tongue stroking over her nub while his fingers filled her again and again.

Rowena tightened her inner muscles and tangled her fingers in his hair. Spasms of pleasure exploded through her, driving all rational thought from her mind. She could only hold on to Dominic and experience the wonder.

The sensations had only begun to recede when he moved up and over her. She bent her knees, drawing her legs up high along his sides. He entered her in one long, smooth thrust. She found his mouth and kissed him wildly as she arched up to meet his downward movements.

"I love you. I love you." They repeated the words over and over, passing them back and forth with their heated breath until they were simply too breathless to speak.

They made the journey together now, and the experience was all the more fulfilling. Rowena felt reality fall away, but Dominic still held her. She hugged him tight, feeling his body moving deeply within her own. Lifting passion-heavy lids, she found his dark blue eyes burning into hers. It was still a bit overwhelming, the fierceness of his desire.

They were beyond words. Rowena reveled in the possessive fire. He wanted her, needed her, and loved her.

The pleasure became so intense Rowena had to close her eyes. Colors erupted behind her lids. She clung to Dominic with her arms and legs, burying her face against the side of his neck. His embrace was just as insistent. They trembled and gasped for breath, too weak to do more than hold on to one another.

With an audible groan, Dominic rolled to his side, taking Rowena with him. One of his arms was beneath her neck, the other encircling her waist. Their legs were tangled, and miraculously his shaft was still sheathed in her body.

"I never want to leave this bed," he whispered. "In fact, I want to remain inside you forever."

She smiled and snuggled a bit closer to him. "You will get no argument from me."

"Good," he mumbled against her damp hair.

She was warm. She was content. Her entire body felt flushed and lazy.

After long leisurely minutes, Rowena stirred. She brought her mouth to Dominic's ear. "Would it please you if I were to have a child?"

He eased away from her, just far enough to see her eyes. "Are you certain?"

She smiled and shook her head. "It's too soon to know."

"But you suspect?"

"I have no rational reason, but I had the strangest dream while I was ill. I saw Fair Fiona."

"What has this to do with our baby?"

"Patience," she chided playfully. "She asked if I were brave, if I were ready, and if I were worthy. I have no idea what that means. But she also said that our son was safe within my womb."

He did no more than study her expression for a moment. "I will be thrilled if you are indeed carrying my son. But this legend nonsense is making us all act like fools. I even imagined that I heard her laughing at me from the trees."

Rowena smiled and pressed her cheek once more against his chest. "I suppose it does sound a bit odd, my lord."

He chuckled and wrapped her tight in his arms. "It is not that I dislike the title, Rowena, but I much prefer the sound of my name on your lips. Say it for me."

"Dominic," she sighed. "My love. My life. Dominic."

"Oh Rowena," he growled, and closed his eyes.

She was not sure what she had done to cause his reaction until she felt his body swell within her. She laughed, delighted by his ready response. "I wish I had known the secret to seducing you was to simply whisper your name."

Shoving against his chest, she soon had him flat on his back.

"You no longer need to seduce me." He chuckled, swept up in her playful mood.

Straddling his hips, she lightly ran her fingernails down his chest. "What I need, *Dominic*, is to feel you moving inside me."

"I live to fulfill your every need." With slow, tantalizing thrusts, he gave her exactly what she had requested.

* * * * *

Despite Thora's frequent insistence that a lady didn't get her hands dirty, Rowena reached down and pulled a weed from among the scraggly herbs and tossed it onto the rapidly growing pile. She didn't care if it was ladylike or not. She loved her herb garden. She loved the rich, verdant smells and the feel of sunlight warming her face.

She couldn't stop smiling. The knowledge that she'd been grinning like a fool for a fortnight did nothing to erase the expression. Her entire body tingled each time she thought about her husband. *Dominic*. Just his name had the power to speed her pulse and melt her insides.

Waking in his arms each morning moved her in ways she had not expected. The security of knowing he was there, knowing he would always be there, left her purring like a contented cat. Life would teach them many lessons, she had no doubt, but with Dominic at her side, she was ready to learn.

When she looked into his beautiful blue eyes and saw devotion and tenderness shining back at her, she wanted to shout from the ramparts that she loved her husband, and he loved her.

Dominic loved her. Her *husband* loved her!

With a happy smile, she returned her attention to the garden. Rowena moved a sprig of parsley to one side so she could extract the weed attempting to choke it out.

"Milady."

She offered Ephraim a distracted wave then her head snapped in his direction. "What are you doing here?" Struggling to her feet in the uneven dirt, she wiped her hands on the cloth tied around her waist. "Who is with…our guest?"

"Our guest promised to remain in his room until I returned. He is desperate for the sound of God's Holy Word, and I am unable to deliver it."

Moving closer to the young man, she lowered her voice. "What does he want?"

"Sir Dominic thoughtfully included a small book of scriptures when he last brought supplies. It has tormented our friend because…"

"You are unable to read to him."

"Would you please come read to him?" He squared his shoulders and looked her in the eyes. "He told me he taught you the skill, so it is only fitting that you use the skill to comfort him."

Rowena laughed. "Those were his exact words no doubt. I must inform Dominic of my destination and change my tunic."

"If it pleases you, I will find Sir Dominic while you attend to the other matter."

"Very well. I'll meet you in the stables."

* * * * *

Fiona drifted on the breeze, greedily absorbing the currents of energy passing through her body. Her strength depleted so quickly here in the human realm. The rhythm of the energy was different, alien to her system, harder to assimilate. Even her father's agreement to release her Fairy abilities hadn't stopped her weakening. This curse was siphoning her essence, fading her to the point of frailty. It must end soon or it would be too late.

They had come so far.

They could not fail now.

Rowena and Dominic had found each other. Their love was growing. She smiled. Figuratively and *literally*. But everything within the universe had its equal and opposite counterpart. Light balanced darkness. Good balanced evil. And a riddle balanced her curse.

Without solving the riddle the curse would never be broken—and Rowena didn't believe in the riddle.

A horse and rider drew her attention from her troubled thoughts. She hissed and twirled out of sight, following Edwin of Llangly as he picked his way through the forest.

Finally, the weasel ventured out. She fluttered from tree to tree, high above his head. No one had seen this creature for nearly a fortnight. She lost interest in where he'd been hiding as she realized where he was bound.

Dashing ahead, Fiona flew into the monastery. Brother Leland sat in silent meditation in one of the monk cells. Knowing time was of the essence, she intensified her Fairy brilliance to devastating intensity. Any other human would have whimpered in pain.

"Who's there?" His voice trembled and his bony hands swiped the air in front of him.

Come with me now! Follow the light. She sent a subtle compulsion along with the words to ensure the friar obeyed.

As if in a trance, Brother Leland rose and followed her down the corridor and into the decrepit chapel on the opposite side of the cells.

Fearsome Dragon! I need you. I need you, now!

The friar followed her into the storeroom and obediently sat down. Her guardian appeared in the doorway.

What is it, Your Highness? You sounded frantic.

Spread your wings, my friend. Conceal us completely. Edwin cannot be allowed to find us.

It is done. He turned his back and spread his mighty wings, making the wall appear unbroken by a doorway.

Fiona flitted nervously. How could she keep the friar quiet once the action began? Not often could she see into the future, but she sensed important events were about to unfold.

Hovering near his ear, Fiona made her voice sound like the musings of his own mind, and began her tale.

* * * * *

Rowena swung down from her horse and rested her arms lightly on the saddle of her palfrey. "I only have one question?" She made her tone dire, her eyes narrowed.

"What, milady?" His ruddy cheeks drained of color, and he gazed at her unblinkingly.

"How did you bear climbing up the latrine?" She shuddered and then laughed at the relief in his expression.

"Don't tease me so. I thought I'd displeased you, and if I displease you, I answer to your husband."

"Nay, Ephraim, you've been delightful and helpful. But you didn't answer my question."

"I breathed through my mouth and climbed as fast as I could. It honestly was not the most unpleasant thing I've ever done. Would you like to hear about the time I—"

"Nay! If it is less pleasant than—"

An arm wrapped around her waist, yanking her back against a tall frame. She screamed and jammed her slippered foot down on her assailant's instep, clawing at the arm banding her waist.

Ephraim drew his dirk and raced toward her, but Rowena felt her head jerked back and a blade pressed against her throat. "Don't come any closer."

Edwin!

The lad froze, his terrified gaze darting to hers.

"You're going to get back on your horse and ride as fast as you can back to the castle. Tell Dominic if he waits too long, there won't be enough left of her to rescue."

"I'm not leaving her!"

"Do as he says, Ephraim." Chances were far greater that Edwin would hurt Ephraim than her. Rowena wanted the boy gone, safely away from the danger.

"But, milady—"

"Don't argue with your mistress. Get!"

Why did Edwin want the alarm sounded? Why did— He spun her around and pressed her against the side of her horse, ending her speculation.

"I'd almost forgotten how beautiful you are."

Her stomach heaved, and she turned her face away. Why hadn't she grabbed a weapon? Why hadn't she been better prepared for... His hand stroked her cheek, his fingers outlined her mouth, and she tasted bile in the back of her mouth.

"Edwin—" She broke off. How could she hope to reason with him? He was obviously mad. What should she do?

"Let's go settle in, shall we?" His hand encircled her wrist, and he pulled her toward the monastery.

Brother Leland! She couldn't let Edwin take her into the monastery. "Nay. You sent Ephraim for Dominic. Let's await him out here."

"What's the matter, Rowena? Are you afraid of ghosts?"

"Aye. Please, I don't want to go up there." She tried to sound pathetic, not panicked, but he didn't seem to care either way. She kicked out at him and jerked against his hold. "I cannot go up there."

He ignored her protests and her struggles. "The only thing haunting this decrepit ruin is an equally decrepit friar."

A new, more virulent wave of panic swept Rowena toward hysteria. Had Edwin killed Brother Leland? Dear God, not now, after all that he had endured.

Edwin said nothing as he tugged her along behind him. There was no railing on either side of the stairs, and his grasp on her wrist was unbreakable. Rowena had no choice but to climb.

The front room was empty, as Rowena had expected. Edwin quickly lit a torch and motioned toward the cells with an insistent nod. She shook her head in mute horror. If Edwin had murdered Brother Leland, she had no wish to view his handiwork.

Edwin's hand clamped down around her upper arm and he gave her a shake. "Call out to him," he whispered. "Identify yourself and tell him all is well."

Hope unfurled with sickening intensity. The friar wasn't dead. When she didn't immediately comply, he twisted her arm up behind her back. Rowena gasped and made a small squeaky sound.

"Now!"

"Brother Leland." Her tone was uneven and raspy. "It's Rowena, you need— Run! Danger! Edwin is with—" Her last warning was cut short by the back of his hand. Rowena landed on her hip, the force of his blow knocking her sideways.

"You stupid bitch! Where will he run? There is nowhere to hide."

Despite the pain throbbing through her head and now her hip, Rowena smiled. She hid the expression behind trembling hands and sat on the stone floor. Edwin stomped toward the cells, the torch held high. He stepped into the first cell, but his sharp curse indicated that Brother Leland was not within. Similar curses followed as he checked each cell. He had to be hiding. There was only one way into or out of the monastery.

"Where is he?" Edwin demanded as he returned to the main room.

"They moved him yesterday," Rowena lied, struggling up from the floor. She was as surprised to find him gone as Edwin. "His condition was much improved, so Dominic had him taken to another location."

"Then why did you cry out to warn him?"

"I'd forgotten, but he's obviously not here."

Edwin seemed to ponder her information for a moment as he anxiously paced the room, the torchlight dancing dizzily as he moved. "No matter. There is nothing he knows that you cannot tell me."

Rowena didn't like the sound of his conclusion, but for the moment Brother Leland was safe. He placed the torch in a wall sconce and returned to her side.

"Edwin it's over." She refused to reveal the terror ripping through her. "I'm happily wed, and you cannot change that."

"You are wrong," he said simply. "I'd hoped to woo you in my own time, but you have made it impossible."

She held perfectly still when his hand cupped her cheek. "In the eyes of the Church you are my father." She spoke calmly, absolutely.

"Only so long as I was married to your mother. You see, I figured it out. If I have my marriage to Yvonne *absolved*, I will be free to marry you."

He was mad. His convoluted schemes had no end. Turning her face away, she stepped back. "Your marriage was not only consummated, but Mother gave you a son."

"She gave me a dead son!" He paused for a breath, regaining his composure. "But you will give me fine, strong sons who will rule Pendragon Castle long after we are gone."

"I will give you nothing. If you hurt me, you will know no peace for the rest of your days." She narrowed her eyes to emphasize the threat.

Fear flickered through his stare. "Do all of the ladies of Pendragon spout curses so easily?"

She didn't respond to his question, but his obsession gave her a weapon.

"Tell me the answer to the riddle, and I will let him live."

"You could never lay hands on the Dragon's Tears even if I did tell you the answer. Do you still not understand? Fair Fiona spoke the curse to *protect* me from such as you."

His eyes turned wild, his head swayed from side to side. "Then it is true. It is all true."

Rowena shivered. Madness shone clearly in his too bright gaze. "Aye." Carefully, she watched his progress across the room and back for any sign that he would turn on her. "Fair Fiona has aided and protected me many times. Why do you think Gaston never touched me? She would not allow it. She speaks to me in dreams."

"Does she?" He stopped pacing and stepped in front of her, his hands coming to rest on her shoulders. "What does she look like? Is she passing fair?"

"She is the most beautiful creature I have ever seen," Rowena whispered, and it was no lie. "As I lay struggling for life, she came to me and comforted me, encouraged me to fight against the poison."

His fingers tightened painfully, and his lips curled back from his teeth in a fierce snarl. "I would have avenged that wrong if the stupid bitch hadn't fallen from her horse."

"The past does not matter now. We need only concern ourselves with the future. Fair Fiona told me I should accept my marriage to Dominic, that it is right and true. She told me our love was strong enough to end the curse for all time. You cannot interfere with that. You would invite the wrath of Fearsome Dragon."

Not trusting his reaction to her exaggeration, she didn't mention the probability that she was carrying Dominic's child. She suspected the knowledge would enrage him.

For just a moment, Rowena's heart pounded with triumph. His expression was confused and then almost sad.

He believed her!

Just as suddenly as the emotions had come, they departed, leaving only hard, cruel determination. "You have ofttimes scoffed at the legend, Rowena. Am I now to believe that you have become a disciple? You mock me. I am not so easily fooled."

One hand moved from her shoulder to the nape of her neck, and he drew her toward him with steady insistence. Automatically, Rowena's arms came up to press against his chest and she turned her head away to avoid his mouth. The Church was right. It felt perverse to be held intimately by a man she had once called father.

"Cease this now!"

He molded her body to his. "I've not even begun," he promised in a throaty whisper.

"You cannot do this. You loved my mother. This is wrong. I'm in love with Dominic." She was sobbing by the time she finished her objections. He was oblivious to her resistance. His arms tightened around her, holding her close as his lips moved over her features.

"Don't fight me, Rowena. I can give you pleasure if you just accept me as your husband."

"You are my father!"

"Nay. I was wed to your mother, but I was only waiting for you to mature."

"I have a husband."

His responding grin was nothing short of evil. "Not for long."

Rowena went wild. She kicked and screamed, tearing at his exposed skin with her nails. He forced her arms to her side and tripped her, toppling them both to the hard stone floor.

They landed with a grunt, Edwin on top of Rowena. His hot breath fanned her face in ragged pants. "It doesn't have to be force. I will be tender with you if you only stop fighting."

"I despise you. I abhor the touch of your hands upon me. It will ever be force. Nay, it will be incest. This is wrong, unnatural, evil. You must not hurt me. I love my husband!"

With an angry hiss, Edwin levered himself off her. "Then we will begin again when you have no husband."

His words sliced through her like a sword.

Chapter Fifteen

"He's not coming," Rowena said softly.

She did her best to sound convincing. There could be any number of reasons for Dominic's tardiness, but she had just thought of a way to use it to her advantage.

Edwin turned from the open doorway where he stood, watching the forest for any hint that his adversary had finally accepted his challenge. "That's ridiculous." He shot her an angry glower. "Why would he not come for you?"

"There is no need." She sat on the floor, leaning against the wall beside the hearth. No fire burned to offer either light or warmth, but she could see the doorway without craning her neck. The torch had sputtered out long ago without Edwin's notice, and his body blocked what little light seeped through the open doorway.

Inactivity had taken its toll on Rowena. She needed to do something, anything. She was going mad just sitting here. Carefully easing her legs beneath her, she stood. She moved several steps closer to Edwin before she continued. "Dominic knows that you gain nothing by harming me so long as he is alive. He will simply wait within the protection of the castle until you have tired of this game."

"Bah," he dismissed, turning back to the doorway. "His pride alone will bring him running. I have something that belongs to the mighty Undaunted. He will come."

Rowena scrambled for another ploy. She couldn't hope to win in a physical confrontation, but perhaps she could outwit him. He had nearly buckled to his own superstitions.

Suddenly, Edwin turned and stalked toward her. "Perhaps he's here already. Perhaps, as you said, he's not moved in to rescue you because he doesn't believe in your peril."

She took one step back for every step he advanced. When his hand reached for the long, jeweled dagger at his side, she gasped. If he had meant to murder her, why keep her here all this time? He meant only to frighten her.

Her back bumped into the dank wall, and Edwin grasped her wrist, cruelly digging his fingers into her flesh. "Scream," he commanded.

"Nay." She automatically rebelled, but the sharp edge of his blade sliced down across her arm and she screamed.

"Again." Once more he punctuated the demand with his dagger.

Rowena screamed and screamed until the stone room rang with the sounds of her terror. Blood ran in hot rivulets from the deep gashes he'd opened on her forearm. She looked down at her crimson-coated fingers and choked back a sob. The stinging pain was nothing compared to the knowledge that she'd aided her enemy.

Dominic emerged from the shadows, sword in hand. His expression promised death.

Rowena whimpered with a hysterical mixture of fear and relief as Edwin let her go. Dominic stood in the doorway, silhouetted by the setting sun, patiently waiting while Edwin drew his sword.

"This has been a long time coming," Dominic said. "You were a dead man the moment you drew her blood."

They moved in step toward the center of the room and each other. Rowena pressed her palm over the throbbing wounds in her forearm, using the fullness of the sleeve to stem the flow of blood. Lightheaded, she slumped against the wall, helpless to do more than watch the drama unfold.

"So the mighty Undaunted finally shows his face," Edwin jeered. "How long have you been cowering in the shadows?"

"Do we talk or do we fight?"

Edwin charged. Dominic was ready, deflecting each strike with his sword. Dominic remained on the defensive, but Rowena watched his eyes. He studied every move Edwin made, assessing his strengths and finding his weakness.

Their swords clashed and scraped and clashed again.

An impotent spectator to the brutal dance, Rowena refused to be a distraction. She stayed against the wall, well out of the fray, fighting a grimace each time the swords sang out in metallic protest.

In a sudden flurry of aggression, Dominic drove Edwin back across the room. Apparently, he'd lost interest in the game. His body moved with practiced grace, forcing Edwin deeper into the darkness.

Dominic sliced Edwin's thigh only inches from his groin. "That is for Rowena's mother."

Edwin howled, swinging wildly in response to the pain. Before he could recover his balance, Dominic cut a deep cross in the middle of his chest. "That is for Brother Leland. And this," he thrust his sword up through Edwin's belly, ruthlessly piercing his heart, "is for my wife!"

Rowena pressed her wounded arm into her abdomen as blood soaked the front of Edwin's tunic and painted the length of Dominic's sword.

"Rot in hell, you vile bastard!" Dominic withdrew his sword, allowing Edwin's body to slump to the cold stone floor.

With mechanical indifference, Dominic wiped his sword clean on the tunic of his fallen foe and returned it to the scabbard at his side. Rowena watched the procedure and shuddered.

Casting one last dismissing glance at Edwin's body, Dominic hurried to Rowena and pulled her into his arms. "It's over, love. It's finally over."

She trembled in his embrace, too overwrought for words.

For a long time he just held her, sheltering her within his arms. He kissed her temple and whispered her name.

"Let me see your arm." He eased her away from his chest.

"Brother Leland," she cried. "What became of Brother Leland?"

"I know not," he confessed, his dark blue eyes filled with tender concern.

"We must find him." Her throbbing arm was forgotten. "He couldn't have fled without assistance, so he must be hiding somewhere."

Milton and several of Dominic's men hovered near the doorway. Dominic ordered them to light torches, but insisted that he examine her injury first. "It will need to be cleaned and dressed when we return to the castle, but I'll bind it now." Ignoring her restlessness, Dominic quickly bound her arm with a strip cut from her other sleeve.

The men had begun to search, but Rowena wouldn't be put off any longer. She kissed Dominic and set off across the main room. He fell into step beside her. The monastery wasn't large, but it was filled with private rooms and prayer closets. Rowena called out Brother Leland's name.

"Here! I am here!"

The cry reached them faintly, muffled and indistinct.

"We can barely hear you. Call out again," Rowena urged.

A small storeroom sat in the far corner of the abandoned chapel. The entrance wasn't easily visible from the arched doorway at the other end of the room. That Edwin had overlooked the doorway wasn't nearly so remarkable as the fact that the friar had managed to find the space in the first place. She gently guided him out into the chapel before she asked him how he found his hiding place.

"I simply followed the light." Brother Leland patted her arm with a characteristic smile.

"What light?" Dominic asked skeptically. "There's no candle or torch with you."

"I saw a bright light and somehow knew I was to follow. When the light faded, I just sat down. I could sense that I was sheltered. Somehow, I knew I was safe."

Rowena glanced at Dominic to see his reaction to the friar's wild tale, but he merely crossed his brawny arms over his chest.

"Is Edwin dead, then?" the friar asked.

"Aye," Rowena said. "He can no longer harm anyone."

As Brother Leland recited a prayer for the passing of Edwin's soul, Rowena guided him down the narrow corridor and out into the common room.

Dominic's men had already removed Edwin's body, but she stared for a troubled moment at the blood-darkened floor.

"Set the dragon free."

Rowena turned to Brother Leland as he spoke the odd command. "What?"

"That's what the voice kept saying as I waited in that room. 'Solve the riddle and set the dragon free.'"

Rowena glanced again at Dominic.

"So, I pondered the riddle as I waited in that room."

"What is always lonely but never alone?" Rowena recited.

Dominic watched them intently, but didn't comment.

"Possesses nothing, but has riches untold?" Brother Leland took up where Rowena had left off. "Speaks only silence, but shares tales far and wide? Remains hidden forever in the shadows of night?"

"Edwin died believing you could solve the riddle," Dominic spoke at last. "Was he right? Do you know the answer?"

"I didn't when he held me captive, but I've spent endless hours in meditation as I recuperated and just now everything seemed to fall into place."

"You've figured it out?" Excitement bubbled within Rowena. So many elements of the legend had proven to be true. Why not the riddle? Her heart pounded with anticipation. "What is the answer?"

"Not what, but whom. No one was ever sure who penned the riddle, but I have always believed that it was Tyrus."

"Lady Fiona's husband?" Dominic asked.

"Aye. The ballad tells the tale from the perspective of Fair Fiona. I think the riddle is just the opposite. It is Tyrus' contribution to the legend."

"But what does it *mean*?" Rowena tried not to be impatient, but her being hummed with enthusiasm. She felt like a child about to receive a precious gift. "To whom was Tyrus referring?"

"To a Carthusian monk, or more specifically to who he became after Lady Fiona left him," said Brother Leland.

"Carthusian monks took vows of poverty and silence. So, he would be lonely, but not alone," Rowena agreed. "Tyrus walked away from vast holdings to join the order, so he would have possessed nothing, but what about the riches untold?"

"Lady Fiona came to Tyrus with a priceless treasure on their wedding day. I have heard that it was one large, perfect diamond, and I have heard that it was a chest filled with sparkling jewels, but one thing is certain—Tyrus refused to part with the treasure when he entered the monastery."

"If he took a vow of silence, then how could he share tales far and wide?" Dominic asked.

The friar smiled, apparently enjoying himself as they worked together to unravel the mystery. "A scribe often copied the Holy Scriptures, and who among us has not heard a tale from the Bible?"

"There is another possibility," Rowena cut in. "The legend itself. Tyrus' and Fiona's tale has been shared far and wide."

"Very well. That still leaves the last line," Dominic said.

"Tyrus is dead, so he remains hidden forever in the shadows of night," Brother Leland suggested.

"And even before his death, he lived here," Rowena reminded. "Except for the front door, there is no natural light in the entire monastery. Every cell here is hidden forever in the shadows of night."

"Then Tyrus is the answer to the riddle," Dominic announced rather skeptically.

"I believe he was referring to himself, aye," Brother Leland agreed.

"Then that leaves only the dragon," said Rowena, her mind already two steps ahead of the conversation. "The voice told you to solve the riddle and set the dragon free?"

"Aye, but only that—solve the riddle and set the dragon free."

She turned to Dominic and smiled. "We've already found Tyrus' dragon."

"Bring torches," Dominic ordered as Rowena turned and headed across the room.

She reached the cell just before the men and stood to one side as they filed in behind Dominic. He handed a thick torch to her as he moved closer to the doorway to examine the stone dragon.

"What is it? What are you looking at?" the friar asked. One of Dominic's men led him into the room, but no one had explained what was happening.

"There's a sculpted dragon's head mounted above the doorway. Dominic and I found it when we were here tending you. We even speculated that it was a legacy from Tyrus, but there didn't seem to be a latch or lever, so we dismissed it as decoration."

"A dragon decorating a monastery?" Brother Leland's brows knitted together in speculation. "That is passing strange."

Stretching up onto his toes, Dominic ran his hands along every edge of the statue, searching again for a latch or lever. He pressed on the fangs; he examined each detail. "I still feel nothing."

"Can you break it off?" Rowena suggested hesitantly.

He chuckled. "I offered to slay it for you then. Everyone stand back."

Rowena guided Brother Leland as far from the doorway as the narrow room allowed. Dominic drew his sword and stepped to one side. Raising his sword in a wide arch, he slammed it down against the dragon's neck. The statue groaned, but didn't move. Dominic swung again and the dragon separated from the wall. He jumped back as it crashed to the cell's floor and obediently split open.

"Is the treasure there? What does it look like?" the friar questioned excitedly.

"I'm not sure, Brother Leland. There seems to be something bundled in oilskin or…" Her description trailed away as Dominic unfolded the bundle across the stone floor. An inner layer of thick black velvet became a pillow for the sparkling jewels. Brilliant diamonds, rubies, sapphires, emeralds, amethysts and golden amber, each stone was identical in shape and size. Rowena reached out and picked up a perfect, teardrop-shaped diamond. "Dragon's Tears." Such a hush had fallen on the room that she whispered the words.

She picked up a fist full of the stones and held them over the friar's open palm. "They're beautiful." She spilled the jewels into his hand. "Every color of the rainbow, and each one is shaped like a tear."

He laughed and explored the smooth, cool stones with his fingertips. "I knew it was real. You have finally done it. You have lifted the curse and freed the dragon."

Rowena glanced at the shattered stone sculpture and then at her husband. Her body thrummed with happiness and relief. They had fought a great battle and emerged victorious.

I love you. She mouthed the words and he grinned, his eyes glowing with responding warmth.

"Are you ready to go home?" She smiled invitingly.

"Aye, my love." He stooped to gather the jewels into the velvet bundle, purposely ignoring the fact that Brother Leland still held a handful.

"You can come back to the castle now, Brother Leland. There is nothing more to fear," Rowena invited.

"I would welcome your hospitality. But in a few days, I want to return to my cottage and my work. Brother Samuel is lost without me."

"You are free to do as you wish."

He held out his hand, offering her the jewels within his grasp.

"Keep them. Put them to use however God directs you. I already have everything I need."

Hearing her statement, Dominic beamed. He motioned one of his men forward and placed Brother Leland's free hand on his arm. "Albert will see you safely to the castle."

Brother Leland nodded.

The same instant Albert cleared the doorway with Brother Leland, Rowena flew into Dominic's arms. They kissed deeply, repeatedly, hungrily. She understood the urgency in his touch. She was desperate for more of him.

"It's over, my love," he promised. "It's truly over."

He couldn't stop touching her and Rowena felt the same. They needed to get back to the castle or they would end up on the cold stone floor.

"Take me home." She whispered the words against his mouth, and he chuckled, understanding her unspoken request.

* * * * *

They met the twilight arm in arm, their hearts soaring, and Fair Fiona watched it from the trees.

"Your father will be pleased," Fearsome Dragon concluded.

"I hope you're right, my friend. They are glorious. I've never seen human hearts so entwined."

"You sound surprised." He hovered near her as the mortals started down the steep trail.

"Not surprised," she corrected, "relieved and impressed. Their lives will be rich and full."

She said nothing for a long while, and Fearsome Dragon grew restless. "You will not be satisfied until you've said goodbye."

Her eyes gleamed with Fairy mischief and she could not help but smile. "My father discourages me from interacting with mortals."

The dragon laughed, shaking his noble head. "And that has kept you from it all these years. I will meet you in the sky."

The human couple finally reached their castle. Dominic set Rowena on the ground as Milton led Majesty away. Fair Fiona waited for just the right moment and then gracefully stepped through the veil.

Rowena's head suddenly turned in Fiona's direction. "Look." Her tone was hushed and reverent.

Dominic followed the direction of her nod and smiled. "Fair Fiona, I presume."

"This is the first you have actually seen her?" Rowena remained within the loose circle of her husband's embrace.

"Aye. But she kissed me once, and I heard her sing."

Fiona laughed, and her nimbus grew brighter, her shape solidified within the light. The wonder in the mortals' eyes amused her, so Fiona decided to sing. Joy, rich and pure infused her song, but Fearsome Dragon was awaiting her.

She kissed each mortal on the cheek and flew around them, speaking ancient words to bless the union of their souls.

"You will flourish, my friends, but I must leave," she said in their human tongue.

Dominic gasped, but Rowena had heard her musical voice before. "Thank you, Fair Fiona, for everything."

"You're welcome. But your lady wife did most of the work. Oh, I almost forgot. Rowena, I'm afraid you'll need to find a new handmaiden. Thora has been…called away." For just a moment, she surrounded herself with the handmaiden's glamour.

Both mortals laughed with delight.

"Will we ever see you again?" Rowena's voice was tinged with sadness.

"I'm not sure, but for now you've no need of me. You'll do just fine on your own."

Rowena smiled at Dominic and love swirled all around them. "So long as we live, you are welcome. I'd be honored to see you again."

"What calls you away?" Dominic asked.

"Another adventure."

She circled them one final time and then disappeared into the cloudless sky.

"Another adventure," Dominic repeated. "I hope the next one ends as well as ours."

Framing his face with her palms, Rowena stretched onto her toes and whispered, "Our adventure hasn't ended, my love. Our adventure has just begun."

Read on for a preview of
Rebel Angels, Book One
Rage and Redemption
By Cyndi Friberg

Chapter One

Krak des Chevaliers
County of Tripoli, Palestine
March 1148

Fidgeting upon the wooden stool, Naomi pushed a lock of long hair behind her ear and concentrated on the manuscript page spread before her. Dust motes danced playfully in the rapidly fading sunlight but she couldn't allow herself to be distracted. The familiar scent of ink and sandalwood soothed her, helping her focus. She shifted the precious vellum folio to a slightly different angle, catching what was left of the light.

To achieve true illumination, a scribe must release light from within the text, not just decorate the margins. Her design was intricate and interesting, but there was no spark or inspiration. No illumination.

Naomi focused on the entwined figures centered on the page and set her quill aside. Eve's long hair concealed everything but her slender limbs. Adam, on the other hand, had only a strategically placed fig leaf to protect his modesty.

"Perhaps without the leaf I could find illumination," Naomi muttered with a mischievous smile.

"I'd be willing to serve as your model."

Naomi twirled about so suddenly she nearly toppled from the stool. Stifling a startled gasp, she stumbled to her feet, pretending the movement had been graceful.

Raising her gaze to the stranger's face, Naomi forgot her clever rejoinder. She forgot to breathe. She forgot everything except the man standing near the doorway.

His features were harsh and angular yet so incredibly beautiful he didn't seem real. Bright with amusement and speculation, his strange golden eyes captured her gaze completely.

"Shall I disrobe?"

The smoky quality of his voice made Naomi tingle. Sleek black hair had been pulled straight back from his face and secured at the nape of his neck. Naomi wanted to trace the slash of his black eyebrows and smooth the faint creases that framed his extraordinary eyes. She wanted to test the resilience of his mouth with her fingertips and...

What was wrong with her?

Shaking away the strange stupor, Naomi forced herself to speak. "I'm not the scribe, my lord, so I require no model."

He walked toward her, his stride long and lazy. "If you aren't the scribe, what were you doing when I arrived?"

Naomi quickly hid her ink-stained hand behind her back. Her sandals scraped against the floorboards as she moved away from the high, angled table. "I was admiring Brother Gabriel's work. He is the finest illuminator in the entire order."

After so many years, the deception shouldn't rankle, but it did. She hated the prejudice that required she deny her accomplishments.

He glanced at the manuscript page then back at her. Who was this man? His garments told her only that he was wealthy. The plush, black velvet surcoat had been elaborately embroidered in gold, and the gray tunic beneath was no less costly. He wore no sword, but Naomi sensed the menace that hovered around men of war.

"What business have you here?" she asked. "Were you looking for Brother Gabriel?"

Before she realized his intention, he reached behind her and grabbed her wrist. His touch sent shivers up her arm and Naomi sucked in a ragged breath. Drawing her arm back in front of her, he turned her hand this way and that, inspecting the calluses and stains.

"You're not a scribe?" he challenged softly.

"The order has been charged with illuminating the Holy Scripts, sir." She avoided his gaze as she continued her explanation. "Some learned men believe women do not possess souls. Almighty God would never bestow talent and inspiration on so lowly a creature. Only a man can be trusted to script the Word of God."

The stranger laughed and Naomi felt her insides clench. He had been beautiful when he scowled. His appeal now made her restless and…hot.

His thumb brushed over her wrist and his gaze settled on her mouth. "Gabriel must have his hands full with you about. Where is he?"

Naomi tried to draw her hand from his grasp but he wouldn't allow it. The soft stroke of his thumb made her pulse jump and her skin flush. "What do you want with Brother Gabriel?"

"What I want at the moment has nothing to do with Gabriel."

Her hand brushed against coarse stone. She'd backed herself against the wall! Her heart fluttered and she found it hard to swallow. "If you have business with—"

"What's your name?" he interrupted.

His shimmering gaze moved slowly over her features. Naomi felt the caress like a physical touch. Coolness from the stones at her back seeped through her clothing in sharp contrast to the heat radiating from his body. She shivered, shifting her weight from one foot to the other.

"I do not share my favors, sir. There are women in the village who are willing to…accommodate your needs."

"What would you know of my needs?"

He sounded odd, as if she had struck some dark, painful chord within him. Naomi's chest tightened and her heart pounded. "Nothing, my lord. I meant only to make clear that I am not a harlot."

He released her hand and moved in closer. Pressing his palms against the wall, he caged her with his body. "I would have your name, damsel."

Fear welled within Naomi but she tried not to panic. The scriptorium was high in a stone tower, secluded and isolated. "Please, my lord. I didn't mean to anger you." She spoke in a calm, even tone.

"I am not angry."

But he looked angry. His golden eyes glittered with determination and the set of his jaw seemed dangerous. He was tall and broad, strong and menacing.

"Who are you?" His voice was barely more than a whisper, his eyes searching.

"No one of consequence." She pushed against his chest, shocked by the inflexibility of his flesh. "Let me go."

He smiled slowly, provocatively. "I think not on both accounts."

Gideon stared down into the woman's bright blue eyes and felt his fangs lengthen. He quickly closed his mouth, unwilling to reveal his true nature. He was hungry, but it had been many weeks since he'd sought the comfort of a woman's embrace. He couldn't decide if he wanted to penetrate her throat with his fangs or feel her feminine core tighten around his shaft.

Perhaps he could have both.

He wrapped his arms around her slender form, pressing her against his chest. She instinctively arched and shoved. This only aligned their lower bodies more intimately. Her eyes widened and the scent of fear exploded in his nose.

"Be still," he commanded with his dark voice and the flash of his eyes.

She went limp in his arms. Her eyes drifting shut and Gideon chuckled. He hadn't meant the compulsion to be quite so powerful. Her head lolled back into the bend of his elbow, exposing her neck and ending his mental debate. He would feed first and then draw her back to awareness as he slowly seduced her senses.

Burying his face in her throat, he inhaled her scent. She smelled fresh and feminine with faint traces of fear and—arousal? Gideon parted his lips and stroked his tongue along her jugular, feeling the rhythmic pounding, the power and life. Intoxicated by her scent, it took him a moment to recognize the subtle sweetness of her taste.

Innocence.

With careful restraint, he pricked her skin with his fangs and then quickly withdrew. He savored the rich complexity of her blood. His heart hammered as her nature was revealed. She was pure of heart. Selfless, devoted and true.

Dark hunger slashed through Gideon and he groaned. The age-old battle within his spirit raged out of control, driving the breath from his body and the strength from his legs. He sank to his knees, maintaining his hold on the woman.

The shriveled remnants of his goodness surged to life, reaching for her, crying out to her. But the evil in him was just as strong. He wanted her as he had never wanted anything or anyone. He threw back his head and roared. Anguish and fury saturated the sound. He longed to drown in her innocence, to gorge on her goodness until…until she was corrupted or dead?

Unsteady and shaken, he sat down on the wood-planked floor and pulled her into his lap, cradling her in his arms like a child. His hand trembled as he brushed the hair back from her face. She looked no different than other humans. Still, something about her held him back. His dark nature demanded that he use her to sate this raw, burning hunger, but he couldn't seem to move.

She shifted within his arms and slowly opened her eyes.

Fear erupted again. He could smell its acrid stench, hear its relentless pounding, taste its bitterness — but it had never been repulsive before.

"What happened?" she asked.

"I frightened you. You fainted."

"I have never fainted." She sounded affronted as she sat up in his lap. She squirmed a bit and then went very still, her hand splayed in the center of his chest.

Her long chestnut hair was tousled, a stray wisp curled against her cheek. She stared up at him with the biggest, bluest eyes he'd ever seen, and Gideon knew he would not ravish her. Seduction, on the other hand, was still a very real possibility.

"Did you pretend to faint so I'd take you in my arms?"

Her eyes lit with indignation and Gideon smiled, his hunger controlled again, at least for the present.

"Why would I need such a ploy?"

"Because you're not yet ready to admit you want me, even to yourself."

She laughed and the hand resting against his chest began to push. "Are you always so arrogant?"

He couldn't bring himself to let her go. Her rounded bottom was doing cruel things to him, yet he ached with the need to touch her. Taste her. "Kiss me and I'll release you." *If you still want to be released once my mouth is moving upon yours.*

Naomi felt like Eve in the Garden of Eden. "I shall scream and you'll be forced to let me go."

"Forced by whom? This chamber is far from the domestic range. We are quite alone."

She didn't move, could scarcely breathe.

Brushing his warm fingers against her cheek, he tucked a curl behind her ear. "Let me taste your mouth. I only want a taste."

She rubbed her palm against his chest, fascinated by the unyielding shape beneath the soft material. Why was she still sitting here? He wasn't really restraining her.

This man was the personification of her darkest fantasies, the elusive, mysterious something that other people whispered about. He was potent, powerful and yet incomprehensible.

His mouth covered hers, driving all rational thought from her mind. She felt the heated slide of his lips and trembled. She felt the sensual glide of his tongue and groaned. His mouth moved over and against hers, his tongue touched and tasted.

She found his sleek hair and sank her fingers into the cool strands. His fingers were in her hair too. She felt his hand close into a fist, carefully controlling her. He tilted her head and his mouth fit more tightly over hers, guiding her lips farther apart.

She accepted the bold thrust of his tongue with a little gasp. Overwhelmed and intoxicated, she felt completely out of control. He was taking too much, moving too fast. She couldn't breathe, couldn't think, could only yield to his passion.

Fear found its way through the haze as he deepened the kiss. He was aggressive now, demanding, his mouth plundering the depths of hers. Naomi shoved against his chest and tore her mouth away.

"More, Naomi, give me more," he growled.

His arms tightened, dragging her flush against his chest. Naomi turned her face away as his words registered. "You called me Naomi."

"Is there some other name you'd prefer?"

His mouth moved to the underside of her jaw and slide along her throat. Shoving hard against his chest, she tried to think, to understand what he was doing to her. He had demanded her name, but she hadn't told him.

Scrambling off his lap, she scurried to the other side of the chamber. "How do you know my name?"

For a moment he sat there staring at her over his shoulder. Then in one fluid motion, he gained his feet and stalked toward her. "You told me your name."

She felt compelled to look at him, to stare into his eyes, but she quickly averted her gaze. "Nay, sir, I did not."

He stood directly across the table from her. It was no real protection. He could easily shove it aside. She sneaked a glance at his face. He was looking at the manuscript page, his expression inscrutable.

"Where will I find Gabriel?"

His voice softly demanded the information and Naomi felt the urge to blurt out his location. "What do you want with Brother Gabriel?"

"Where will I find him?"

He looked up and their gazes locked before she dragged hers away. Naomi felt hot and then cold. "I've no idea. You need to inquire with the castellan. His name is Brother Aaron."

Suddenly he was beside her, his palms framing her face, and Naomi had no choice but to meet his penetrating stare. "What is Gabriel to you?"

She struggled against the need to tell him every detail of her relationship with Brother Gabriel. Keeping her mouth firmly closed, Naomi fought the bizarre compulsion. Never would she do anything that would endanger her mentor and closest friend, but the need to speak became overwhelming.

"He is a member of the Holy Order of St. John. Surely you knew that before you came here."

"What is he to *you*?"

Stubbornly closing her eyes, she allowed Brother Gabriel's kind, serene face to form within her mind, driving back the dark compulsion. "Why have you detained me?"

"Because you're lying." His hand slid down along her jaw, his thumb stroking back and forth across her bottom lip.

A hot, golden haze burned through her mind, consuming the image of Brother Gabriel. Naomi's eyes flew open. It was as if he were controlling images inside her head!

"You lied about being a scribe. You lied about Gabriel. You not only know where he is, but he is important to you. What is the connection?"

Someone had to end the stalemate. Although he could easily find out about her, his identity and purpose would be far harder to learn. "Brother Gabriel is the nearest thing to a father I have ever known. He is a friend and mentor. What is he to you?"

"Gabriel is my brother." With an enigmatic smile he turned and left the room.

She stared after him for a long moment, her mind filled with questions. Why had Gabriel never mentioned having a brother? Was the stranger a mercenary or had he come simply to visit his brother? His interest seemed somehow…menacing.

How had he known her name?

An odd combination of fear and excitement pulsed through her entire body. She had never met a man who made her tingle with just the intensity of his gaze.

She must tell Brother Gabriel a man claiming to be his brother had arrived at the Krak des Chevaliers, but he was in the chapel attending Vespers. As she should have been, she realized with a small, rebellious smile.

It was all so very strange.

She turned her attention back to the manuscript page, determined to banish thoughts of the stranger from her mind. His striking features refused to stay suppressed. With a helpless sigh, she reached for a scrap of vellum and began to sketch.

* * * * *

Naomi angled her sketch of the stranger toward the lamplight and felt heat spread across her cheeks. Just his image caused her senses to respond. It was ridiculous.

"I missed you at Vespers," Brother Gabriel said from somewhere behind her. "What kept you so occupied that you neglected your evening prayers?"

Carefully keeping the scrap of vellum turned away, Naomi pivoted on the stool and offered her warmest smile. "Adam and Eve. Well, mostly Adam."

Brother Gabriel chuckled and Naomi tried to release the tension gripping her abdomen. She studied her mentor with new interest as he crossed the scriptorium. There was nothing she didn't know about this man or so she'd believed until a short time ago.

He wore a long-sleeved black robe emblazoned with the distinctive white cross identifying him as a member of the elite Order of St. John of Jerusalem. Naomi felt proud to be part of such an important order. The Knights of St. John had been serving Western pilgrims as they traveled through the Holy Land for well over a century. One of their grandest accomplishments had been building a hospital in the heart of Jerusalem. Now members of the order were often called Knights Hospitaller.

Naomi focused her attention on the man within the robe. Gabriel's neatly trimmed hair was a bright blending of silver and gold, nearly opposite from the raven-black locks of the man claiming to be his brother. His eyes were a warm brown, but there were shards of gold Naomi had never noticed before.

"Is something troubling you, Naomi? You stare at me as if I have sprouted horns."

"Who is this man?" She handed him the scrap of vellum.

His eyes widened for just a moment before he concealed his surprise. She watched his throat work as he swallowed awkwardly. "Where did you see him?"

"He just left. You may have passed in the bailey."

He set the sketch aside and grasped both of her hands. Fear shone in his eyes as he searched her face and person. "Are you well? Did he harm you? Threaten you?"

Naomi nervously licked her lips. "I'm fine. But why would that be your first assumption? Is he your brother as he claimed?"

Releasing her hands, Brother Gabriel averted his face for a moment before he spoke. "Tell me exactly what happened."

"Nay, not until you tell me why he frightens you. I have never known you to be afraid of anyone or anything yet I see fear in your eyes."

"Gideon can be dangerous, Naomi. I cannot pretend otherwise. He—"

"Gideon," she whispered. "He didn't tell me his name."

"What *did* he tell you?"

"Only that he is your brother. He asked where he could find you and when I wouldn't volunteer the information, he became annoyed." She had to fight back a smile as she remembered the heated embrace they had shared. "He can be quite intense."

"Did he touch you?" He took a step toward her. "You said he didn't harm you."

"He didn't harm me," she said reassuringly. "What does he want with you?"

"I'm not certain."

"Why did you never tell me you have a brother?" The faintest edge cut through her tone despite Naomi's effort to conceal her disappointment.

"It never occurred to me that you would meet." He turned toward the door. "I must find him. His coming can only mean trouble for both of us."

* * * * *

Gideon leaned against the stone wall of the mercenary barracks and stretched out his legs along the narrow cot assigned for his use. Crispin had chosen the cot on his left while the one on his right remained unoccupied. The barracks were spacious and surprisingly clean. Gideon had arrived with eight mercenaries and the castellan of Krak des Chevaliers had extended them hospitality without hesitation. The compound was massive. Ten additional inhabitants would hardly be noticed.

Men of every shape and variety milled about the open room conversing with each other, some sharpening weapons. Gideon watched them with dispassionate interest in the smoky lamplight, his mind distracted by his encounter with Naomi.

She had been lovely and spirited. Still, her emotional connection to Gabriel was what interested him most. Who was she? How had she come to be in Gabriel's care? Did she know her "father's" true nature?

"Does he know you're here?" Crispin asked.

"I've yet to speak with him, but it's only a matter of time. As soon as the girl tells him I'm about, Gabriel will come running."

Gideon had quickly learned having a human under his control was more than just convenient. It was necessary. Crispin safeguarded Gideon whenever he was vulnerable. Gideon didn't allow him to remember many of the things they did together, but Crispin was loyal. A preternatural compulsion assured his loyalty.

"This girl, is she comely?" Crispin asked with a characteristic grin.

"She is wondrously fair." Gideon felt his hunger stir as he remembered her sweet taste, so pure and innocent. "Her dark hair has just a hint of fire and her eyes hold the blue of an endless summer sky."

"How poetic," Crispin teased him.

The raucous sound of numerous conversations diminished suddenly, drawing Gideon's attention toward the main entrance to the barracks. A Knight Hospitaller stood in the doorway, his dark monastic robes decorated only by the large white cross on his chest.

Gideon suppressed his unconscious reaction to the symbol. Revulsion, fury and fear rolled through him. Breathing in through his nose and out through his mouth, he managed to keep his expression composed. He focused on the individual clothed within the robes and ignored his discomfort.

Nearly a century had passed since he last saw his brother face-to-face. The confrontation was long overdue. Drab robes didn't distract from the purity of Gabriel's features or the bright splendor of his gilt-colored hair. Gideon watched as he crossed the barracks. Gabriel managed to maintain a serene expression yet his gaze revealed his uncertainty.

"Gideon," he greeted calmly as he reached the cot.

"Gabriel," Gideon replied, his tone mocking.

"What brings you to the Krak?"

Before Gideon could answer, Gabriel noticed Crispin's avid interest. "May we speak outside?"

Gideon smiled. "Why? Do you have words for me that would make my friend uncomfortable?"

"Making people uncomfortable seems to be your goal not mine."

He narrowed his eyes. How much had Naomi confessed? Surely she hadn't shared all the details of their meeting. Swinging his legs to the floor, Gideon rose and followed his brother out into the night.

Moonlight caught on the large cross atop the chapel's bell tower, casting a dense shadow across Gideon's path. His steps faltered and his stomach clenched. With a surge of stubborn determination, he marched through the shape and into the darkness beside the barracks. He didn't stop until they were well away from curious ears.

"How did you find me?" Gabriel asked.

"It's a simple thing to find someone who is following you. Did Michael dispatch you or do you willingly participate in my punishment?"

"There is only one participant in your punishment, Gideon, and that is *you*." Gabriel's voice was firm, his expression guarded. "I am here. You cannot change that fact. When did you become aware of my presence?"

"I saw you in Jerusalem. I thought you had some manner of assignment, but the more I thought about it, the more suspicious I became. How long have I *been* your assignment?"

Gabriel smiled and glanced away. "You have been more like a command center from which I am dispatched to other assignments."

"So you spy on me unless He has something of more importance for you to do?"

"For the most part," Gabriel agreed.

"And you are only to observe? Not give me guidance?"

"Would you accept my guidance should I give it?"

Gideon chuckled, resting one shoulder against the barracks outer wall. "You're nearly as good at avoiding questions as am I. You can speak only truth so tell me now. What role has Michael set for you?"

Gabriel fidgeted. "I have been told to monitor your situation."

"And report back to Michael no doubt. How is the study coming? Have I learned my lessons well? How much longer am I to be banished from the Light, expected to live off these mortals?"

"That is and has always been up to you. All Michael did was release your constraints. You claimed that we are slaves so Michael set you free."

"There is no freedom in what I have become," Gideon sneered.

"You are a creature of your own making. If you are not content, then change."

They glared at each other for a long moment.

"Have all these years taught you nothing?" Gabriel asked.

Anger boiled up within Gideon, tasting foul in the back of his throat. He folded his arms across his chest and began to pace. "Oh, my time with mankind has taught me many things. I've learned to be ruthless and to deceive. I've learned to manipulate others to my own will. I've learned to lust and covet. I've learned —"

"Nothing you needed to know," Gabriel interrupted impatiently. "Have you not seen the sacrifices they make for each other? Their tenderness and their loyalty, their courage and honor?"

"Honor?" Gideon scoffed. "Honor is as much a myth as love."

"You have known love, Gideon. I love you unconditionally. You must learn how to *give* love, not how to *be* loved."

Gideon looked away from the hope and the expectation in his brother's eyes. He gazed out into the night, drawing strength from the darkness.

"Are you in love with her, Gabriel?" he asked in a quietly provoking tone. "Do you feel the full range of human emotions as I do, or did Michael spare you that torment?"

"We speak of Naomi now?" Gabriel asked.

"She is quite remarkable. The most intriguing combination of innocence and lush, feminine promise."

Gabriel took a step forward, anger hardening his features and brightening his gaze. "Leave Naomi alone. She has nothing to do with any of this."

Gideon grinned, amazed at how well he had guessed what his brother was feeling. "No wonder you masquerade as a monk. Your very nature makes the role effortless. Piety, selflessness and chastity are routine for an angel. You do not burn with lust, do you? You feel protective and responsible, but you feel nothing more for this girl."

"I have cared for Naomi since she was a babe." Gabriel sounded defensive. His bright eyes narrowed in his perfect face. "Her mother died in my arms, and I have taken responsibility for the child ever since."

A deep chuckle rumbled in Gideon's chest. "She is no longer a child, *Brother* Gabriel. And I will continue her education from here."

"Why are you doing this?" Gabriel demanded, frustration clear in his melodious voice.

"Because I can," Gideon snapped in return.

"I don't understand."

"Aye, you do. That is the reason you stink of fear. You understand exactly what I intend for your precious 'daughter'." Gideon started back toward the barracks.

"Will it ease your pain to hurt Naomi?"

"That's what I intend to find out." He tossed the words over his shoulder without turning around.

"She has done nothing to deserve this, Gideon. I will do everything in my power to protect her from you."

"Good." He paused at the corner of the building. Penetrating the shadows with the golden intensity of his glare, he knocked Gabriel back a step. "I welcome the conflict, *brother*. I have grown quite accustomed to war."

Anything-but-Ordinary is Cyndi's creed and her writing reflects her dedication to the concept. She writes in a variety of genres, but seems happiest in outer space. Her books have been nominated for numerous awards, and *Taken by Storm* was named Best Fantasy/Science Fiction Romance of the year by Romance Reviews Today.

She lives in Colorado with her high school sweetheart turned husband of many years. With a pampered cat curled on the corner of her desk, she dreams of fascinating words and larger than life adventures -- and wouldn't have it any other way!

Website / Blog: http://www.cyndifriberg.com

www.ingramcontent.com/pod-product-compliance
Lightning Source LLC
Chambersburg PA
CBHW062023170626
46813CB00001B/266